The velvet wings fluttered closer and closer

Chase sat quietly on the grass, cupping a pool of sugar syrup in his palm. A huge Kamehameha butterfly hovered around him in a slowly closing spiral. It settled, fled, settled and fled again. Chase didn't move at all, not even to present his lure more openly. He waited motionlessly. Finally the butterfly rested completely, safely, in the palm of his hand, drinking deeply of the sweetness that he offered.

Nicole knew the exact instant when the butterfly trustingly drank, because that was when Chase's gray eyes looked up and found her hidden among the green shadows, watching a butterfly cherished within the hard curve of his hand.

Dear Reader,

When two people fall in love, the world is suddenly new and exciting, and it's that same excitement we bring to you in Silhouette Intimate Moments. These are stories with scope, with grandeur. These characters lead the lives we all dream of, and everything they do reflects the wonder of being in love.

Longer and more sensuous than most romances, Silhouette Intimate Moments novels take you away from everyday life and let you share the magic of love. Adventure, glamour, drama, even suspense—these are the passwords that let you into a world where love has a power beyond the ordinary, where the best authors in the field today create stories of love and commitment that will stay with you always.

In coming months look for novels by your favorite authors: Maura Seger, Parris Afton Bonds, Elizabeth Lowell and Erin St. Claire, to name just a few. And whenever you buy books, look for all the Silhouette Intimate Moments, love stories *for* today's women *by* today's women.

Leslie J. Wainger
Senior Editor
Silhouette Books

IMRL-7/85

Fires of Eden

Elizabeth Lowell

Silhouette Intimate Moments

Published by Silhouette Books New York

America's Publisher of Contemporary Romance

SILHOUETTE BOOKS
300 East 42nd St., New York, N.Y.   10017

ISBN: 0-373-07141-8

First Silhouette Books printing May 1986

ELIZABETH LOWELL

writes in several fields. When friends ask her why she decided to write "*romances*, of all things," she just smiles. She has been married for eighteen years to the only man she has ever loved. How can she help but write novels that celebrate love and life?

Chapter 1

You've never seen anyone like her."

Chase Wilcox's only response to his younger brother's enthusiasm was a sideways look and a grunt that could have been interpreted as either agreement or disinterest. Chase's expression gave no clue as to his feelings. He was a man who had learned the hard way that emotions could be treacherous, particularly where women were concerned.

And a woman was most definitely concerned tonight.

Chase had first seen Nicole Ballard three weeks before, in a photo his brother, Dane, had taken and sent to Washington. The snapshot had been all color and grace and movement, Nicole's long golden-red hair streaming out as she spun around with a delighted child in her arms. Chase had been riveted by the combination of intelligence and pleasure in the woman's face and by the sensuous, fiery cloud of her hair concealing her body and that of the tiny seven-year-old child laughing in her arms.

The picture had haunted Chase, but it hadn't been a pleasant haunting. Lately, Dane's infrequent letters had been full of praise for Nicole. Everything Chase read made him more uneasy. The snapshot had made him... angry. Dane's wife was no match for the red-haired temptress who was worming her way into the family's daily life. No woman would have been a match for Nicole. Even the blurred snapshot had been like a fist to Chase's heart, sending a shock wave through his body. He had looked at that photo again and again and, with each look, his anger had increased. Dane couldn't stand against such temptation for long.

No man could.

Chase had come to Hawaii as soon as possible. He hadn't even unpacked before Dane had dragged him to the Kipuka Club to see "Pele" dance. Now Chase was tired, irritable and angry beneath his dark, calm exterior. With his black hair and tanned face, Chase could have been taken for a true native of Hawaii—until he turned and the ice-pale flash of his gray eyes was revealed in the club's dimly lit interior.

Covertly Chase studied his younger brother, who was eagerly awaiting the appearance of Pele. As he watched Dane, Chase wondered how deeply the red-haired predator had her claws into his trusting brother.

Not as deeply as she wanted them, that's for sure, or he'd be getting a divorce, Chase told himself grimly. *Well, she's too late. The show's over. She'll just have to take her home-wrecking act on the road and find another rich fool.*

Chase waited impatiently to get on with it, to get close enough to Pele to find the weakness that would allow him to drive in a wedge and break her wide open, ending the threat to his brother's marriage. As Chase waited, his jaw ached with the effort of restraining his rage. He was careful to keep his fury to himself, knowing that Dane believed the woman to be virtuous, intelligent, warm, loving, kind, and all the other lies and lures females use to attract gullible males.

But Chase wasn't gullible anymore. His former wife had cured him. Any lingering delusions he might have had about the true nature of the female character were resolved when Lynnette had called him four weeks ago and announced that she was tired of their daughter and he could have her back. For good. It was typical of Lynnette that Lisa had been standing nearby, listening as her mother dumped her.

Just the memory of Lynnette's casual cruelty made Chase's whole body tense with rage. Chase had married because he'd wanted a child. Lynnette hadn't wanted Lisa at all, but she had demanded custody because that was the only foolproof way to keep the pipeline to the Wilcox wealth open. The judge had been taken in by Lynnette's tiny, heart-shaped face and soft-voiced lies about motherhood, but Lynnette had held onto Lisa only long enough to find a wealthier fool to marry.

Chase was profoundly grateful to have his daughter back, in spite of the fact that it couldn't have come at a worse time for him professionally. Mount Saint Helens had been swelling and rumbling with promises of new eruptions, and he had been within weeks of finishing up the first phase of a long-term study of the return of life to the volcano's devastated slopes. It was no place for a thin, shy seven-year-old. He had been on the point of abandoning his project when Dane's wife had called and asked if it would be all right for Lisa to stay in Hawaii with them for the summer. It had been typical of Janet that she acted as if Chase were doing her a favor when he agreed.

Bloody fool, thought Chase angrily, looking at his brother's handsome profile. *Don't you know what an incredibly rare treasure you have in Janet? She's the exception to the rule that all women are whores. So what in hell's name are you doing panting after a glorified shimmy dancer?*

Chase looked at his clenched hands and wished that he were on Hawaii only as a professional vulcanologist and not as an unwanted marriage counselor. To him Hawaii wasn't the Big Island; it was Volcano Island, the burning Eden that was the site of the world's biggest and most active volcanoes. He belonged up on the mountain, not in a dim club, waiting to meet the woman his younger brother was making a fool of himself over.

"—my brother, Dr. Chase Wilcox."

Automatically Chase brought his attention back to the moment and smiled as Dane introduced him to yet another volcano observatory scientist, university ethnologist, or Hilo native. The Kipuka Club was a private supper club supported by a mixture of university types, volcano crawlers, and native Hawaiians such as Bobby Kamehameha, the club's owner and the drummer for the dancers.

As Chase stood up to meet the man, he felt a fleeting moment of surprise. At six feet five, with a naturally powerful build, Chase was accustomed to being the biggest man in any room. Bobby was bigger. A lot bigger. Six feet eight, at least sixty pounds heavier, with the deceptively smooth, almost soft-looking physique that full-blooded Polynesians often have. Chase knew better than to believe the satin surface. Bobby's power showed in his eyes and in the hard hand gently gripping Chase's.

"I could have used you in college," said Chase, his smile becoming less professional and more personal. "The defense kept pounding me into the grass."

"You play pro?" asked Bobby.

"Nope. Too small."

Bobby laughed. "More like too smart. Dane told me about the Mount Saint Helens project, among others. Hawaii is honored to have you." The big man grinned suddenly. "Even if you are another rich haole."

Chase laughed and released Bobby's hand, only to have the big Hawaiian grab it again. Broad, blunt fingertips traced the lines of calluses on Chase's palms and finger-tips.

"You no tell me he drum," complained Bobby, slipping into the easy rhythms of pidgin as he turned to Dane. It wasn't the island's true pidgin, which would have been nearly incomprehensible to nonnatives. Rather, it was the languid, slangy version of English that was developing in the islands' seething cultural and linguistic stew.

"You no ask," shot back Dane.

Bobby said something in melodic Hawaiian that Chase suspected was distinctly unmusical.

"Friends," continued Bobby with great dignity and perfect enunciation, "should not have to ask about matters of such great, even grave, importance." He threw a thick arm around Chase's shoulders. "You me brudder. Long stay island, sure-sure."

Chase looked at the array of modern bongo drums set out on a corner of the stage and smiled. "At least you're not hung up on tradition here."

"My ancestors lived as well as they could, as often as they could, taking the best that was available to them at the time," said Bobby, amusement and intelligence gleaming in his black eyes. "That's the only Hawaiian tradition I care about. I leave the sixty-pound surfboards and poi for the crazy haoles."

The lights flickered wildly.

"The haoles," said Bobby gravely, "are restless tonight. I don't blame them. Pele's back. She's enough to make Mauna Loa's stone rivers melt and run again."

Bobby released Chase and went to the stage.

Dane looked at his rather bemused older brother. "Bobby has a PhD in medieval iconography. His second one is in nonverbal communications."

"I believe it. After meeting him, I'd believe anything." Chase had a sudden thought. "Is he Pele's lover?"

Dane's surprise showed on his darkly elegant face. Like his brother, Dane was taller than most men, although he was inches shorter, and quite a bit more slender, than Chase. Unlike his brother, Dane didn't mistrust the world in general and women in particular.

"Bobby's married," said Dane.

"Since when has that bothered a woman on the make?" asked Chase, his voice as sardonic as the hard line of his mouth.

"Nicole's not like that," said Dane simply.

"She's a woman, isn't she?"

Dane winced at the cynicism in his brother's words. "Nicole doesn't sleep around."

"Are we talking about Nicole, 'Pele,' or an alabaster saint?" asked Chase sarcastically.

"Yes," retorted Dane. "Pele is just a nickname Bobby's mother gave her when they met—goddess of the volcano."

Chase looked away and felt his hands balling into fists at the laughter and affection in Dane's voice. His brother was heading for disaster and didn't even know it. It was all Chase could do not to turn and hammer home a few truths about the inevitable relationship between women and betrayal into his naive younger brother's head.

"What does Janet think of this—dancer?" Chase asked tightly, substituting the word *dancer* at the last instant for the much coarser name he had in mind.

"She's Nicole's biggest fan," Dane assured him.

Chase's caustic curse was lost beneath a flurry of drumbeats. The illumination in the club went from dim to zero. Spotlights bloomed and focused in shades of gold on the small, raised stage.

Nicole Ballard saw the sudden sword's edge of light coming through the crack in the green velvet curtain and smiled encouragingly to the seven teenagers lined up in front of her. At her signal they turned and faced the closed curtain. She rested her hand for an instant on the shining chestnut hair of Sandi Wilcox, silently reassuring the nervous girl. She and her friend Judy had been practicing in secret for months, wanting to surprise their fathers. With a final gentle touch to soothe Sandi, Nicole left the stage, her bare feet making no noise on the floor.

Janet stood in the wings holding the hand of a small, almost frail girl with pale gray eyes and hair as black and shiny as volcanic glass. When Nicole approached, the little girl held out her free hand. Nicole took it and then waited with breath held, nearly as nervous as the girls on stage. The hula would tell a very old story of feasting and sly gods and shrewd men. The dance had been passed through countless generations of Hawaiians until it had lodged in the files of the university's ethnology department. Nicole had found the amusing dance, had reconstructed it with the help of Bobby's mother and had taught it to the children.

The girls wore neither shiny cellophane skirts nor authentic ti leaves for their dance. In keeping with Bobby's eccentric idea of true tradition, the girls' costumes were more Samoan than Hawaiian—the best available, rather than the most "authentic." Short, wraparound, silk, splashed with vivid flowers against a dark background, the skirts, which Polynesians called lavalavas, emphasized the grace of the body's movements rather than offering a rustling striptease with every swing of hip. Each girl wore a matching halter top, a hibiscus flower over her ear and a lei woven of fragrant native flowers.

Bobby had been quite firm about purple orchid leis. They did *not* constitute a modern enhancement of the "best available" tradition of Hawaii. They stank. They were not allowed past the front door. It was the same with the islands' famous steel guitar and ukulele music. No way. Never. Period. No matter how passionately the patrons pleaded or argued, the wailing, twanging music was forbidden within the Kipuka Club's carved wooden walls.

Nicole had always been grateful. Cellophane and steel guitars were not her favorite things. Orchids, however, did *not* stink. They were delicate, gorgeous, sensual and...not among the most fragrant of Hawaii's flowers. Yet she considered the beautiful orchids well lost if it meant retaining the crisp, exotic rhythms of bongo drums, Bobby's bass chants and the husky, eerie notes of the Bolivian panpipes that Bobby loved and played every time he could find someone else for the drums.

The driving, attention-getting rhythms of the drums changed beneath Bobby's hands into a more fluid beat. He began chanting softly, telling the story of the hula in liquid Hawaiian as the curtain parted to reveal the seven girls. There were muffled sounds of surprise from the audience when parents recognized their offspring beneath the colored lights.

Nicole smiled, knowing that hearing their names whispered through the audience was all the reward the girls needed. The audience's surprise was complete, and it would increase as the girls danced. They had worked hard. It showed in the unforced grace of their hands describing legends in the dusky room. The hula was slow, fluid, each motion a separate phrase in an unspoken language.

When the music ended the girls received enthusiastic applause from aunts, uncles, fathers, mothers and neighbors. Smiling, giggling, Sandi hurried off the stage and threw her arms around Janet.

"Did you see your dad?" asked Janet.

Sandi shook her head. "The lights were too bright. But I heard him. And I heard Uncle Chase laughing."

"Not at you, honey," Janet said quickly.

"Oh, I know that," she said, her voice confident. "He was teasing Daddy about something. I could tell. Honestly, they're worse than me and Mark."

Janet hid her smile as she bent and picked up Lisa. Around them, university students began filtering onto the stage. Nicole gave Sandi a quick hug, touched Lisa's cheek and looked questioningly at Janet.

"Are you staying?" asked Nicole.

Janet shook her head. "Dane will take you home. I've got to get Lisa to bed and finish the proposal."

"What is it this time?"

"Eden in Shades of Green."

Nicole tilted her head thoughtfully, then nodded. "That should be a welcome switch from their usual academic titles. I like it."

"I hope the Pacific Rim Foundation does, too. It will cost a bundle to do right. Did you know that no one has done a comprehensive, scientifically accurate botanical survey of these islands yet?" demanded Janet. "When you think that—"

A flurry of drumbeats tugged at Nicole. "Let me know if you want to send a few drawings with the proposal," she said hurriedly. "I've got some of Waimea Canyon that are just that—shades of green." She kissed Lisa quickly. "See you tomorrow, honey." She turned to Sandi and said, "You were beautiful. I'm going to be out of a job."

Sandi's smile was almost as bright as the spotlights bathing the stage.

Nicole took her place at the back of the raised wooden floor just as the curtain went up. In front of her were the advanced Polynesian dance students, who earned pocket money and learned audience skills working in the Kipuka Club on the weekends. Men and women alike wore colorful lavalavas wrapped low on their hips, and fragrant leis around their necks. Even though Nicole stood well out of the spotlights, the audience discovered her immediately. Murmurs of "Pele" rippled through the crowd.

Chase found himself leaning forward, straining to see the woman who dominated the stage even from the shadows. He saw nothing but a dark shape silhouetted by fire that twisted and shimmered with each liquid movement of her body. Then Chase realized that it wasn't fire he was seeing—it was hair the color of flames, a glorious fall of incandescent, red-gold strands. Her arms lifted sinuously, smooth golden flesh framed by the silken violence of her unbound hair.

Goddess of fire.

For a moment Chase was afraid he had spoken aloud. Then he realized that, even if he had, no one would have noticed. The men and women around him were intent upon the stage.

Bobby's deep bass chant and gently throbbing drums wove in and out of the dancers' motions as he pursued his eclectic idea of "traditional" entertainment. The result was an elemental synthesis of ancient and modern. At times Bobby would switch his narration from English to pidgin, or to a rhythmic combination of the two that was uniquely and humorously his own. The audience laughed as the dance and Bobby's chants told of men outwitting gods and one another. People clapped in time with the triumphs of men over the sea and watched in rapt attention as two lovers were tricked by a jealous spirit into throwing themselves into a lake of lava burning within Kilauea's black mouth.

Chase watched as intently as anyone in the audience, riveted by Nicole's graceful motions. He didn't notice the other dancers. For him, they simply didn't exist. There was nothing but the woman with fiery hair and golden skin. He leaned forward even more, trying to make out details of her appearance. It was impossible. She was too well concealed within her softly curling hip-length hair and the shadows at the back of the stage.

Gradually the rhythm of the drums changed from the stately dignity of the Hawaiian hula to the playful, sensual rhythms of Tahiti. One by one all of the dancers except Nicole stepped forward to display the few minutes of Tahitian dancing that each had chosen to perform. The movements were graceful, rapid and strenuous, calling for equal parts of coordination and strength. Bodies began to gleam like polished gold or mahogany, and the darkness resonated with the beat of drums.

The rhythm increased in both intricacy and speed, challenging the dancers to equal its driving presence. The men and women who couldn't maintain the pace drifted to the side of the stage and sat like participants at a feast, calling out encouragement to the remaining dancers. The number of dancers dwindled to five, then four, then two—Nicole and a Polynesian man, whose name was Sam Chu Lin. He was barely taller than Nicole's five feet, ten inches. Like her, Sam wore a short lavalava. Unlike her, that was all he wore. His superb physical conditioning showed in every rippling muscle of his body as he faced her, swaying provocatively, challengingly.

For the first time, Nicole stepped fully into the spotlight. Her hair blazed suddenly, vividly, drawing a low sound of surprise and pleasure from the audience. Her body swayed rhythmically as she answered the male dancer's challenge with movements that exactly echoed his. Bobby gave a short cry of encouragement and shifted the rhythm into an even more rapid pace. Sam answered with sinuous, repeated, powerful movements of his hips. The motions were as difficult to achieve as they were frankly sensual. With each intricate movement of his hips, Sam inched closer to Nicole's teasing, gleaming body.

Nicole didn't retreat. She moved her hips in a figure-eight motion that was so quick that the print of her lavalava seemed to run and blur. Her hair flew out as she turned her back suddenly to Sam, giving him an unobstructed view of her wildly moving yet perfectly disciplined hips. She smiled over her shoulder at him, and it was a smile as old as Eve, a feminine challenge as fiery as the flame-colored hair that enhanced each sensuous movement of her body.

Pulsing, driving rhythms poured out of the drums beneath Bobby's flying hands. Sam leaped into the air as Nicole turned to face him again. When he came down lightly on the stage, his urgently moving body was so close to hers that her hair licked over him like fire and clung to his gleaming skin. He smiled at her, an elemental male smile whose intent was as unmistakable as the potent motions of his body.

Nicole answered with a wild, impossible quickening of the dance.

Chase's breath came in with a thick sound and wedged in his throat. It became very clear to him that in Tahiti, dance was an erotic ritual in which both partners displayed their physical lures—strength, discipline, grace and a primal sensuality that was literally breathtaking to watch.

As the drumbeat thickened and increased yet again, Nicole and Sam danced toe to toe, their bodies moving so rapidly that individual motions were a blur. Sweat glittered on Sam's dark skin and gave Nicole's an almost iridescent quality. There was no sound but the rapid, primitive thunder of the drums and the soft thud of bare feet meeting wood with each shift of the dance. Sweat gathered in golden rivulets and ran from Sam's body as the beat increased relentlessly. His breath came in labored gasps as he fought to keep pace with Nicole's incandescent dance. But finally he could not. With a hoarse cry he dropped down among the dancers who were sitting on the stage.

Nicole never hesitated in her dance. With a provocative snap of her hips, she turned and held out her hands to Bobby as though inviting him to replace her spent partner. Bobby's answer was yet another quickening in the pounding beat of the drums. The rhythm swept through Nicole, exploding into passionate movements of her body that were both dance and something far older, as deeply rooted in the human psyche as life itself. Fiery hair flying, body gleaming, her smile flashing, Nicole gave herself wholly to the hot, sensual dance.

Bobby's hands became a dark blur over the drums, yet still he could not keep up with her. He held the violent rhythms at their peak for a long instant, then with a hoarse sound, he surrendered to the woman who burned wildly in the center of the stage. With a throaty, triumphant cry, she danced on alone, accompanied by only the wild beating of her heart and the audience calling "Pele! Pele!" as they celebrated her victory.

Suddenly Nicole was standing motionless within the pouring golden spotlights, her breasts rising and falling rapidly, her arms held out as though to an unseen lover, her skin shimmering with heat, her hair the red-gold of Pele's own burning lava fountains.

The room was plunged into darkness. The audience continued calling for Pele, but no one answered. After a time the lights came up and men and women settled back around their tables and began talking again. Even so, currents of excitement still rippled through the room where the fire goddess had danced.

Chase felt as though he were on fire himself. He was grateful that the light level in the room remained low, for his own savage arousal was all too apparent. He cursed his body silently, futilely, for its betrayal. The only thing that answered him was the hot drumming blood through his veins. With narrowed gray eyes, he looked at the faces of the other men in the room, wondering how many felt as he did. He saw a variety of expressions—pleasure, excitement, humor, appreciation—but nowhere did he see a reflection of his own violent response to the sensual dance.

His only consolation was that Dane, while he had obviously enjoyed Nicole's performance, had not been deeply aroused.

"Is it time to say 'I told you so'?" asked Dane smugly.

"Just what did you tell me, little brother?" asked Chase, his voice rough.

"That you've never seen anything like her."

Chase shrugged, then smiled sardonically. "Outside of a red-light district, no, I can't say as I have."

"Chase Wilcox, closet puritan," Dane said in disbelief. "Say it again, brother. I still don't believe it. Tahitian dancing is a little sexy, sure, but it's not smutty. Look around you. The Kipuka Club is rated P.G.''

Chase forced a smile onto his lips, knowing his brother was right. There were families gathered all through the supper club, enjoying the abundant food and good will that were the Kipuka's hallmark. If he had found Nicole's dance to be incredibly arousing, the problem was with him rather than with the dance itself. He'd seen Tahitian dance performed before—but not by anyone like that fire-haired goddess.

These men must be as blind as stones not to see the wildness in her, the hunger. And the heat. My God, the heat! On the heels of that thought came another, one that made Chase's mouth curl slightly beneath the thick black sheen of his mustache. *The women must be blind, too, or they'd grab their men whenever Pele came on stage and take off like bats out of an erupting volcano.*

"When does Nicole make her rounds of the tables?" asked Chase.

"Make her rounds?"

"Yeah. You know. Go to each table and smile and press the flesh and get tips stuffed into her lavalava."

Dane shook his head. "You've been keeping the wrong company. You keep acting like this is a strip joint and Nicole's some kind of exceptionally well-coordinated tart. If you try to stuff money in her lavalava, you'll lose your hand."

"I don't notice Janet dancing here," said Chase dryly.

"Try next Wednesday," shot back Dane. "That's amateur night. But if I catch your hands anywhere near her lavalava, I'll hire three men and break your arm!"

Chase tilted his head back and laughed, releasing some of the tension that had built so explosively in him. The sound of his laughter was contagious, making people nearby look around and smile at him for no better reason than their pleasure in hearing him.

"I'm glad to see you have enough sense to be jealous of Janet," said Chase.

"Just cautious," amended Dane. "Women fall into your hands like summer rain. Janet makes life very comfortable for me. I don't want her too close to your lethal charm. After fifteen years of staid married life, she might get itchy."

Like you're itchy? asked Chase silently. Aloud, he said, "Women never exactly avoided you. You're so damned civilized and elegant you're almost pretty."

Dane smiled widely. "Yeah. Ain't it grand?"

As long as it isn't Nicole chasing you, yes! There's no way you could have a very discreet, very meaningless affair with her and then go back to Janet a wiser man. But you don't know that and you aren't listening to what I'm trying to say. Listen, damn you!

Even as Chase silently urged Dane to open his ears, he conceded to himself that there wasn't much hope of words getting through. Except for Janet, Chase had never known Dane react to a woman the way he did to Nicole. If Chase had thought yelling at his brother—or hammering sense into his thick head—would work, he'd start yelling and hammering. But those approaches had never worked with Dane. He did things his own way, in his own time, and the devil take the hindmost.

No, words wouldn't do it. Action would. For that, Chase needed to know more about the woman who was so fascinating to his very married brother.

"Does Nicole do anything but dance?" asked Chase.

"Like what?" asked Dane, his eyes narrowing.

"Work for a living."

"There speaks a man who's never tried Tahitian dancing," retorted Dane. "Didn't you see Sam Chu Lin? He was sweating like a Turk in a sauna, and it wasn't because he's out of shape. Hell, if I had his muscles, I'd burn mine."

Chase made a noncommittal sound. His ice-gray glance roved the room restlessly, searching for a flash of fire and grace and supple strength. Pele. Nicole. By either name, a woman to match the burning mountain.

"She's an artist," said Dane.

Chase gave his brother a sidelong look, hardly able to believe what had just been said. "That's what all the, er, exotic dancers say."

"Yeah, but I'll bet none of them strut their stuff in a bona fide gallery."

The arch of Chase's left eyebrow rose in a silent question.

"Didn't I tell you? Nicole does line drawings and watercolors that are accurate enough to illustrate scientific texts and original enough to be sold as art." Dane signaled a passing waiter, pointed at the two empty beer bottles on the table, and returned his attention to Chase. "But you'll see that for yourself. She'll be working with you on *Islands of Life*."

"She's capable of scientific illustration?" asked Chase, trying to keep his voice from revealing his disbelief. Since the perfection of the 35mm camera, few artists had the inclination, the ability and the control required for meticulous recreations of nature such as Audubon had made famous.

"Did you see the *Volcano Portfolio* the observatory put out a year ago?" asked Dane.

Chase nodded.

"The illustrations were all Nicole's."

Chase thought of the talent, drive and discipline that were required for someone to perfect both a gift for drawing and the more physically challenging gift of dance. He remembered the drawings for the *Volcano Portfolio*. He had been struck at the time by the artist's ability to capture both the scientific facts of an erupting volcano and the more elusive emotional truth of a volcano's awesome reality.

A chill slowly condensed in Chase as he measured the clear pride and appreciation in his brother's blue eyes while he extolled Nicole's accomplishments. He sounded like a doting parent—or a man falling in love. *Christ. What chance does Janet stand against a woman like Nicole? Intelligence, grace and a fire that could burn a man to his soul. Pele incarnate.*

Hoping that he was wrong, afraid that he was not, Chase began to question his brother in earnest about Nicole Ballard. Everything Chase heard made the chill condensing in him colder, more numbing.

"She's great with kids," continued Dane, warming to his theme. "Takes them on long hikes nearly every weekend, back up in the kipukas on Kilauea's slopes where nobody else goes. Bobby's kids showed a batch of kipukas to her and it was love at first sight. Lisa follows her around like a gray-eyed shadow. Nicole's teaching her how to draw." The flow of words became a groan. "Oh hell, that was supposed to be a surprise. Forget I said anything."

"So Nicole dances and paints," said Chase with an easiness he didn't feel. *Great with kids, huh? Yeah, sure. Lynnette made a lot of noises about motherhood, too. You've picked a real winner, Dane. Just like your rock-stupid older brother. Now I've got to find a way to convince you before you make the worst mistake of your life. Like I did.* "Sounds like a hand-to-mouth way to make a living."

Dane shrugged. "She wasn't born lucky, like we were."

"Lucky as in rich?" suggested Chase dryly.

"Yeah. Nicole pays her bills and not much more. She's not losing any sleep over it, either. She likes her life the way it is."

Don't you believe it, little brother. She's setting up to clean your pockets right down to the lint in the seams.

"Well, I suppose her lovers take up the financial slack from time to time," said Chase, throwing a bill onto the waiter's tray and picking up an icy bottle of beer.

"Nope," Dane said confidently, grabbing a beer for himself. "No lovers, no live-ins, no 'friends,' no nothing. Everybody's sister and nobody's woman."

"Bull," said Chase succinctly, forgetting he had meant to be tactful.

"Same to you, buddy," retorted Dane. "I'm the one who knows her, remember? And I say she's alone."

Chase closed his eyes, concealing the sudden rage he knew would show in their gray depths. *Alone? Never. Without a man to share her fire, she'd burn herself to ash. But she really has you fooled, doesn't she?*

"How long have you known her?" asked Chase.

"Long enough. She's as unattached as they come, and it isn't for lack of offers."

"I'll bet," agreed Chase dryly. "I'll also bet that if she's turning men down, it's because they aren't rich enough. Scientists and university types aren't noted for the gold rolling out of their pockets. A woman like her is expensive."

"You're way off base," said Dane, an edge to his voice.

"I'll bet I'm not," Chase said softly. "I'll bet I can get your perfect Ms. Ballard in bed before the end of the month."

"Not even you, Chase. She hasn't dated since I've known her."

"How many rich men have tried her?"

There was a long, taut silence. Then Dane's hands relaxed from the fists they had formed. Almost curiously, he looked at his hard-faced older brother. "None that I know of," said Dane. "Why?"

"Like I said, there aren't many rich men around."

Dane took a long slow breath—long enough to count to ten. "Every woman isn't like Lynnette," he said firmly, "out for money and willing to do damn near anything to get it."

Chase shrugged and said, "The proof is in the pudding, little brother. You got lucky with Janet. A lifetime of luck. All you have to do is not screw it up." Then, before Dane could say anything, Chase pinned him with a pale crystalline glance. "Relax. If your Nicole is such a bloody perfect saint, then I'll be the first to apologize to you. And if not—" He smiled ferally. "Well, live and learn, right?"

Dane's lips stretched into a rather hard smile. "You're on, brother." He laughed softly. "Janet is going to love this. She's been wanting to go on a vacation without the kids. I'll set it up for July first, because you'll be paying off your lost bet by two weeks of babysitting!"

So Janet wants a second honeymoon, does she? thought Chase. *Or does she just want to get you away from that hot little goddess for awhile?*

"Win or lose, I'll take Sandi and Mark for two weeks this fall," said Chase coolly. "Janet could use the break. She's looking tired."

Or like a woman worried about keeping her thick-headed husband from making a fatal mistake.

"Oh, you'll lose," said Dane confidently. "Nicole's not like the women you're used to. You'll see."

Chase simply leaned back and smiled. Nicole Ballard, alias "Pele," was exactly like the women he was used to.

And he would prove it.

Chapter 2

The flower-splashed grounds of the Kamehameha family estate tumbled down to a black sand beach and the turquoise sea beyond. Paths wound softly among ohia and jacaranda, coral and rainbow shower trees. The first vivid rush of summer blossoms was still hidden within the living silence of the trees, waiting for just the right moment to come unwrapped in the sun. Then the buds would throw off their darkness and burn like colored torches against the intense green of the forest canopy. Even now the petals were swelling beneath their dark wrappings.

That was what Nicole wanted to capture in a sketch—the tender, terrifying moment when the bud first came apart and gave itself to the sun.

Nicole stopped suddenly and looked over her shoulder, thinking she had heard someone call her name. The path leading toward the big house was all but hidden by foliage. So were the small cottages that circled the house like eccentric moons. The cottages were very private and were reserved for members and friends of the sprawling Kamehameha family. Nicole lived in the cottage that was closest to the sea. She had lived there since she had discovered a very young, disheveled, defiant Benny Kamehameha standing at the edge of a frozen black lava river overlooking a kipuka halfway up Kilauea's rough slope. He had run away from home after his first day of kindergarten because he couldn't bear being teased about his limp by the other children.

Nicole had been working part-time at the volcano observatory long enough to have heard of the Kamehamehas and the Kipuka Club, so she knew where Benny belonged. She also knew that he wasn't ready to go home yet. She talked quietly with him, sketching as she talked, working quickly to catch the aura of anger and intelligence she had seen on his thin face as he stood and brooded over the green land falling away at his feet. When she finished, she talked him into walking back down the mountain with her.

Despite his limp, Benny had an ease with and understanding of the land that was uncanny. Nicole told him so, pointing out that none of the kids who had teased him could have matched his pace on that broken ground. By the time she returned him to his worried parents, Benny had been thoughtful rather than defiant. When she had given him the sketch of himself, standing like a prince on black lava ramparts, Benny had been transfixed. So had his parents. They had also been horrified to learn that Nicole was still living in a hotel, waiting for an apartment to become vacant in Hilo. They had decreed on the spot that she was to have her pick of the three vacant cottages within the Kamehameha estate and was to live there as long as she wished.

That had been more than three years before. Nicole had come to love the spacious, gently wild grounds of the estate and the tiny cottage that was tucked just up the hill from the beach. Most of the year, the cottage was private to the point of isolation, perfect for her temperament and artistic needs.

But not when school was out.

The sound came to Nicole again, a high cry like the wind rushing through a narrow lava canyon.

"Niiii-colllle. Waaaiiit."

A thin, wiry body catapulted down the path with an uneven gait that was surprisingly fast. A sketch pad and pencils were clutched in one of the child's hands.

"Slow down, Benny," she called. "I'm not going anywhere."

Barefoot, nut-brown, with a flashing smile that rarely failed to soothe Nicole's impatience at being interrupted, Benny was one of her favorites among the island children who gathered around her like clouds around a mountain whenever they spotted her alone.

"Picnic?" asked Benny, excitement making his black eyes shine with life.

"Not today, honey," said Nicole.

Benny's eyes shifted to her sketch pad. "Watch?"

"Quiet?" she retorted, smiling, enjoying the coded exchanges that Benny used, as though there weren't enough time in his young life for him to waste it on anything as mundane as speech.

Without another word Benny fell in line behind Nicole on the path. He knew the rules when she was working: The first time he interrupted Nicole was "free." Sometimes other interruptions were tolerated, particularly if they were very few and the questions concerned painting or the plants themselves. After that, an interruption had better mean something urgent, like Kilauea splitting a seam and pouring liquid fire over the face of the land. Anything less important, and the chatty child was invited to go talk to the honeycreepers flitting brightly through the trees five thousand feet up Mauna Loa. The rules had never bothered Benny as they did some of the other children. Silence came easily to him.

Nicole went to her favorite spot, a small lava prominence overlooking a crescent-shaped beach. At the edge of the sand, coconut palms swayed and dipped in the breeze like stately dancers. The ocean was alive with unimaginable, unnamed tones of blue and green. Surf smiled and then laughed whitely over black sand. It wasn't the Eden-like perfection of the beach that drew Nicole, however. It was the concentration of flowering trees that had been planted there by Bobby's grandmother.

All but the scarlet-blossomed ohia tree grew in other climates and continents, yet all of the trees seemed to reach a peak in the gentle Eden of Hawaii. Coral trees blazed with color, their clusters of flowers rising from each naked branch tip like a handful of flame. The shower tree was named for the fantastic cascades of blossoms that covered the branches. In other places, shower trees came in single colors—white or yellow or pink or pale orange. In Hawaii, the trees had cross-pollinated to become what the natives called a rainbow shower, a tree that produced flowers of all colors in soft-petaled rainbow drifts that had no equal on any continent.

Rising above the other trees was a cluster of jacarandas. With their smooth dark trunks, fernlike leaves and delicate lavender flowers, the jacarandas were Nicole's favorites. She loved to lie beneath the trees at the height of their bloom, to see sunlight glowing through pale purple blossoms, and to have sweet, spent petals swirl down around her in a fantastic amethyst snow. But that particular glory was in the future. Today the jacaranda branches were naked and gleaming in the moist air, the wood smooth except for buds swelling silently into the tropic sky.

Once, Nicole had thought of herself like that—a bud swelling in silence, waiting only for the right conditions to bloom. Once, but no longer. She had learned that the sensual flowering was a futile dream. The years from thirteen to seventeen had been a nightmare for her. Other girls had budded and bloomed all around her, while she had grown

tall and then taller still, with no more curves than a fence
post. Nor had she been pretty. Her light brown eyes, pale
skin and fiery hair did not go well with most color com-
binations. Other girls had boyfriends and admiring glances
and bathing suits that revealed a lush feminine flowering.
Nicole had simply kept on growing taller until she'd felt
like a red-headed clown on stilts.

Then her body had begun to change in a wild rush, as
though realizing that the blooming season was passing by.
She was too intelligent not to make the connection between increasing bra size and increasing masculine attention. Unfortunately, boys were no more interested in her
as a person than they had been before her breasts had
grown. After the novelty of being whistled at wore off, she
decided that round was as bad as flat—both left her feeling like a stranger in her own body. The boys who looked
at her now weren't interested in anything but getting their
hands on her at the earliest possible moment. When she
objected, they called her a tease, or worse.

Cynicism had come early to Nicole, and had stayed. She
learned to fend off blunt advances with the same breezy
humor that she had previously used to hide her hurt at
being ignored. Then she had met Ted. He had kept his
hands to himself. He had appeared interested in her
thoughts and dreams. Later, she'd realized that it was her
family's money that had attracted Ted, not herself. He
hadn't been a gentle lover. Her virginity had been an un-
welcome surprise. He had dumped a few state-of-the-art
sex manuals in her lap and told her to study up on what
men liked, there would be a test later. She had failed that
test, and others, as well.

Four years later, her father had gone bankrupt. Ted had
walked out. To prevent being judged for what he was—a
fortune hunter—he informed their mutual friends that the
marriage had been a disaster due entirely to the fact that
Nicole was a closet lesbian and refused even to have children.

Nicole hadn't waited around for the postmortems. She had fled as far as she could, as fast as she could, leaving behind girlish dreams and marital disaster alike. The instant she had stepped off the plane at Hilo, she had felt a sense of homecoming that had nearly overwhelmed her, as though the island itself had reached out to enfold her in a welcoming embrace. The island hadn't cared that she was too tall to be truly feminine, or that despite the outward promise of her body she was too cold to respond to a man. Hawaii had simply wrapped her in fragrance and warmth, asking nothing in return.

"Sad?"

The soft word penetrated Nicole's preoccupation with the past. She realized that she was standing with her sketch pad tucked under her arm, staring at nothing. Automatically her free hand went out to stroke the smooth black hair of the child who stood beside her.

"Mainland sad," she said huskily. "But I'm in Hawaii now."

"Always-always," said Benny quickly, repeating himself for emphasis.

"Yes, I'm staying," Nicole reassured him.

She settled lotus fashion onto an oversize chaise lounge. A simple wooden table stood within arm's reach to one side. The furniture had appeared in the stand of jacarandas the day after Bobby's mother had discovered Nicole propped awkwardly against a tree, spare pencils clamped in her teeth, frowning and sketching madly before the incoming afternoon rains veiled the trees in mist. She would have sat on the ground, but even the profusion of ferns couldn't blunt the hard edges of the lava beneath the green cloak of plants.

Benny settled just behind Nicole on the big chaise, making no more disturbance than a falling leaf. He positioned his own sketch pad and began to draw. There was no sound but that of the distant surf blending with birds calling from the ohia's highest branches. Nicole sketched her favorite jacaranda. Though it was tall, it was beautifully proportioned and somehow essentially feminine. Every time she saw it, she thought of the ancient legends in which women were turned into trees.

Today the jacaranda was reduced to its pure, naked lines. No profusion of amethyst flowers blurred the essential strength of the tree. No sighing, delicate, lacy leaves distracted from the endurance of the trunk itself. In this pause between cycles, the tree called to Nicole's intelligence as well as to her senses, reminding her that the jacaranda's lush flowering was made possible only by the strength and resilience of the trunk itself. Without that quiet power as a support, the buds pushing tightly from branch tips would never know the instant of blooming.

After a long time Nicole looked up from her sketch pad, stretched and realized from the sun's position that she had been working for several hours. At the edge of her concentration, she had been aware of Benny coming and going as quietly as a breeze, sketching with her, then roaming for a while before coming back and sketching some more. At ten, Benny had learned the kind of patience that some adults went a lifetime without knowing.

"Eat?"

The soft question came from the direction of a wildly overgrown path leading to the big house.

"Eat," agreed Nicole.

"Back."

There was a rustle of foliage, then the soft, uneven sounds of Benny running up the abandoned path. Soon he would be back, lugging a basket of food that would feed five people. The first few times Benny had appeared with food, Nicole had gone to the big house and protested that it wasn't necessary; she could certainly get her own lunch. The elder Mrs. Kamehameha—who refused to be called anything but Grandmother—had simply smiled and had continued sending huge lunches down to the beach whenever Benny appeared with a hopeful grin and an empty basket.

Nicole had finally realized that the Kamehameha family had adopted her, treating her like the daughters, nieces, aunts and mothers who came and went from the estate in numbers too great to count. The Kamehamehas would accept no money for rent or for any of the other less obvious things they did for Nicole. She repaid the family in the only way they would accept. She became one of them. She taught their children ancient and modern native dances, showed them a few basic drawing techniques and gave her own drawings to anyone who looked at one of them more than once.

And she danced in the Kipuka Club, unknowingly bringing to its small stage the same sensual yearnings that the Tahitian dances expressed so vividly.

"Picnic," announced Benny, popping out of one of the shortcuts he managed to find in even the most tangled, rugged places.

Nicole laughed, realizing that he had managed to finagle that most prized of things—a private picnic with the redheaded haole who the island children half believed was actually Pele incarnate.

"Picnic," she agreed.

Without regard for his sketches laid out on the chaise, Benny started to unload the basket, which was laden with food.

"Wait, you'll ruin your sketches," said Nicole, snatching up the sheets.

Benny's thin shoulders moved in a shrug. "Bad," he said, commenting on his sketches.

"Good," she countered firmly.

As Nicole spread out the sketches Benny had made of the jacaranda trees, she felt tiny, immaterial fingertips whisper up her spine. As always, there was something in each sketch that made the landscapes unreal. Sometimes it was a subtly oversized blossom. Sometimes it was a tree whose leaves were upside down. Sometimes it was the suggestion of a face in the clouds. Often it was something that couldn't be defined, as unique as the thin-faced boy who was now dividing fruit, bread and smoked chicken between two plates.

One sketch was stunning. It embodied an eerie, beautiful sense of being caught within a grove of maidens quivering on the point of becoming something they couldn't imagine. Like Nicole, Benny had sensed the essential femininity of the jacaranda trees. Unlike her, he had been able to translate his intuition into a unique vision of a time and a place where myth, man and nature were one and the same.

"Good-good-*good*," Nicole said, catching Benny's chin in her hand, holding him gently until his big black eyes met hers. "You have a gift, Benny. You see what no one else can, and then you capture that vision on paper."

"Not like your tree," he said, abandoning his one word discourse for the moment, telling her how important drawing was to him.

"Do you look like me?" she asked softly.

He laughed and gave her a look that reminded her that he was very much Bobby's son. "No-no-*no*."

"Then why should your work look like mine?" she asked reasonably.

Benny looked from his sketch to the tree, then from her sketch to the tree. "Different."

"Very much so. That's how it should be. I like your drawings. They make me see back into time. Eden. Paradise." She grinned suddenly. "Hawaii before haoles. No one else can make me see that. Only you."

The boy gave her a sudden, brilliant smile.

The memory of that smile stayed with Nicole all during the bus ride up the mountain. Usually she would go to the volcano observatory. She worked there as a research assistant whenever any of the scientists needed her. Actually, "research assistant" was a catchall title used to keep the bureaucracy happy. What she did defied pigeonholing. She organized projects for those scientists who couldn't organize their own wallets, much less something as complex as the logistics of getting men and materials in place for some of the elaborate experiments being conducted on the volcanoes. Sometimes she filed papers. Sometimes she typed them. Sometimes she poured coffee and watered plants.

And sometimes she went into Kilauea's fire pit and scooped scalding steam into containers for later analysis.

Always Nicole learned, soaking up the good-natured arguments around her, listening, asking questions of the more patient scientists. She had discovered that the more she knew about the mysterious, majestic volcanoes seething beneath her feet, the more depth her drawings took on.

Nicole got off the bus near the original volcano observatory, which was perched on the caldera rim, overlooking what once had been a lake of lava. The old frame house was preserved now as a historic site. Other than a few ferns and struggling bushes, there were no plants on the rim.

The path to the observatory was marked by occasional rock cairns and by the many feet that had worn off the original glossy finish of the pahoehoe lava that made up much of the caldera's floor. Nicole left the path and scrambled across a patch of rough aa lava, smiling to herself as she remembered how the Hawaiian names for various kinds of lava had been explained to her. Pahoehoe had the same easy-flowing, liquid sound to it as the lava itself. Aa lava, on the other hand, was rough and thick and sharp and thus had made its own name as the Hawaiians walked barefoot over it, saying "Ah-ah!"

Nicole still doubted the derivation of the names, but she loved the story. And she was grateful for the tough hiking shoes she wore. They looked rather startling contrasted with her flowered halter, as did the sturdy khaki shorts she used for hiking. Her hair was braided and pinned securely on top of her head, emphasizing the clean lines of her face.

After a few moments Nicole found a relatively comfortable perch on a mound of pahoehoe. The lava, which had once been thin and quick-flowing, had hardened into smooth billows and swirls with a nearly mirror-bright finish. Bracing her sketch pad on her knees, she began a study of the old house that brooded over the frozen lava lake. She had been meaning to complete her series on the house but something had always intervened. Now that Dane's brother had come to Hawaii to lend his name to the *Islands of Life* project, she knew that time to work on sketches simply for herself would become even more rare.

Not that she minded working on *Islands of Life*. She was in love with kipukas, survivors of past volcanic eruptions. Their endurance and beauty in the face of overwhelming odds had always fascinated her. It had been the same for the gradual colonization of life on cooled lava slopes. The grace and tenacity of returning life never failed to inspire her. She was looking forward to working with Dr. Chase Wilcox, a man who had made the study of volcanoes and emergent life his specialty. For a moment she wondered if Chase would be as funny and friendly as his brother, Dane. She hoped so. As long as Chase wasn't a womanizer, she'd be content.

It wasn't that she couldn't handle herself if he were on the make. She could. It was just that she would have to spend a lot of time out in the various, very isolated kipukas with him. If he were an octopus in drag, life would get tedious before he gave up and went hunting elsewhere. But she was confident he would give up. They all did, sooner or later. She just kept smiling and wisecracking and saying no. Even good old Fred had given up, eventually.

A shadow fell over her paper. Nicole looked up, blinked and decided that thinking of the devil was as effective as speaking of him. All six feet two inches of God's gift to Hawaiian women stood in front of her.

"Hello, Fred," she said absently, wondering for the hundredth time what women saw in him. His sunstreaked hair and wide blue eyes simply didn't raise a quiver in her. She took that as another sign of her innate frigidity. Fred Warren had set more hearts pounding on the island than anything except a massive eruption.

"Hi, babe. Saw you drawing and you looked lonely."

"I'm not," said Nicole cheerfully, and then changed the subject in the one way guaranteed to deflect a scientist—asking about his work. "She singing in harmony yet?" asked Nicole, referring to Kilauea's record of having harmonic tremors before most eruptions.

"Getting there. Quakes are coming in swarms, but they're not really lined up in a row yet. She's working on it, though. Getting hotter and readier by the second."

"Must have heard you got back from vacation."

"Miss me?" he said, showing Nicole a double row of perfect teeth.

"I died for you—didn't you get the funeral invitation?" Nicole asked, holding her head to one side as she considered whether to add a bit more shading along the north side of the house.

"You don't look dead," he said, frankly appreciating the healthy curves filling out Nicole's hiking clothes.

"Miracle drugs. You survive, it's a miracle." She put her hand on Fred's leg and pushed firmly. "You're gorgeous, but you aren't a historic monument yet. Move it, huh?"

"This better?" he asked, crowding against her knees, giving her a close-up of his brief hiking shorts and muscular thighs.

"Only if you shave your legs."

Fred laughed and backed up, shaking his head. "You dancing at the club tonight?"

She nodded.

"When are you going to do a solo in my bed?"

"Same as always—just as soon as you can dance or drum me right off the Kipuka Club's stage."

He groaned. "No fair. Even Bobby can't do that, and he's as strong as a mountain."

"Takes more than strength."

"Yeah? Like what?"

"Endurance. Finesse. Determination." She looked up at Fred suddenly. "And red hair."

"I'll dye it."

"A few pounds off wouldn't hurt," she agreed innocently.

Fred groaned and gave up. "See you tonight, babe."

"Yeah, but I won't see you."

"Why not?"

"Spotlights blind me."

"Ever heard of braille?" he asked.

"On your perfect body?" Nicole said, holding the back of her hand across her eyes as though overcome. "Be still my beating heart." She lowered her hand and changed the subject again. "Marcie wants to know if the hotshot pool for this month is closed."

"Marcie?"

"The new haole from Washington State. Ph.D. Seismologist. She's sure she can predict eruptions from the quake patterns better than anyone else."

"Marcie," muttered Fred, trying to place her. Every summer there was an influx of personnel ranging from visiting VIPs to graduate student gofers.

"Blonde," said Nicole. "Cleavage from chin to navel. Green eyes that only women ever notice."

"Oh, *that* Marcie." Fred smiled to himself. "So she wants to play, does she?"

"I don't know about that," said Nicole dryly, "but she does want to get some money into the hotshot pool."

"Thanks, babe. I'll, er, check her out for tremors."

Shaking her head, Nicole watched Fred stalk off over the lava in search of more willing game. She forgot about his relatively genial lechery as soon as her glance fell on the north side of the house again. Her sketch definitely needed more shading to catch the aura of age and weathering. She lifted her pencil and worked swiftly, losing herself once again.

Only the insistent cheeping of her watch alarm called her out of her concentration. She muttered a few words, sighed and shut off the alarm. If she hurried, she had just enough time to get home, shower and race to the Kipuka Club. She would miss the student performers, but she wasn't worried about them. They were all excellent dancers. They didn't need her to hold an audience's attention.

The bus was late. Nicole raced through her shower, pulled on her dance costume and ran out of the cottage without looking in the mirror. Her hair swirled around her like a warm cape. Too warm. If she hadn't liked the scent and the feel of her hair brushing against her skin, she would have cut off the long strands. But there was something delicious about her hair's softness and silky weight and the way it echoed every movement of her dance.

Why couldn't it have been black or brown or blond? she asked herself silently. *Because it's red,* came the swift reply—the words her mother had used every time Nicole had complained about her bright mop of hair.

Nicole slipped in the back door of the Kipuka Club just as the students began their final hula. From behind the stage, she couldn't see either the students or the musicians. She heard the exchange of chants between the dancers and knew that they were doing one of their more traditional numbers. She went to the small room backstage and pulled traditional wrist and ankle decorations from a drawer.

Just as Nicole bent over to pull on her softly clashing shell anklets, the drums began a rhythmic pulsing. She froze, sensing instantly that Bobby wasn't the drummer tonight. The sound was different. Cleaner. Quicker. More intense. Bobby was good, but the new drummer was extraordinary.

Anticipation bloomed silently in her as she pulled a ginger flower lei from the refrigerator. The cool petals made a wonderful contrast to the heat of her body. The flowers heightened the golden cast of her skin and deepened the fiery lights in her hair. The sunny color of the flowers on her lavalava and halter were repeated in the thick tassels of dried grass she carried in each hand. A cross between a long, soft brush and a small pompon with a handle, the grass tassels rustled and snapped with each hand motion, emphasizing and enhancing the rhythms of the dance.

Behind the curtain Nicole moved to the slow, sinuous rhythms of the hula, warming her body for the strenuous Tahitian dance to come. Instead of accompanying the dancers with a chant, Bobby was playing Bolivian panpipes, an instrument made by natives of the high Andes mountains of South America. The pure, husky sounds of the pipes tugged at Nicole's imagination. Bobby played two pipes at once, each pipe containing half a scale. Harmony was possible, but difficult. He was forced to move his mouth very quickly and blow in short, sharp spurts. The result was a ghostly staccato that evoked spirits chanting to one another across a bottomless mountain chasm.

Shivers of pleasure coursed over Nicole's skin as the primal drums and husky pipes called urgently to the dancers. She timed her entrance to coincide with the darkness that came at the climax of the hula. There wasn't enough light for her to see the drummer as she slipped onto the stage. All she could make out was the silhouette of a broad-shouldered, powerful man whose hair was even darker than the lightless stage. He could have been haole or Hawaiian, old or young or in between. After the fleeting impression of sheer size came an awareness of the contrasting delicacy of his fingertips smoothing a sensual, pulsing rhythm from the drums.

Each beat was echoed in Nicole's blood, in her rippling anticipation of the moment when she would turn and challenge the mysterious, powerful drummer on a stage empty of other dancers.

When the lights came up, Nicole's hair blazed from crown to hip as though each strand were truly made of fire. Murmurs of "Pele" raced through the audience. The panpipes unleashed a husky exuberant sound that was more electrifying than a shout. The drummer hesitated fractionally, then settled in with the assurance of a river of molten stone running swiftly down to a waiting sea. Nicole found herself almost impatient for the others to dance and be gone, leaving her and the drummer alone.

As the act progressed, the dancers came forward to challenge one another, then fell away one by one until only Sam was left to face Pele. The drums slowed to a languid, almost taunting rhythm that exactly echoed the lithe motions of Nicole's hips as she danced barefoot into the spotlight. Grass whispered and rustled rhythmically in her hands, underlining each fluid movement of her torso. The ginger lei swayed with her breasts, caressing her skin with its smooth, cool petals.

The rhythm changed subtly, picking up speed without losing either clarity or its oddly taunting quality. Nicole danced for a few moments with her back to the drummer, her hips gracefully swaying, before she turned the stage over to Sam with a flip of the thick grass tassels she held in her hands. The panpipes picked up the challenge, urging Sam to greater and greater exertions. He smiled and moved sinuously, quickly, with the muscular grace and potency possible only for a male dancer. Nicole copied his motions, smiling, her hands speaking teasingly to him with every rustle of grass, her hips easily keeping pace with his.

The drumbeat reached a peak, paused, then began again with redoubled speed. Sweat began to gleam on Sam's body, making him look like a polished wooden idol. He leaped up and came down closer to Nicole, his body speaking to her of the joys that would come to both of them when she stopped leading him on this endless chase.

She turned her back and danced, letting him see the grace and power of the hips that would never belong to him, for he was merely mortal, and Pele demanded something more of her lovers.

With a low cry, Sam jumped in front of Nicole again, trying to entice her to cede the contest and herself to him. At each beat, each rotation of his hips, he came closer to her, coaxing her senses with his display of strength and grace and sensuality.

Smoothly, heartlessly, the goddess Pele flicked her hips and picked up the pace in the same instant that the drummer did. For her the sensation of neither leading nor following the rhythm was extraordinary, as though drummer and dancer were one. Her eyes closed, her head tilted slightly back and she smiled like a woman held deep within her lover's arms.

Nicole didn't see Sam's eyes narrow in male response, nor did she see the sudden tension in the drummer's body as her sensual smile ripped through him. She did sense that the rhythm would change soon, becoming even faster, drumming Sam right off the stage. Even as the change came, she met it. Her body shimmered with life and sensual fire. Her hips described flashing, rhythmic arcs that were so quick that no individual motion could be seen. For a few moments Sam stayed with her; then he gave a hoarse cry of defeat and sank to the stage with the other vanquished dancers.

There was an instant of hush, like a missed heartbeat, as Nicole turned to face the unknown drummer. Suddenly staccato rhythms poured out of the drums with renewed speed and potency, taunting her. Her torso moved in response, matching each beat, answering the male challenge with feminine grace and endurance. And then she surpassed the wild drumbeats with a sinuous surge that brought cries of "Pele!" from the audience. The sounds were echoed by the panpipes' husky, primitive harmonies.

Without hesitation the drummer equaled the increased speed of the dance. Nicole had known intuitively that he would. A sense of inevitability, of uncanny rightness, burst softly inside her. She forgot the audience, forgot the stage, forgot everything but the dance, giving herself entirely to the primal rhythms called forth by the stranger's hard, skillful hands. She was no longer Nicole Ballard, haole. She was Pele, alive among the volcano's fires, calling for a lover to equal her dance.

And the drummer answered.

Thunder poured from the drums, a wild breaking wave of sound composed of individual beats. Each pulse was met by a sinuous motion of Nicole's body, as though the drummer were the heart beating within her. The panpipes issued short notes, their panting cries telling of human endurance stretched to its breaking point. The beat increased yet again, and she became an incandescent shimmer of motion and color, a fire goddess burning within the sensual incantations of the drums. She was Pele, inexhaustible; and the drummer was her more-than-human lover.

Suddenly Nicole sensed the fatigue in her own body, the almost subliminal blurring of the clean motions of the dance. It was the same for the sound of the drums, a slurring of perfection. She knew then that she didn't want to dance the drummer off the stage. He deserved better, for he had brought out the best in her in a way no one else ever had. He had called out both the discipline and the wildness, letting her burn within his primal rhythms.

Now those rhythms were faltering.

With a soft cry she turned to face the drummer, holding out her hands in triumph and supplication. Even as she turned, the drumming peaked. Simultaneously the stage lights vanished, leaving drummer and dancer equally unvanquished, sharing the victorious midnight.

Into the silence and darkness came applause like storm waves breaking. Nicole didn't hear anything but her own heart, her own breath. She felt a man's arms come around her, felt her own hands sliding over his hot skin and then their mouths joined as though they were lovers separated since the beginning of time.

Chapter 3

Chase pulled Nicole against his body in the same instant that his lips took hers. There was no hesitation, no awkwardness, simply a hot certainty that this woman belonged in his arms. Her mouth was as exciting as her dance had been. The taste of her exploded through him, shattering his normal control. His arms tightened around her, bending her like a bow beneath the elemental power of his embrace. His tongue claimed her mouth fully, penetrating deeply, repeatedly, until he heard her moan and felt the sweet pain of her nails scoring his naked back.

Dimly he heard Bobby's hissed warning.

Only the knowledge that the stage lights would be coming back on allowed Chase to end the wild kiss. Even then he kept holding Nicole, letting the sensual perfume of crushed flowers and warm woman mingle with the heady taste of her on his tongue. His heart beat as rapidly as though it were a drum beneath his hands, and his blood was a hot rush through his even hotter body. He had never wanted a woman the way he wanted Nicole at that moment. He hadn't even known such wanting was possible. It was all he could do not to pull her down onto the floor and bury his hard, aching flesh deep within her untamed body.

With a wrench, Chase moved away from Nicole just as the lights came on. Beneath the flaming veil of her hair, his long fingers held her wrist so tightly that he felt the bones move beneath her flesh. He tried to ease his grip, but could not. An irrational part of him was afraid that she would flick her hips tauntingly at him and disappear into the island's legendary past like her namesake goddess, leaving him to burn alone.

Nicole felt his heat and power radiating through her skin as she bowed to the cheering audience. She sensed his determination to hold on to her in the callused fingers locked around her wrist. She was a tall woman, and her body was conditioned by the rigors of dance and of hiking through Hawaii's wild country, yet she knew that if she fought his grasp she wouldn't be able to free herself.

Nor did she really want to. Not yet. The siren cry of the dance was still hot within her, making her tremble. Or it could have been the taste of him that was sending waves of sensation through her, the taste and the memory of how it had felt to be bent like a bow beneath the power of his sensual demands, to feel him shudder in return as her nails tested the strength of his naked back.

Bobby walked out on stage, gestured toward the hard-faced man holding on to Nicole, and said softly, "Welcome to Hawaii, brother." The big Hawaiian turned toward the audience, put his hand on Chase's shoulder and said, "Dr. Chase Wilcox, vulcanologist, biologist and the hottest damn drummer I've ever heard!"

The audience cheered wildly. For the first time since Chase had seen Nicole's flame-colored hair at the back of the stage, he was truly aware of the people beyond the footlights. His mouth curved up at one corner as he realized how close he had come to giving them a spectacle they would never have forgotten. While he bowed in acknowledgment of the audience's fervor, he felt Nicole tugging discreetly against his hard grasp. He didn't slacken his grip on her. Her skin felt too good against his palm for him to risk her escaping.

Nicole glanced sideways at the tall man who held her wrist. Other than an unmistakable stamp of masculinity, there was no expression on his face. She was having a difficult time accepting that this skilled, passionate drummer was the renowned scientist Dr. Wilcox, the man who had been selected to author a big, glossy book about Hawaii's kipukas.

With a curiosity she couldn't conceal, Nicole weighed the man standing so close beside her. Chase had dense black hair and surprising, ice-gray eyes quickened by intelligence and cynicism in equal measure. His face was angular, tanned, defined by twin black slashes of eyebrow and a midnight gleam of mustache above a mouth whose heat and sensuality she had already discovered. His shoulders were broad and heavily muscled. His naked chest was darkened by sun, thatched with curling, glossy black hair and gleaming with sweat. A black lavalava rode low on his lean hips. The cloth's scarlet flowers only heightened the almost overwhelming effect of male potency. Everything about him was hard, from the line of his chin to his fingers which were clamped just short of pain around her wrist.

The curtains closed, freeing the stage from scrutiny. Bobby stretched his arms and briskly rubbed lips nearly numbed by the panpipes' demands. A huge dark hand reached out and wrapped itself around the back of Nicole's head. Automatically she braced her free hand on his thick shoulder and came up on tiptoe to receive his congratulatory kiss.

"Hell of a dance, Pele," said Bobby, smiling down at her from his greater height. "Damn near set the place on fire."

Chase's eyes narrowed as he sensed the ease implicit in Nicole's automatic acceptance of Bobby's embrace. That kind of mutual physical assurance came only from being siblings, longtime friends—or lovers. Logic dictated the latter. It wasn't a logic that Chase enjoyed. The flare of anger he felt was as irrational as his refusal to let go of Nicole's wrist, and he knew it. He also knew that unless Bobby's big hand released the silken fire of Nicole's hair soon, Chase would be tempted to make an issue of it. His normal discipline and control had vanished in the primal thunder of drums and the sensual heat of the dance.

"You should thank Dr. Wilcox, not me," Nicole said, kissing Bobby's cheek in return. "His drumming was as primitive and wild as Kilauea itself."

"Call me Chase," he said, smiling rather thinly at Nicole. "Anyone who dances like you do can't be long on formality."

Bobby let go of Nicole and gave Chase a swift, speculative look.

"Just how do I dance?" asked Nicole neutrally.

"Like Eden on fire," he said, his eyes narrowed, intense.

"Sounds dangerous," she retorted, her smile almost as narrow as his eyes.

"Yes," agreed Chase. "And sexy. Untamed. Goddess of the unleashed volcano. But you know that already. That's why you dance."

Nicole laughed. "Thank you—I think. But my name is Nicole, not Pele. Other than my hair," she added matter-of-factly, "there's nothing startling or unusual about me."

Chase gave Bobby a sidelong glance. "Does she expect me to believe that?" asked Chase.

"You bet, haole. Why not? She believes it."

Chase's eyes went from the fiery crown of Nicole's head, past her supple, womanly curves and down to her bare, golden-brown feet. He had seen more conventionally beautiful women. He himself preferred women who were small and delicate rather than tall and firmly curving. At least, he had always thought he preferred fragile and petite. Yet he had never felt anything quite so exciting as Nicole arched against him, fitting him perfectly, soft matched with hard, heat with hunger.

And she had known it.

Dangerous. Sexy. Untamed, thought Chase grimly. *But not for long. You've met your match, Pele. You'll burn in my arms, not Dane's. You won't even know that you've lost your chance at a rich husband until it's too late.*

"Did you get your stuff moved in?" asked Bobby.

Chase pulled his attention from Nicole's flushed, moist lips long enough to realize what Bobby was talking about. "Yes. Thanks. The cottage is perfect. Your mother was a bit difficult, though."

"Talked your arm off?" asked Bobby, smiling.

"Stubborn. Refused to accept cash, credit or traveler's checks."

Bobby's laugh rumbled like a sleepy volcano. "We don't charge rent to family."

Chase's mouth softened into a whimsical smile. "Bobby, even if you checked all the way back to the Garden of Eden, I doubt you'd find any blood relationship between us."

"So? You need a transfusion or something?" When Chase would have objected further, Bobby added, "Ask Nicole about blood and family. She's lived with us for years." He clapped Chase on the shoulder. "Talk to you later," Bobby said, and disappeared through the curtains into the seething conversations that were the Kipuka Club's hallmark.

Chase looked at Nicole measuringly, more certain than ever that he had been right. She and Bobby were lovers or had been in the past. It hadn't stuck, though, or she wouldn't be hunting Dane. Perhaps Bobby hadn't been wealthy enough, or perhaps his wife had dug in and fought

for her man until Nicole had shrugged and gone looking
for easier prey.

Pity Janet isn't a fighter, thought Chase. *But she isn't.
She's too gentle to fight. If Dane wanted a divorce, she
would give it to him even though it broke her heart. Besides, what woman could measure up to Pele in a fight, in
a bed or anywhere else? Any way I look at it, Janet loses,
unless I can get Nicole in my bed and out of Dane's hair.
And after that kiss, I don't think it should be too hard.*

Belatedly Chase realized that Nicole had said something to him. "What?" he asked.

Nicole's wrist tugged against his encircling fingers. "You
have something of mine," she pointed out reasonably.

"This?" he asked, smiling and holding up her wrist as
though he had just discovered it attached to his fingers.

She put her left wrist alongside. "Must be. It's a perfect match with my other one. See?"

"Perfect indeed," he murmured, running his fingertip
from wrist to elbow along first one of her arms and then
the other. He saw the visible shiver of her response and his
breath shortened again. "It's hard to find such perfection," he said, looking into her eyes.

For a moment Chase forgot what he had been saying—
Nicole's eyes were a startlingly pure gold in the light slanting from the stage wings. The color was as vivid and as
unexpected as the silky blaze of her hair. "Very hard," he
said huskily. "But I'm feeling generous tonight. I'll give
your wrist back if you'll use it to have a drink with me."

Normally Nicole would have turned aside the invitation
with a smile and a humorous excuse, but there was nothing normal about tonight. There hadn't been since the
moment she had heard Chase's fingers stroking the drums,
calling forth a sensual resonance that still quivered deep
within her. He was a stranger, yet during the dance she had
felt as though she had always known him, always searched
for him, always yearned toward the instant in time when

he came to her out of the darkness and wrapped his power and his hunger around her.

"I—" Nicole forced herself to look away from the clear, crystal depths of his eyes. She couldn't think when Chase looked at her like that. She could only feel and what she felt was a sense of fire and rightness that would have frightened her if her mind had been working at all. "All right," she said, her voice almost as husky as his. Then she realized that she must still look hot and disheveled from the wild dance. "I'll shower and meet you back here in ten minutes."

"It takes longer than that to get to the Kamehameha estate and back," pointed out Chase, not letting go of Nicole's wrist.

"There's a shower backstage here."

"Big enough for two?"

Chase felt the instant of stiffness that went through Nicole and cursed himself for a fool. Just because she was in the business of selling herself to the highest bidder didn't mean that she was easy or even cheap. Coming on to her like a boy who had just discovered a built-in Erector Set wasn't the way to make her want him more than she wanted Dane. Dane had always been smooth and civilized, handsome and elegant.

"Sorry," murmured Chase. He released Nicole's wrist reluctantly, letting his fingertips slide across her palm. "I'm hot and sweaty and must smell like old socks, but I'll wait my turn."

Nicole closed her eyes for an instant, savoring the sweet brush of his fingers, regretting the reflexive stiffening that had come to her at his half-serious, wholly sensual invitation. "You don't smell like old socks," she said in a low voice.

"No?"

"No."

Chase smiled slowly, relieved that she wasn't going to make him pay for rushing her. "How do I smell?" he asked teasingly.

"Like a man who enjoys the strength of his own body."

Chase's eyes widened. He had been expecting a saucy double entendre or outright flattery. Nicole's honesty and perceptiveness surprised him. "Do you?" he asked as she turned away and walked into the wings.

"Do I what?"

"Enjoy the strength of a man's body."

There were long moments of silence. Chase heard Nicole's footsteps retreating and then a faint husky murmur that could have been the word *once* or *tonight* or both together. But that didn't make sense, so he assumed that he had heard incorrectly. He called out again, his voice low and resonant.

There was no answer except the vague rush of water against glass as Nicole turned on the shower. She coiled her hair on top of her head, wrapped a towel around it and stepped into the warm water. With her eyes closed she stood beneath the pulsing spray, enjoying the rhythmic slide of water over her body. When her skin felt cool and sleek to the touch, she stepped out of the shower, dried herself and went to the long cupboard where Bobby kept a supply of lavalavas of various sizes. She picked out an emerald-green cloth with black orchids and a matching black halter. After a moment's hesitation, she pulled out an indigo lavalava that looked like it would fit Chase's lean hips. She left the cloth draped conspicuously on the sink.

It took just a few moments more for her to weave her hair into an elegant mass that added defiant inches to her height. Once she had chosen the style simply because it kept men at a distance. She had discovered that there were few things men liked less than a woman who was taller than they were. But tonight she wasn't worried about height or sensual distance. She wore the hairstyle because it was cool, and Hawaii was always warm. Besides, even if she wore heels, Chase would still be taller than she was.

From her purse Nicole took a small vial of perfume whose fragrance had haunted her since she had first discovered it a year before. The scent was like a breeze whispering from a rain-swept tropical garden—delicate, tantalizing, quintessentially feminine—all the things that Nicole felt she lacked as a woman. As a last touch, Nicole picked up two slender ivory chopsticks that had tassels made of strings of tiny golden bells. Once the chopsticks were anchored securely in the coils of her hair, the bells shimmered and chimed sweetly with every movement of her head. The sounds reminded her of the past Christmas, when the Kamehameha family had given her the beautiful hair ornaments.

"Your turn," said Nicole, brushing past Chase in the semidarkness behind the stage. "I'll be at Dane's table."

The fleeting caress of soft skin, the elusive fragrance, the delicate whispering of bells exploded silently in Chase's senses. For an instant he was too stunned to move. Then he spun and opened the bathroom door with a jerk, angry at himself for being taken off guard yet again by Nicole's compelling sensuality.

My hat's off to you, little brother, thought Chase grimly as he turned the shower on full. And cold. *How you've held out this long is more than I can imagine. Even for Janet.*

Chase didn't linger in the icy shower. He had no intention of leaving Dane within reach of Nicole's fire for an instant longer than necessary. Ignoring the lavalava Nicole had laid out, Chase wrapped a towel around his hips and retrieved his own clothes from Bobby's office, where he had exchanged them earlier for the lavalava he had worn on stage. His slacks were black cotton and his shirt was the same icy gray as his eyes. He kicked into a pair of black beach walkers, settled his damply curling hair with a few impatient swipes of a comb and stalked out to rescue Dane.

Chase was just in time to see Nicole leave a table full of laughing, appreciative men and go to Dane. Rage flickered through Chase as his brother stood and enveloped Nicole in a hug.

"They're going to pass a law against you," said Dane, shaking his head as he released Nicole. "Whew! I still don't believe it."

"Blame it on your brother," retorted Nicole, smiling.

"Yeah, he plays a mean set of drums," agreed Dane. "How are you getting home?"

"If she needs a ride, I'll take care of it," said Chase coolly, stepping between his brother and Nicole.

Dane knew Chase well enough to recognize the hostility beneath the words. He gave his older brother an odd look, shrugged, and said, "Fine."

"Where's Janet?" asked Chase bluntly.

"Working on the proposal," said Dane.

"Maybe she could use some help."

"I'm staying out of her hair," Dane said, smiling. "What more could she ask?"

"Moral support?" suggested Chase, his voice both soft and cold.

"What's eating you?" asked Dane in exasperation. "You know Janet—all she wants when she's working is peace and quiet. Hell, I'm the same way. The last thing she needs is me hovering over her asking if I can help every five minutes. She's had enough trouble with this proposal as it is. Now that school is out, the kids are always underfoot."

Chase said nothing, but he wondered if the proposal was taking so long because Janet was spending more time worrying about her husband and a certain redheaded temptress than she was about grant language and sponsors. Rather grimly, Chase congratulated himself on arriving in Hawaii just in time to keep his brother from making a fool of himself.

"Hey, babe, that was one hot dance!"

The voice came from halfway across the room. The distance was closed rapidly as Fred towed a very buxom blonde through the crowd toward Dane's table. Though small, the woman could hardly have been described as petite—certainly not from the waist up.

"Hello, Fred," said Dane, smiling wryly as he took in the blonde. "Is this your latest entry into the haole summer sweepstakes?"

Fred grinned. "This is Dr. Marsha Sumner. Seismologist. You can see why—she walks through a room and everything quivers." He winked broadly at the blonde, who wasn't the least ruffled by the teasing. "Marcie, meet Dane Wilcox, Nicole Ballard and Dr. Wilcox."

"Chase," he corrected, holding out his hand. "It's a pleasure, Dr. Sumner. I saw the article you did for *Scientific American*. Very impressive."

Marcie smiled. "From you, that's praise indeed. And call me Marcie."

"Marcie," murmured Chase, releasing her hand slowly.

Nicole watched the introduction and found herself wondering how the blonde would look in a luau pit with an apple in her mouth. Then Nicole reined in her baseless irritation and smiled at the other woman, reminding herself that it wasn't Marcie's fault that she was eight inches shorter than herself and therefore infinitely more feminine in the eyes of men.

Be honest, Nicole told herself bitingly. *You wouldn't care if Marcie sent every man in the room into a frenzy— as long as Chase wasn't one of them.*

"Hi, Marcie," said Nicole. "Did Fred initiate you into the hotshot pool?"

Marcie gave Fred a sideways glance out of very green eyes. "Did he ever," she murmured. Then she looked at Nicole again. "You know, when I met you last week I couldn't believe that you were Pele. No offense.'' Marcie shrugged. "You just didn't come on like a professional hula dancer. But tonight—whew! Bet they registered that performance on every seismograph from here to the mainland.''

"It was Chase," said Nicole, glancing at the tall man beside her. "He added something extra.''

Marcie looked at Chase with frank appreciation. "I'll just bet you did. You're enough to start harmonic tremors in granite. Speaking of which," said Marcie, turning back to Fred, "have you seen the paper from four to six P.M.? Swarms of the sweetest little shakers you'd ever want to see. The mountain's warming up, no doubt about it.''

Fred looked unconvinced. "Maybe, babe. Maybe. Remind me to show you some of the paper from last September. She shimmied and she shook, and she looked like she was going to come in six kinds of harmony. No juice though. Not even any decent moans. Same thing happened later. I think the old fissure zone is plugged solid and Pele's going to show us a few new tricks.''

A man at the next table overheard the discussion and offered his opinion as to the size and disposition of the magma pool that enlivened Kilauea's heart. Fred and Marcie turned toward him and were soon lost in a three-cornered argument that rapidly escalated to other tables, becoming the kind of scientific free-for-all that was the Kipuka Club's major attraction for its varied clientele.

Chase listened to the voices raised in eager, insistent, sometimes belligerent conversation just a few feet away. He smiled and shook his head. "And to think you left home to get away from scientific disputes," he said to Dane.

Dane smiled crookedly. "And I promptly married a botanist who has a flair for writing grant proposals. Talk about being able to line up arguments in support of your position! Janet in action is awesome." He looked at Nicole. "Mom and Dad are both physicists. Used to drive me crazy with their arguments. I mean, how the hell can an intelligent human being get hot under the collar about particles of maybe-matter so small that they can be mathematically proven to exist only when they move backward in time?" Dane looked down at the table. "On the other hand, maybe that's what happened to my beer," he said thoughtfully.

"It moved backward in time?" asked Nicole, trying not to laugh.

"Yeah. All the way to Prohibition." He looked mournfully at the empty bottle.

A waiter materialized in response to Chase's signal—three fingers and a bottle of beer held over his head. Nicole sat down gratefully, feeling almost light-headed from the long workday and the strenuous, exhilarating dance. The waiter returned with three beers, plus a large pitcher of water and a glass that he set in front of Nicole.

"Thanks, Pete," said Nicole, smiling up at the young waiter. "You just saved my life."

Pete flashed her a pleased, appreciative smile that made Chase shift restlessly.

Nicole poured a glass of water and drank it with swift, delicate greed. Chase watched each motion of her throat, the dark pink flick of her tongue licking up stray drops and the smooth golden gleam of her breasts curving above the black halter as she sighed her pleasure at having her thirst slaked. Hunger swept through him, an almost violent need to touch Nicole, hold her, know again the wild sweetness of her taste in his mouth.

"What?" Chase responded absently, aware that Dane had asked him a question.

"I just wanted to be sure you could spare the two weeks," Dane said, his voice smooth and smug. He had been worried by the currents of sensuality flowing between his brother and Nicole during the dance. It wasn't the loss of a bet that upset Dane; it was the knowledge that Chase had used up more than his share of women since his divorce. He was the wrong man for a woman to give her heart to, especially a woman whose heart had been as badly bruised as Nicole's. Dane had had an urge to take her aside after the dance and warn her that Chase was way out of her depth. But once off the stage, she had treated Chase just as she treated most men—pleasantly and aloofly, like a family cat greeting a guest.

"What two weeks?" asked Chase.

"When you take Mark and Sandi," explained Dane.

Chase's head snapped around as he gave Dane his full attention. "Counting chickens?" he asked dryly.

Dane just smiled.

"What chickens?" asked Nicole.

"Chase and I have a bet," said Dane. "When he loses, he takes the kids while Janet and I go on vacation."

"Oh." Nicole sensed the emotions that seethed just beneath Chase's careful exterior. She turned toward him and impulsively rested her hand on his lower arm. "I know how busy you must be, and Dane's kids can be a handful. Not to mention Lisa." Nicole smiled at the thought of the shy and stubborn child who had Chase's gray eyes. "Don't worry. If you lose, I'll help out. They love picnics in the kipukas."

The affection Nicole felt for the children showed in her voice and in the smile that came and went like the flicker of flame in a wind. Chase's expression settled into grim lines as he saw Dane's pleased response. Chase knew from bitter personal experience that the second fastest way to a father's heart was to seem interested in his children.

You don't miss a trick, do you, Pele? If Dane hasn't gotten the message your body is sending out, you can always make a fuss over his kids. Chase grimaced. That was exactly what his last girlfriend had done. She had oohed and cooed over every snapshot of Lisa. But the instant it had become clear that the child, rather than a handful of pictures, was going to live with Chase, the girlfriend had wished him luck and vanished to find another rich fool whose only responsibilities lay with his stockbroker. *Lures and lies. But some of those lures are damned irresistible,* he admitted, looking at the smooth, elegant fingers resting on the tanned skin just above his wrist.

Nicole realized that she had left her hand too long on Chase's hard forearm. With Dane or Bobby, it wouldn't have mattered. They were married, and friends. Chase was not. He was something new, something entirely unknown. Touching him made her…restless. Being touched by him made heat race through her. The feeling was both intriguing and upsetting. She knew from past experience with her husband that she wasn't a sensual woman. At best, sex with Ted had been an uncomfortable event for her. At worst, it had been painful.

And it was her fault. Her very experienced husband had made that clear to her on the night he had left her and moved in with a petite divorcée who had enough money to keep him in the style to which he had become accustomed. The divorcée was also a skilled, responsive lover. Nicole, on the other hand, was neither skilled nor responsive in bed, as Ted had pointed out on more than one occasion.

Other than your hair, there's not one damned thing hot about you. You're a walking example of fraud in packaging.

Ted's cruel words still echoed in Nicole's mind on those nights when being alone became loneliness, when her youthful dream of a loving partnership with a man became a nightmare of emptiness too painful to bear. The rational part of her mind didn't doubt the truth of her husband's summation of her womanhood. Ted, after all, had been an acknowledged connoisseur of women.

Yet a part of Nicole had always hoped and dreamed that with the right man she would respond. With the right man, she would know the heat of passion and the peace of companionship. With the right man, she would be able to share herself mind and body, and share his mind and body in return. With the right man.

And it felt so very right with Chase.

It had felt right since the first instant she had heard the drums speak beneath his hands. The single kiss on the darkened stage still sang in her blood, urging her to touch him again, to know again the fierce perfection of being in his arms. Instinct told her that the act of love with Chase wouldn't be painful or humiliating. She sensed that as surely as she had sensed the shifts in his drumming the instant before they had actually occurred. There was an elemental rapport between her and Chase that defied rational explanation. He was right for her. She knew it. She was right for him.

Did he know it?

Chase sensed that Nicole was watching him. He turned and caught her speculative amber gaze. In that instant he wanted to draw her close and kiss her until they were both breathless, but he knew that the time and the place were wrong. Seduction was accomplished better in privacy than in the genial, almost familial, and certainly loud atmosphere of the Kipuka Club on a Saturday night. Too many people—and one of them was Dane. Chase didn't need his younger brother overseeing every detail of male advance and female retreat with amusement in his eyes.

Chase found himself reaching for Nicole's water glass instead of for her lips. He needed to touch something that had touched her, to be closer to her in some primitive, indefinable way. The knowledge that she had held the glass, that her mouth had touched it, that the water had slid caressingly over her tongue, combined to make the glass irresistible to him.

"May I?" he murmured, picking up the glass without taking his eyes from hers.

Wordlessly, Nicole nodded. The delicate sounds of golden bells pierced the blur of surrounding conversation. The sweet music sank into Chase like tiny, sensual claws, pricking him into full physical awareness. He poured a clear stream of water into the glass, put his lips on the rim where hers had so recently lingered, and drank. He knew that she was watching him as intently as he had watched her. The knowledge was a sudden thickening of the blood in his veins, a heavy beat of desire swelling.

Dane took a swallow of beer and set down the bottle with a thump. "I know you're going to accuse me of hedging my bets," he said, looking apologetically at Chase, "but I'm going to have to impose on you for a ride home. No hurry, though. I've got some table-hopping to do."

Chase shot his younger brother a jaundiced look. "Something wrong with your car?"

"Janet thought she'd be able to come here later, so I caught a ride in on the bus. But she called while you were on stage and told me it's slow going for her tonight. I was going to bum a ride with Nicole—"

"Sure," she interrupted, smiling wryly. "There's always room for one more on the Hilo bus."

"Car's on the fritz again, huh?" asked Dane, both sympathy and amusement in his voice.

"How did you guess?" she said, her voice dry.

Dane grinned. "Psychic. That and the fact that your car is old enough to vote."

"But far too stupid," retorted Nicole. "It doesn't know first from third."

"Told you the transmission was going," said Dane, giving Chase a sideways glance.

With a stifled curse, Chase accepted the inevitable. The only consolation was that he and Nicole both lived on the Kamehameha estate. It was logical to drop off Dane first, which would leave them alone. Finally. The night wouldn't be an entire disaster in the seduction department.

What's the rush? he asked himself bitingly. *You've got until the end of the month.*

There was no answer but the heavy beat of his own blood. He wanted her. Now. Right now. Even though he knew it wasn't going to happen tonight, probably not for many nights, that didn't still the hot rush of desire focusing in him.

Dane, Chase asked silently, *how in hell did you hold out this long?*

It was a question that Chase was still asking after Dane had pulled himself out of the low-slung passenger seat of Chase's rented sports car and had vanished into his own house.

"Care to try for more comfortable quarters?" asked Chase, looking over his shoulder at Nicole. Against his wishes, she had insisted on taking the cramped rear seat, which was more a luggage compartment than anything else.

Nicole's mouth turned down at one corner at the thought of struggling out of the back seat beneath Chase's very interested gaze. Suddenly the back seemed more spacious than the front. In the passenger seat she would be practically on top of Chase. He was a big man even in normal surroundings. In the intimate confinement of the car, he was huge. It was more than simple size, though. She had ridden in sports cars with Bobby, who was truly a giant, and had never felt the sense of risk and sensual alertness that was simmering in her blood now.

Chase waited, sensing that Nicole was suddenly wary of him in a very female way. She looked very female, too, like a particularly lush piece of amber nestled in black velvet folds. Fragrant amber. In the soft, humid darkness, her scent whispered to his senses, telling him that a living woman was only inches away from his touch. He wondered if, like amber, she would generate electricity when rubbed with silk.

Nicole brushed stray tendrils of hair away from her mouth and flinched inwardly as she saw the slight smile beneath Chase's smooth mustache. She had no doubt that she looked like two pounds of hamburger stuffed into a one-pound bag. For the nth time in her life, she wished that she had been born into a more delicate body.

"Not much help for it, is there?" muttered Nicole.

Chase got out of the car and walked around to the passenger side. With real pleasure he held out his hand as he watched Nicole's supple body uncoil from the confining back seat. Most of the women he had known would have looked awkward scrambling out of the Porsche's tiny compartment, but Nicole's dance-trained body had both strength and grace. Even when he tugged her forward unexpectedly, pulling her off balance into his arms, she caught herself with a speed that would have done credit to a cat.

And she felt exquisite pressed against him, a resilient warmth that went from throat to toe. As his arms closed around her, he found himself wondering why he had always thought he preferred small women. What a waste. No matter how close a man of his size held a tiny woman, part of him always went begging. Not with Nicole, though. She filled his arms just as she filled his senses. Completely.

"Chase—" said Nicole, seeing his head tilt toward hers, a warm shadow closing out the sky.

"Shhhh," he murmured, nuzzling her lips. "I just realized that all my life I've wanted to kiss a tall woman wearing moonlight and fragile golden bells."

Chapter 4

The memory of that kiss was still on Nicole's lips three days later as she led the way along an unmarked path that ended in a small kipuka. When Chase had kissed her, she had been infused again with a sense of rightness. He hadn't been put off by her size or the subtle hesitations that came from her fear of not pleasing him. He had taken her mouth smoothly, hotly, completely, as though it were his by right. Frissons of warmth had shivered through her as they had the first moment she had heard the drum speak beneath his hard and caressing hands.

She hadn't been experienced enough to know that the tiny tremors singing throughout her body were delicate harbingers of the possibility of deep passion. She had only known that she felt sleek and soft and very feminine held against Chase's powerful body.

A passing car had reminded them that they were standing locked together beneath a streetlight in front of Dane's house. Chase's eyes had been narrowed, nearly silver, and he had released her very reluctantly. Once out of his arms,

Nicole had become uneasy. She told herself that at a rational level she barely knew Chase. At a deeper, irrational, level she was sure that she had always known him. The contrast between the two feelings was unnerving, like walking across a barely congealed flow of lava and sensing heat welling up beneath the ground, telling of the seething, barely contained molten rock just below the cool surface of reality.

When Chase had parked his car at the Kamehameha estate, Nicole had smiled, whispered her thanks for the ride and slipped off into the darkness of the overgrown trails before he could touch her again. She had seen Chase at the observatory the next day while she was talking with Dr. Vic about the landscape she had done for his wife's birthday. Dr. Vic had been delighted by the jacaranda tree. He had given Nicole a resounding kiss on her cheek and a check that she had argued was too much by half. He had ignored her, turning away to call out to Chase. When she'd turned around, too, Chase had looked at her with something close to anger and contempt in his eyes. In the next instant the look was gone. He was smiling, shaking Dr. Vic's hand and inviting Nicole to have a cup of coffee with him.

Chase had taken her to dinner at the Kipuka Club the following night. Once there they had quickly been surrounded by her admirers and his colleagues. Other than giving her lingering looks that made her heart beat erratically, Chase had done nothing to increase the sensual tension between them. Nicole had been grateful. She needed some assurance that he felt the same sense of rightness that she did when they were together, a rightness that was based on far more than their mutual physical attraction. She needed to know more about Chase in a rational way as well as in the instinctive, almost overwhelming way that only he had ever made her experience.

When Chase had suggested that Nicole show him a few of her favorite kipukas so that they could begin selecting the ones that would be featured in *Islands of Life*, Nicole had been delighted. There were so many personal questions she wanted to ask Chase, but it was impossible to ask even one when they were surrounded by observatory personnel wanting to talk to Dr. Wilcox. She needed time alone with Chase. She needed to reassure herself that he was real, that she hadn't dreamed him up from the depths of her own need and that he wanted to know her on as many levels as she wanted to know him.

A glance over her shoulder assured Nicole that Chase was having no trouble following her. The trail was little more than a memorized series of twists and turns across a portion of Kilauea's rough slope. The volcano itself wasn't steep-sided. Hawaii's volcanoes were shaped like gently convex shields, unlike the steep, cone-shaped volcanoes of California, Italy or Japan. But repeated lava flows, especially of the thicker aa lava, lay like massive, carelessly thrown ropes across the Hawaiian landscape. Chunks of congealed lava that once had floated on liquid rivers of stone were now frozen in place, sharp corners sticking out every which way, ready to snag the unwary traveler.

There was little foliage on the particular stretch of the trail that Nicole and Chase walked over. The lava flow was largely pahoehoe, whose smooth, nearly mirror-finish surface resisted being broken down so that seeds and roots could find places to take hold. The trail showed as a slightly dull thread twisting over the shiny surface of the land. The black lava reflected the misty tropical sunlight, redoubling the heat.

Sweat gathered on Nicole's forehead and in the shadowed valley between her breasts. She didn't really notice. Between Tahitian dancing and many hours spent climbing black lava slopes, she was accustomed to her own body. To her, perspiration was simply the way bodies tried to cool themselves in Hawaii's moist, enveloping warmth.

Chase watched the deceptively slim legs ahead of him. Nicole was hiking across the rough land at a pace that would have left a lot of men gasping and looking for a place to sit in the shade. He sensed that she wasn't trying to challenge him by walking him into the ground, nor was she even trying to show off her own lithe body. The pace was her normal one. It showed in the regularity of her breathing and the grace of her walk. The implicit promise of feminine endurance and flexibility made his breath shorten as he thought of the sensual possibilities.

How the hell can a woman look sexy in sawed-off hiking shoes, ragged khaki shorts and a faded halter top with frayed ties? Chase asked himself half whimsically, half savagely.

The only answer was the elegant, elliptical motions of Nicole's hips as she walked up the trail.

Rather grimly Chase brought his attention back to the shadowy trail. As a field geologist, he was accustomed to rough-country hiking, but Kilauea's slopes had some rather special traps for the inattentive. Sometimes ground that looked perfectly solid turned out to be a thin roof left by a fast-moving stream of molten lava long ago. Sometimes the ground was an even thinner bubble of congealed lava surrounding nothing more substantial than air. If a foot broke through the roof, the hiker stood a good chance of collecting everything from a few cuts to a broken ankle.

Yet despite its inherent dangers, Chase enjoyed hiking Kilauea. The landscape was magnificent, an austere testament to the living force of the earth itself.

"Have you ever seen Pele's hair?" asked Nicole, stopping next to a particularly shiny formation of pahoehoe.

"A few nights ago," said Chase, looking at the braided red blaze that was almost concealed beneath the white scarf that Nicole wore gypsy style on her head. "It was beautiful. Like fire."

Nicole met the compliment with a quick, almost shy smile, trying at the same time not to hear her former husband's words: *The only thing hot about you is your hair.*

"I meant a kind of volcanic rock that's called Pele's hair," she explained, bending down and pointing to a small hole. Inside was something that looked like a flattened tangle of silver-gold hairs. "Look in the pukas—the holes."

Chase squatted on his heels next to Nicole and touched the shining hairs with a gentle fingertip, careful not to disturb their fragile beauty. "No," he said. "I haven't seen this outside a specimen drawer or the pages of a geology text. It's a miracle that something this delicate can come from such a violent thing as the earth splitting and bleeding molten stone."

For a moment Chase looked beyond the shining hairs to the unusually clear sky. Against the horizon, the massive, gentle, smoothly curving slope of Mauna Loa far overshadowed Kilauea's smaller mass. As he measured the high volcano, his eyes were unfocused yet clear, the gaze of a man seeing something within his mind.

"What are you thinking about?" asked Nicole softly, needing to know something more about Chase than his desire for her. Other men had desired her—or, to be precise, her body—but she had never wanted them in return, never wanted to explore them mind and body. She wondered what it was about Chase that made him seem so different to her, and she wondered if asking him questions would somehow let her answer the only important one: *Could she trust herself to him?*

Chase gestured toward the smooth, brooding mass of Mauna Loa. When he spoke his voice was husky, slow, as though he were thinking aloud. "Did you know that if you measure Mauna Loa from its base, it's the biggest mountain on earth?"

"But—" began Nicole, remembering that Mauna Loa wasn't even fourteen thousand feet high, and Mount Everest was twice that.

"Mauna Loa's true base," continued Chase, pinning her with his clear gray eyes, "is three miles below sea level. Its crown is more than thirteen thousand feet above sea level. Nearly thirty thousand feet total. Taller than Everest. As for mass, Mauna Loa makes up ten thousand cubic miles of the island of Hawaii. Kilauea is little more than a swelling on the big volcano's side, and the other companion volcanoes on Hawaii are eroding away even as we talk. But Mauna Loa is still alive, still growing, the reigning queen of Earth.''

Chase looked away from Nicole's amber eyes to the indigo curve of Mauna Loa. "The only mountain we know that's bigger than Mauna Loa is called Olympus Mons. It's on Mars. Olympus Mons is fifteen miles high. It, too, is a volcano. So far as we know, it's extinct and has been for millions and millions of years. What we see now is the eroded remains of an incredible, once-living mountain whose base would have stretched from Los Angeles to San Francisco.''

Chase fell silent, trying to imagine what it would have been like to see Olympus Mons erupt, to see a mountain fifteen miles high spewing immense rivers of fire while the surface of Mars itself trembled and swayed. Did vapor form on the volcano's slopes, condensing into rain that ran in boiling torrents seven miles straight down to an empty ocean? Or had there been water on the surface of Mars then, clouds and streams and rivers, even life swimming in a doomed sea?

In the silence that followed Chase's words, Nicole closed her eyes and tried to visualize a mountain nearly eighty thousand feet high and four hundred miles across at the base. *What would it be like to stand on the lip of its awesome crater and see Mars spread out below like a painting done in infinite tones of rust?*

And then she heard Chase's deep voice say, "I'd sell my soul to have seen that mountain erupt. I'd sell my future for a chance to stand on its slopes even now.'' Then he stood abruptly, with a sound that could have been a laugh. "But I was born far too late for the eruption and too soon for the exploration. I'll be dead long before man stands on any part of Mars."

The buried yearning in Chase's voice made emotion thicken in Nicole's throat. She wished suddenly that she could give Chase his impossible desire, could see his face as he stood on a mountain fifteen miles high and saw an alien planet spread at his feet.

"You have Hawaii," Nicole said, her voice husky, intense. "It's not as high as Olympus Mons, but it's alive. You can hear its breath in the deep volcanic fissures, feel its warmth, sense its heartbeat beneath your feet. And sometimes you can see Hawaii's blood pouring out, setting fire to everything, even stone."

Chase looked into Nicole's golden eyes and saw himself reflected, his own buried dreams and sad acceptance of what could not be. *I'll never stand on Mars. I will, however, stand on a living mountain with the goddess of the volcano at my side. I'm standing there now, and she is here, burning, making me burn.*

"Yes," he said deeply, "I have Hawaii and Pele is my guide. What more could any man ask?"

Silently the answer came to him: he could ask to trust his guide. *Oh, but you can,* he assured himself sardonically. *You can trust her to be like other women, selfish to the core. Hawaiians worshiped Pele, but they didn't love her. No fools, those men. They knew that a woman's heart is fickle.*

"How much farther is the kipuka?" asked Chase briskly, breaking the intimacy of the moment when he had believed that he saw his dreams reflected in a woman's eyes.

"Twenty minutes, maybe a bit more."

Chase looked dubiously over the rumpled, furrowed landscape. There was nothing there that he could see but lava, lava and more lava.

"It's there," she assured him. "See what looks like a tiny smudge of green on the far side of that lava flow?" she asked, pointing across the black land. "Those are the tops of ohia trees."

"You're hallucinating," Chase said flatly.

Nicole laughed and set out across the volcano-sculpted landscape again. She walked until she came to a broad, congealed stream of rough lava. It was a tough scramble up and across, which was why she rarely came to this particular kipuka. She scraped her palm, grazed her leg and picked up a few other small wounds before she stood on the far edge of the flow and looked down into an improbable swatch of green surrounded on all sides by more recent lava flows that were largely naked of plant life.

Less than ten acres in extent, the kipuka was an island of survival dating from a lava flow that was many decades old. On the uphill side of the kipuka, a slight irregularity in the land had divided the lava flow. It had combined again on the downhill side, clearly separating the kipuka from the rest of the devastated land. While the remainder of the green countryside had been inundated with molten stone, these few acres had been saved.

Ohia trees grew in tall profusion, bearing the first scarlet flowers of summer among their graceful branches. Ferns in more shapes and heights and kinds than Nicole could name crowded over the hard rocks, sending slender fronds toward the life-giving sun. Every growing space from ground level to treetop was taken up by some form of plant. The explosion of life was all the more startling for the empty land surrounding it.

Sensing Chase beside her, Nicole turned toward him. He was studying the lush greenery with a bemused expression that made her wish that she dared to take out her sketch pad and draw him.

"I've seen all kinds of freak survivals from volcanic eruptions," said Chase slowly. "Trees standing while others only inches away were blown to splinters; flowers blooming where nothing had any right to survive at all; the tracks of mice that had burrowed out from under a blan-

ket of hot ash. All unexpected. Freaks of fate. But kipukas are normal in Hawaii, not freaks. They're the
inevitable result of lava rivers flowing slowly over slop-
ing, uneven land.'' He laughed. ''And having said that,
I've got to admit that it still looks like magic to me.''

''Yes,'' murmured Nicole. ''It's as though Pele couldn't
bear to burn all of life while she was building her island
home, so she saved a few places and plants that were
special to her.''

Chase pulled a notebook from his backpack and began
making cryptic entries about the height, width and kind of
lava flow. Nicole retrieved her own sketchbook, flipped to
the back, and began to draw. The lines she made with a
black pen were as intense and unflinching as the face of the
man looking into the miraculous Eden enclosed by a destroyed land. She worked quickly, almost furtively, not
wanting to share the sketch with anyone yet, even Chase.
Especially Chase.

After a time he asked without looking up, ''Is there a
path into the kipuka?''

''Not that I know of,'' said Nicole, putting away the
sketch hastily. ''I went partway around the perimeter once.
It's pretty much the same as here. At least waist-high aa
lava, uneven and sharp as the day it was made.''

Chase grunted, stowed his notebook and scrambled
down into the kipuka. He turned at the bottom and held
out his arms to help Nicole. She was grateful for his
strength bracing her as chunks of lava crumbled and
turned unexpectedly beneath her feet. His hands closed
around her waist as he lifted her and set her down on the
kipuka's more even footing.

''Thanks,'' said Nicole, her voice too tight, almost
breathless. She hadn't expected to be picked up so easily.
She thought of herself as substantial, not petite. The feeling of relative smallness was both sensually intriguing and
mentally unnerving, as though reality had shifted subtly,
changing her perspective of herself and the world.

Chase looked down into Nicole's startled golden-brown eyes, wondering what had surprised her. The question faded because no answer could be nearly as interesting as the feel of her supple flesh inside the circle of his hands. He flexed his fingers slightly, testing the resilience of her body.

"You know," he murmured, shifting his glance from her eyes to her slightly parted lips, "I'm finally beginning to understand why men throughout history have paid a lot to have dancers for their mistresses."

Nicole's normally quick wit deserted her, reducing her to a one-word question. "Why?"

"You feel good," he said simply, closing Nicole's wide eyes with a gentle kiss on each lid. "God," he muttered, flexing his fingers again, more deeply. "That's a lie. You feel incredible. You make a man wonder what it would be like to—"

Chase managed to rein in his words, but not his thoughts. *What will it be like to have all of you wrapped around me, moving with me, wanting it as much as I do? I wouldn't have to worry about crushing you or frightening you or being too big for you. You'd fit me like a hot satin glove.*

The sudden dilation of Chase's pupils was the first outward sign of the direction of his thoughts. The second was the heavy beat of his pulse beneath the tanned skin of his neck. The third was unmistakable, pressing hotly against Nicole as he pulled her hard into his arms.

"Chase?"

"Don't talk," he said in a thick voice. "Just kiss me. It's not enough, not nearly enough, but—"

As he took her mouth, his arms tightened as they had on the darkened stage, bending her supple body like a bow, arching her into him with a force that would have been painful if she hadn't come to him willingly. He knew that he should slow down, that this was the first, rather than the last, stage of seduction, but when her mouth opened beneath his probing tongue, he shuddered and thrust deeply into her, wanting all of her. Here. Now.

Part of Chase wondered at his own lack of control when it came to Nicole, but most of him cared only for the sweet feel of her against his body. She was resilient and warm and so soft that he groaned from the depth of his hunger for her. With barely restrained urgency his mouth moved over her face and neck and smooth, naked shoulders. Lips and tongue traced the small marks his teeth had left.

The combination of caresses that were both hard and soft, consuming her, was like nothing Nicole had ever known. Nor had she expected a man to tremble at the delicate touch of her teeth on his jaw as Chase did when she returned the wild, biting kisses he was giving to her. The salty taste and slightly rough texture of his cheek expanded through her senses, making her wonder how many other tastes and textures he had for her to discover. The thought of all the possibilities made her breath catch. She had never felt quite like this before—hungry to know all of a man in every way she could.

The sudden tightening of Nicole's body was felt by Chase as though it were his own. He found her mouth in a fierce kiss as his hands slid down her spine, cupped her firm buttocks and rocked her against his thighs. Her shudder of response was as exciting as the tiny sound she made at the back of her throat when his hungry flesh stroked her softness slowly, again and again, silently promising her both passion and release. With each motion of his hips, his tongue moved over hers, claiming her mouth. The deep kiss continued while his hands peeled away her halter, leaving her half-naked.

Automatically Nicole's hands came up to cover herself. Chase was surprised by the defensive gesture, for she had been as involved in the passionate love play as he had. Then he remembered that he was supposed to be doing just that—playing. This was supposed to be prelude, not culmination. Yet he barely had enough control left not to take her down onto the rough ground and to hell with cuts and bruises. His own lack of control shocked him, cooling the unexpected, raging fires of his passion as nothing else could have.

"You're right," he said, his voice almost harsh. "This isn't the time or the place. Turn around."

When Nicole obeyed, Chase replaced her halter with deliberate motions, first waiting patiently for her to remove her hands from her breasts. She stood, trembling, as he fastened both ties very carefully. She took an uneven breath, wanting to tell him that she hadn't meant to stop him, that she had covered herself without thinking, because her husband had nearly always hurt her sensitive breasts in his attempts to force a response from her.

And that had been only the beginning of the hurting.

She wanted to tell Chase about it, but she couldn't. The words simply wouldn't come to her lips. She was too ashamed of her past failures as a woman to stand in the brilliant sunlight and discuss them with the first man she had ever really wanted. The thought of saying something that intimate all but paralyzed her. Numbly, silently, she waited for the angry male words and gestures that had always come when she had failed her husband sexually.

Chase felt the stiffness of Nicole's body as he put his hands on her shoulders. Silently he cursed himself again for his baffling lack of control with her. He had seduced enough women to know how it was done—and how it wasn't. It wasn't done on a bed of prickly ferns and lava sharp enough to cut to the bone. It also wasn't done by letting things get out of hand to the point that both people were frustrated and angry when the lovemaking stopped short of its goal.

Great going, hotshot, he congratulated himself sardonically. *You've just nominated yourself for the Rutting Jackass of the Year award.*

"Sorry," he murmured, brushing his lips across the soft skin at the nape of Nicole's neck. "Are you okay?"

For a moment she couldn't believe that either the gentle caress or the quiet words had happened. Her breath came out in a long, ragged sigh. Wordlessly she nodded.

Chase turned Nicole around, saw that she wasn't angry and felt relief spread through him. The relief was as uncharacteristic as the all but uncontrollable passion had been. Since his divorce he had chosen sophisticated, superficial, and sexually satisfying relationships with women. Except for returning the physical pleasure women gave to him, Chase hadn't been concerned with their emotions. Nor had the women been concerned with his. By and large the arrangements had worked well enough for his purposes. Until now. The magic of the redheaded witch's body had brought him to the point of eruption with only a few kisses.

Remember what you're here for, Chase told himself. *You're here for Dane, not for a quickie in the underbrush. And if you keep coming on to Nicole like you've never had a woman, she's going to decide that gentleman Dane looks like a better deal—wife and all.*

Abruptly Chase turned away from Nicole. "Has anyone done a formal survey of this kipuka's biota?" he asked, his voice normal. Controlled.

For a moment there was no answer. Chase fought the impulse to turn around and look for emotions on Nicole's face. He shouldn't care whether she was happy or sad, relieved or tight with need. He knew that she had wanted him, but not to the point of losing her head as he almost had. It was up to him to raise the level of her need until she was like Kilauea on the eve of eruption, trembling on the brink of a hot, mindless release that only he could give her. Afterward he would go to Dane, tell his brother that he had lost the bet, and—

And then?

There was no answer to Chase's silent question except the heavy beating of his heart when he remembered how it had felt to press himself against Nicole's disarming softness.

"No one has done a truly disciplined study," said Nicole, looking at the broad line of Chase's shoulders silhouetted against the kipuka's foliage. "Not here. Mauna Loa's kipukas are better known though. Especially Puaulu."

When Chase pulled out his notebook again and began writing, Nicole felt the remainder of her tension drain away. For a moment, while his back was turned, he had seemed angry with her. Now he was focused on the work at hand. She could understand that and accept it without feeling slighted. She was the same way when she danced or painted; she used every bit of her concentration.

"Spell Puaulu, would you?" asked Chase, frowning. "I'm even less used to the Hawaiian language than I am to shield volcanoes."

Smiling, Nicole spelled the word. Then she asked, "What kind of country are you used to?"

"Cone volcanoes. I've been working on Mount Saint Helens since a few months before the first major eruption."

Chase looked up from the notebook long enough to estimate the size of the larger trees in the kipuka. His eyes were clear, nearly transparent, with hints of blue and silver condensed around the pupil.

"Where did you live before that?" asked Nicole.

"Iceland. I worked on the Heimaey Island volcano, with time out for Surtsey Island and for the huge fissure fields on Iceland itself." Chase's pen paused over the page for a moment before he resumed talking. "At first it was enough just to study the violence of the eruptions. There's nothing as exciting as feeling the earth shudder like a ship in a storm, hearing a sound greater than any thunder breaking over you. And then the fire. It's unbelievable, like being in on the birth of the world. And, in a way, that's exactly what it is. Birth. Without volcanoes, a lot of earth's land simply wouldn't exist."

"Or water?" asked Nicole softly, remembering fragments of conversations overheard in the observatory. "Although it seems impossible that the oceans could have come from cooled volcanic gases."

Chase looked up from his notebook, pleased that she understood something about the volcanoes that had always fascinated him. If present theories were correct, volcanoes were literally the fountainhead of Eden. "It's true, though," he said. "Volcanoes are immense, complex chemical factories. Even the air we breathe probably came from beneath the crust of the earth. As if that weren't enough, volcanoes make wonderful evolutionary laboratories."

"How?" asked Nicole, curious about the paradox of new kinds of life resulting from the fiery devastation of volcanic eruption.

"In many ways, Hawaii is truly Eden. The islands' isolation from other land masses has allowed life to develop here in forms that are unlike any others anywhere else on earth," explained Chase, looking at the lush vegetation growing up out of the dark lava. "Plant seeds that came here from the mainland didn't have to fight animals in order to survive, simply because there were no animals in the beginning. A seed can be carried on the wind or float in currents or be carried in a bird's body. Animals—other than the smallest insects—can't."

Chase paused over an entry in his notebook, crossed it out and went on speaking as he wrote. "Once a plant seed survived and took root here, it changed. The plant had been adapted to an environment that was thick with competing forms of life. Hawaii was different. There wasn't anything but bare rock waiting to be covered." He looked up again, watching the kipuka's varied greenery shift beneath the wind. "It's estimated that the seventeen hundred flowering plants the islands have today are the result of less than three hundred ancestral colonists."

Gray eyes searched the boundary between lava and life, black and green. "If we were above four thousand feet, this kipuka would be alive with the songs of honeycreepers. But their ancestral finch colonist wasn't immune to avian malaria or pox. When European man arrived with his barnyard animals, and mosquitoes hatched from ships' water barrels, most native birds died. The mosquito introduced couldn't survive above four thousand feet, or you'd have lost all of Hawaii's endemic birds. You may still lose them. There are other species of mosquitoes that can survive high altitudes. So far, they haven't found their way to the islands. They will, though. There's world enough and time. And men are careless of their Edens."

As Chase's notebook snapped shut, Nicole sensed the emotion underlying his neutral tone. "That's why you agreed to do *Islands of Life*, isn't it? You're afraid that Eden is living on borrowed time."

"I *know* that Eden is living on borrowed time," Chase said, looking at Nicole with gray eyes that had seen too many things lost before they had even really been found. "And yes, that's why I'm here. I knew that this would be my only chance to see landscapes and life-forms that exist nowhere else on earth. Hawaii is proof that life bows to no odds. And that doesn't always mean 'nature red in tooth and claw,'" he added. "This was a gentle Eden. Most Hawaiian plants have neither thorns nor poisons to discourage browsers. Not even bad smells."

Chase gestured to the kipuka's lush greenness, so startling against the dark lava surrounding it. "The Hawaiian islands are gigantic kipukas, havens for land creatures in the midst of a huge, hostile environment we call the sea. Because there was no need to be aggressive—to fight for water or sun or survival—plants, and even animals, changed to meet the softer circumstances of this Eden. Birds and insects that came here on the wing often lost the ability to fly, for taking to the air is useful only when the alternative is being eaten. Otherwise, especially for birds, flying is a waste of calories that could be better used for making babies. No land predators meant that flight wasn't required, even for nesting in trees."

"Eden without snakes," murmured Nicole, remembering that none of the islands had native snakes.

"Except for the two-legged variety," agreed Chase dryly.

"Ah well," she said, smiling wistfully, "nothing is perfect. I'll take Eden however I can get it."

Including a rich Adam? thought Chase. Though he said nothing aloud, his mouth flattened at the reminder of what Nicole was really after. When she listened to him so attentively, asked intelligent questions and watched him with her brilliant, nearly gold eyes as though he were the only man on earth, it was hard to remember that he was supposed to be the predator in Eden, not Pele.

Chase looked away from Nicole's clear eyes, toward the wind-ruffled kipuka. Scents drifted up to him from exotic shrubs and flowers that were like nothing he had ever seen outside of botanical gardens. Yet nothing smelled as good as the woman who stood so close that he could hear her quiet, even breathing and sense the warmth of her skin.

There was a flower the size of Chase's palm growing near the edge of the kipuka. Its pale petals were smooth and creamy. He stroked the blossom from crown to cup, making the flower shiver and sway as though at a gentle breath of wind. The petals were exquisitely soft, fragrant, flawless. Yet he recently had caressed a woman's lips that were more smooth, more perfect, and he knew those sensual textures would be surpassed by the hidden places of her body. The thought of exploring her satin depths rippled through him like a swarm of tiny, harmonic earthquakes.

"Do you know of any endangered biota here, in this kipuka?" asked Chase, his voice too husky to be quite normal, his fingertip caressing the softly shivering flower.

"No," said Nicole, unable to look away from the intensely feminine flower being so lightly stroked by Chase. Then, silently, she added, *Just me. Do I count? I'm on the edge of losing my heart to a man I've known only a few days. That qualifies me as endangered, doesn't it? No? Then how about stupid?*

But Nicole couldn't even convince herself of that. It didn't feel stupid to trust Chase. It felt inevitable, like the plants losing their thorns and poisons when they found Eden. When she was with him, she discovered new things about herself. Each time he touched her, the discoveries multiplied. Like now. She had just discovered that she was jealous of the flower that was trembling so softly against his fingertip.

"Then it would be all right for us to explore this?" he asked, his voice deep, his eyes watching her rather than the flower.

"Do we have a choice?" Nicole asked huskily.

"There are other kipukas."

"Not here, not now."

Gently Chase picked the flower. "You're right." He inhaled the delicate scent before his tongue flicked out to try the deep, interior smoothness of the blossom, where its whiteness graded into a deep scarlet. Once, twice, three times, he tasted the flower before he caught the edge of a petal with exquisite care between his teeth. After a moment he released the creamy softness. There was no mark to show the sensual testing. "Nice," he murmured, turning toward her. "Do you know what this is?"

Nicole said the first thing that came to her mind. "A flower."

A smile curved beneath the midnight slash of Chase's mustache. "You're sure?" he asked, his voice deep, teasing.

Color crept beneath the golden tan on Nicole's cheeks. "It could be a morning glory that doesn't know it's nearly noon," she muttered.

"Actually, I think it's a hibiscus," said Chase.

Nicole touched one of the curving petals. "Actually, you're right."

Smiling, Chase tucked the blossom gently into the V of Nicole's halter. Then he bent and tasted the flower again. Shivers coursed over her as his black hair brushed against the rising curve of her breasts.

"I'm going to enjoy finding and tasting all the flowers," he murmured, brushing his lips over her warm golden skin.

"Chase—" she began, her voice trembling.

"That's what we're here for, remember?"

"Tasting?"

"And learning."

Nicole closed her eyes and thought of all the things Chase and this gentle Eden could teach her, things she had almost given up hope of ever being able to learn.

Suddenly she knew that if Chase asked for her, she would give herself to him. If she held back, she would spend the rest of her lonely life wondering what might have been, hating herself for not having the courage of the living things that changed to meet a new environment. There was no reason to hold on to fear any longer.

She was his. She had always been his. She just hadn't known it until now.

Chapter 5

The next weekend, as Chase settled into position behind the drums at the Kipuka club, he told himself that the days he had spent camping on Mauna Loa's slopes with other observatory scientists had allowed him to get his desire for Nicole under control.

And then Nicole stepped out onto the small stage. Spotlights turned her skin to molten gold and her unbound hair to fire. Her hips moved with liquid ease, describing sensual arcs that made Chase's blood pool thickly, hotly, focusing and hardening his desire with every rapid beat of his heart.

He took one look at Pele burning in the darkness and knew that he had to have her tonight. His hands first whispered and then pounded out the elemental truth on the resonating surface of the drums. He acknowledged no other dancers, drumming them off the stage with ease, seeking to be alone with the woman who danced like fire unleashed.

And then they were alone on the stage, thunder and lightning perfectly matched in dazzling display. Instinctively each knew when the other would peak, when the perfect match of sound and motion would begin to blur. There was a soft cry and suddenly silent drums, midnight closing around as applause broke over the stage.

Nicole found Chase just as he reached to enfold her. His mouth was hard, hungry, hot, like the powerful body beneath her hands.

"Come with me."

"Yes," whispered Nicole without hesitation, for she had wanted to be with him every minute of the days he had been gone.

When the curtains opened, the stage was empty.

Chase heard the startled silence and the spreading murmur just before the club's back door shut quietly behind him. He guided Nicole toward his Porsche, his hand firm on the small of her back. He was reluctant to speak, to break the feeling of triumph and relief that had come to him when she had simply whispered "yes" and followed him through the darkness. He had been afraid even to think about the possibility that she didn't want him as much as he wanted her.

Nicole was grateful that Chase didn't want to talk. She was having enough trouble coping with the nervousness that had come to her the instant she was no longer in his arms. She didn't think she could carry on a conversation without giving away her fear. As she walked with Chase, she wondered if Hawaii's first thornless plant had shivered with apprehension as it unfolded its vulnerable leaves.

As Nicole got into the Porsche, she pulled her hair forward over her shoulder until the long strands rippled and shimmered in her lap like flame. The car started with a feral sound of power and leaped out into traffic, telling Nicole that she was captured as surely as any woman thrown over a raider's saddle and carried away into the night. And in some ways that was how Nicole felt. Captured. Helpless.

Eyes closed, Nicole reminded herself of the moment Chase's teeth had closed with such delicacy on the fragile flower. The image had haunted her the whole time he was gone, whispering to her that a man capable of such ravishing gentleness wouldn't hurt her if she failed to please him with her response.

A few quick glances at her as he drove told Chase that though she'd given her consent, Nicole was uneasy. It didn't surprise him. They shared a mutual desire, but they didn't know each other very well. He was much bigger, far stronger. If he chose to hurt her, there would be little she could do to protect herself. Under the circumstances, it was only natural that she would be uneasy. But he didn't want that. He wanted her to be as she had been on the stage, coming to him without hesitation, burning for him.

Chase ran his fingertip from Nicole's shoulder to the back of her hand. "It's all right," he said gently. "I won't be rough with you."

She gave him a look out of startled gold eyes that told him he had guessed accurately what was on her mind. Then she smiled and touched his cheek with her palm.

"I know," she whispered. "I'm just—nervous."

Silently Chase caressed Nicole again. He decided that she would feel more at ease in her own cottage than in his. Neither one of them spoke as he handed her out of the Porsche and they walked toward her home. Beneath the moon's brilliant silver illumination, concealed spotlights glittered among the foliage like captive stars. The wind smoothed through the trees, which made soft sounds in response as though stroked by a lover's hand. The scent of flowers and sea mingled in the warm night, making yet another kind of caress on Nicole's heightened senses.

The door of the cottage opened. Moonlight poured through the wall of windows that faced the sea, giving an eldritch glow to the room's interior. Nicole's furniture was

both minimal and elegant, patterned after Japanese de-
signs for living. A futon was stacked along the glass wall,
waiting to be unfolded into a bed. Scattered cushions, a
dining table big enough for two and a desk completed the
furnishings.

Chase's hand swept along the wall to the right of the
doorway. Recessed lights glowed suddenly, gently illumi-
nating the room. Subdued flames seemed to twist and
shiver in Nicole's long hair. He caught a handful of the fire
that was falling over her shoulder and between her breasts.
He lifted the silky hair to his lips, gently pulling her closer.
He sensed the moment of hesitation before she put her
hands on his shoulders and stood on tiptoe to be kissed.

"I don't blame you for not wanting to get close," said
Chase, smiling crookedly, his teeth a flash of brightness
beneath his dense black mustache. "After all that drumming, I need a shower."

"That's not—" she began, then lost the words as his lips
fitted over hers.

His tongue dipped into her mouth as delicately as
though she were a flower. The tip of his tongue tasted her
once, then withdrew.

"Shower," he murmured.

Suddenly Nicole's halter fell away from her breasts. She
hadn't even been aware that Chase had untied the cloth
until she felt the air moving over her hot skin. Reflexively
she brought her hands up to cover herself. The reaction
puzzled Chase, for Nicole had no reason to be embarrassed about revealing herself to him. Her breasts were as
firm and lush as her hips, and the narrowness of her waist
was a temptation for any man's hands. Just looking at her
was enough to arouse him.

"Chase," she said softly, wanting to explain her retreat, not knowing where to begin.

"How did you know," asked Chase, bending down until he could nibble on her hand, "that hide-and-seek was
one of my favorite games?"

His tongue traced the fingertips of her right hand with hot, darting touches, and his mustache nuzzled against the sensitive skin between her fingers. With the same ravishing care he had used on the flower, his teeth closed on her index finger. He nibbled delicately down the smooth skin, then inserted his tongue between two fingers, caressing them and the soft breast beneath.

Nicole made a small sound of mingled surprise and pleasure as Chase continued teasing her, teaching her how very sensitive her skin could be. Each time his tongue slid between her fingers to her breast, her breath caught. Each time his teeth tugged tenderly at a finger, her breath came out in an uneven rush. She didn't realize that he was gently, inevitably nuzzling aside the barrier until he licked between her fingers and found the pink crown of her breast. With a thick sound of satisfaction, he traced the areola with his tongue.

For a moment Nicole stiffened, expecting to be hurt. Nothing came but the firm, moist tip of Chase's tongue exploring her textured nipple. The gentle caress continued until she shivered and felt herself changing, her nipple tightening into an erect bud. Still he touched her, drawing her into a taut peak and then tugging on that peak with his lips until Nicole forgot the hurtful lessons of the past, feeling only the pleasures of the present rippling through her. Her fingers opened until she was offering herself to him rather than protecting herself from him.

A low thread of sound came from Chase as he took what she had given to him, drawing her into his mouth deeply, suckling her with a rhythmic motion that made her feel almost dizzy. Her breast tightened even more, shaping itself to his insistent tongue, sending tiny quakes through her body with each sweet tug of his mouth. She closed her eyes and gave herself to the sensations as she had already given herself to him.

"No," she breathed when she felt his mouth leave her breast. "Not yet."

The words were too soft for Chase to hear, but it didn't matter. He wasn't ready to end the tantalizing seduction any more than she was. With equal care he nibbled and nuzzled and probed the hand that still shielded Nicole's other breast. If her fingers seemed reluctant to move aside this time, it was simply because she wanted to prolong the sweet anticipation of the moment when his tongue would curl caressingly around her, urging her to sensations that she had never felt before. When at last his tongue slid between the barrier of her fingers, her nipple was already hard, waiting for his mouth, wanting it.

Nicole couldn't control the throaty cry of pleasure that came when Chase captured the taut prize. The sound set off sensual quakes all through Chase's body, threatening his control. He released her, only to find that the sight of her nipple rising tautly between her fingers was as erotic as her tiny cry had been.

"Shower?" he asked, his voice deep. Then, huskily, "It's now or never."

Even as Chase spoke he touched each nipple with a hungry fingertip, wanting only to taste her in his mouth again, to feel the sensual trembling take her, to hear her sweet cries. Nicole opened eyes that were almost dazed. She looked down at herself as though she couldn't believe that it was Nicole Ballard standing half-naked in the living room, offering her breasts to a man.

No. Fully naked. Chase's fingers had loosened her lavalava while his mouth caressed her. Now he had opened his hands and the cloth was sliding down her body to the floor. Her silky underwear followed before she could draw the breath to object. When Chase saw her, his eyes narrowed, and he made a sound as though he had just been struck.

"Fire goddess," he said hoarsely, looking at the pale perfection of Nicole's skin and the burnished flame marking the apex of her legs.

Chase closed his eyes, knowing that if he looked at Nicole again he wouldn't be able to wait. Already he had rushed her more than he'd wanted to, more than she was comfortable with. Yet he couldn't help it. His hunger for her was as unruly as magma on the edge of eruption, seething and testing the boundaries that barely restrained its hot release. He felt as though he had waited years for this moment. The pressure for relief was nearly unbearable.

Yet she wasn't ready. Not the way he was. Feeling as though he were made of twisted ropes of flesh. Aching for it.

"Shower?" asked Chase, opening his eyes, looking only at Nicole's face. He didn't know whether to smile or swear as her expression registered on him. She seemed dazed, almost edgy, lost, surprised—everything but ready for him.

"There," she said, looking toward the opposite side of the living room where a small door opened into the bathroom.

Chase dropped to one knee and lifted first one of Nicole's feet, then the other, removing both the shell anklets and the panties that had slid down under his urging. The scent of her made him want to tease apart her legs to find the hidden textures just as he had nuzzled apart her fingers earlier. But he knew if he did that, they wouldn't make it to the shower. They wouldn't even make it to the bed.

"Do you—" Nicole looked down at Chase's thick black hair, which lay like a shadow just below her navel. She sensed the warmth of his body radiating against the sensitive skin of her inner thighs. Suddenly she felt disoriented, almost weak. "Do you want to go first?" she asked in a rush.

"First?" he asked, looking up, startled. Then he smiled slightly. "No," he said. "And I don't want to go second, either."

"Then what—oh," she said, understanding.

"Is 'oh' the Hawaiian word for two in a shower?" asked Chase politely. "If so, then most definitely, *oh*."

Nicole felt a flush climbing up from her breasts and fled toward the shower before Chase could see her heightened color. She felt completely out of her depth. She knew what it was like to have sex with a man, but she had never shared a shower with one.

You'd never been naked in your own living room with a man, either, she reminded herself, *and that didn't hurt, did it?*

Nicole's breasts tingled at the memory of Chase's hot, gentle mouth. No, it hadn't hurt at all. It had been like nothing she had ever known. She drew a steadying breath and turned on the water, letting it warm up as she divided her hair into two halves and pulled one over each shoulder. She began to braid the right side with swiftly flying fingers.

"That looks like fun," said Chase's deep voice from the doorway. His eyes took in the picture she made standing nude in front of the mirror, her hair spilling over her creamy skin, concealing most of her body like a fiery cloak. "Can I help?" he asked, his voice as light as he was determined to be. She had looked almost frightened as she had fled to the shower.

"Can you braid?" Nicole asked in surprise, looking over her shoulder.

"Of course," Chase said, giving her a wounded look. "The first thing they taught us in summer camp was how to braid key chains for our fathers and necklaces for our mothers. I always thought it was the damnedest waste of time—until now."

His hand stroked the long fall of hair that covered Nicole's left breast, tumbled in loose swirls to her waist and finally blended with the fiery hair between her thighs. At the first touch of his fingers, the tip of Nicole's breast hardened so swiftly that it was almost painful. Almost, but not quite. The difference was a stroke of sensual fire that was a revelation to her. Her eyes widened and her breath came in sharply. Chase bent down until the tip of his tongue just touched the nipple that had responded so immediately to his touch.

"Hello," he murmured, nuzzling the taut peak. "Do I know you?"

Nicole was torn between laughter and a moan as Chase's mouth tugged gently at the nipple. His sensual teasing was as new to her as the sensations radiating from her breast to the center of her body. Ripples of heat shimmered through her with each movement of his tongue.

"Yes," said Chase, lifting his head, admiring the tight, glistening peak, "now I recognize you. We met just a few minutes ago. You have a friend nearby, don't you?"

Nicole made a throaty sound that was part laughter, part pleasure as Chase nuzzled between the fiery strands covering her other breast. She let go of the braid she had been working on and threaded her fingers into the much more satisfying thickness of Chase's hair, unconsciously holding him against her, wanting to prolong the sweet caress. His long fingers slid beneath her hair to curl around her breasts, taking their weight in his palms.

For an instant fear returned to Nicole, a reflexive withdrawal from intimacy. Her husband's hands had been even more careless of her delicate flesh than his mouth had been, especially when he was aroused. And she had little doubt that Chase was aroused.

Chase sensed the tiny flinching as his thumbs caressed the hardened peaks of Nicole's breasts. Reluctantly he removed his hands from the firm curves, wondering why she had retreated. "Sorry. I'd better concentrate on something I'm good at," he said, going back to braiding her hair.

"That's not it," she said after a moment, her voice strained.

"You mean I'm not good at braiding?" he asked, brushing his lips over the nipple peeking out from between strands of hair.

"That's not—" Nicole's breath came in swiftly. "It's just that—"

"Did I hurt you?" interrupted Chase, his voice quiet.

Nicole shook her head.

His index finger tilted her chin up until she had to look him in the eye. "Tell me if I do," he said simply. "I know that a man my size can make a woman—nervous."

She searched his gray eyes for a long moment, then nodded, relaxing again.

By a deliberate act of will, Chase confined himself to braiding Nicole's hair, ignoring the ruby-tipped temptations so close to hand. Her hesitations and withdrawals puzzled him, for while he might have rushed her, he was a long way from overpowering her. And she was a long way from being unwilling.

Suddenly Chase realized what was making Nicole hesitate. She must understand as well as he did that the moment she went to bed with him, any possibility of seducing Dane away from Janet was gone.

No wonder you're nervous, Chase thought, admiring the long, dark eyelashes concealing Nicole's eyes as she looked down at the hair she was braiding. *From what I've seen, Dane really likes you, but he hasn't bedded you yet, or you wouldn't be here with me. Dane's better looking than I'll ever be, civilized, rich, more than half in love with you— but he's married. And you're gambling all that on a toss in the hay with a man who is rich, not very civilized, hasn't said a thing about liking or loving you—but is unmarried and more than willing to take you to bed.*

You're hoping that I'll still want you afterward, but you're too hungry to wait and be sure. That's quite a risk you're taking on me, Pele. More than you know. More than you're going to know until you wake up alone, with no rich Wilcox to comfort you, and no hope of one. But there are other rich fools in the world. You'll find one to take care of you. Women like you always do.

Chase finished the braid and backed away from Nicole. As she lifted her arms over her head to tuck her braids into place, the elegant sensuality of her body was fully revealed for the first time. *God, I almost envy the man you finally sell yourself to,* thought Chase, desire flowing through him in hot, rhythmic surges as he looked at her.

Nicole anchored the braids on top of her head with the skill of long practice. As she worked, she sensed Chase standing behind her, watching her in the full-length bathroom mirror. The look on his face sent both fear and a strange heat through her. Often her husband had looked at her like that when she was naked, and then he had taken her quickly, roughly, as though punishing her. She had come to fear that expression on a man's face.

But Chase had been very gentle with her. He had also given her more pleasure than she had ever known. The fact that he wanted her didn't automatically mean that he would hurt her. Besides, the picture he made standing behind her, naked but for the lavalava riding low on his hips, made her body tingle in hidden places. It was a new, delicious sensation. Hesitantly she smiled as she met his eyes in the mirror.

With a single sinuous motion, Chase stripped off his clothes. He didn't notice her eyes widening in surprise and returning fear when she saw his full nakedness in the instant before he came to stand behind her. She couldn't control a slight flinching when his hands came up to her shoulders.

"Like I said," Chase murmured, brushing his lips across the nape of Nicole's neck, "sometimes I make a woman nervous. It's all right, Pele. I know my own strength. I won't hurt you."

Chase's hands went from Nicole's shoulders to her hips as though the skin of his palms could taste her if he just went very slowly, very gently. He repeated the caress, but this time down the front of her body, shaping her breasts and waist and the resilient curve of her thighs. The pressure of his hands eased her against his body until there was nothing between them.

"Don't worry, little one," he said huskily, kissing the curve of Nicole's neck as his hands caressed her thighs. "We'll fit together very well."

Chase turned away, opened the shower door and stepped in. The endearment echoed in Nicole's mind as she stared after him, too surprised to move. *Little one.* She shook her head as though to wake up from a dream. *Little one!* She had never thought of herself as small in her whole life. But then, compared to Chase, most people were just that. Little.

Bemused, Nicole followed Chase into the shower, her nervousness fading beneath the novelty of being considered small. The fact that he understood her fears reassured her that she had been correct in trusting her instincts: Chase was the right man for her. The first few times with him might be difficult, for nothing could instantly remove reflexes learned in the past at such cost. But even so, the tension in her body at that moment owed as much to anticipation as to anxiety. She was no longer afraid that Chase would hurt her and keep on hurting her until he found his own satisfaction.

Warm water spilled down Nicole's body as Chase moved aside to make room for her. Ginger-scented soap filled the steamy enclosure with fragrance. Lather slipped from Chase's hands down his body as he soaped his shoulders. The glistening white stream made a sensual contrast to his tanned skin and the midnight mat of hair curling down his torso.

Nicole wanted to run her hands beneath the lather, to know each swell of muscle and length of tendon, to feel the heat of Chase's body beneath her palms. After the first instant of temptation, she controlled the urge to touch him. In the early months of her marriage, when she had tried to please her husband, she had quickly learned that touching him only shortened the time before he took her. She didn't want that tonight. The anticipation she felt was too new, too fragile, too sweet to lose simply because she couldn't control her own foolish impulses.

When Nicole reached for the soap, Chase shook his head and turned her so that she was facing away from him, shielded from the full force of the water by his broad back. Warm, soapy hands began rubbing Nicole's skin. Strong thumbs traced the length of her spine with long, caressing motions. Broad palms first stroked and then cupped the full curve of her hips, savoring her wordlessly, making her feel sleek and very feminine. When his long fingers traced the shadow cleft at the base of her spine, she shivered. He touched her hidden warmth once, then retreated with a slowness that sent stirrings of fire through her.

Chase closed his teeth very gently on the nape of Nicole's neck. He smiled as a shiver of response coursed over her. His hands slid around her body, seeking other pleasure points. With his fingers spread, he pressed one palm just above her fiery nest of hair, as his other hand found and kneaded her breast. Both hands moved slowly, skillfully, while his teeth caressed her sensitive nape. Caught between the loving movements of his hands and his mouth, Nicole trembled. Her body moved in languid response, increasing the sweet pressure.

She wished that she could touch Chase without bringing a hurried end to the delicious, sensual play. For the first time in her life, she wanted to caress a man as intimately as she herself was being touched. The heat of Chase's body was an irresistible lure, and his strength intrigued rather than frightened her now. Even feeling the hard length of him pressed against her hip didn't frighten her. With his hands stroking her so sweetly, learning her, knowing her, there was no room for fear. All she could feel was heat rising slowly in her, radiating through her, making her tremble with tiny, secret ripples as a lifetime of undiscovered sensuality stirred and began to awaken beneath his gentle touch.

When Chase sensed the softening of Nicole's body, both triumph and desire ripped through him. He believed that she was no longer worrying about choosing the wrong rich brother. Instead, she was beginning to want him, beginning to come apart in his hands. For a moment Chase was afraid that the feel of her hips moving slowly was going to cost what self-control he had. Having her move against him like that was what he had wanted since the first time he had seen her dance to the slow beat of Bobby's drums, her hair swaying in fiery counterpoint to the stately elegance of the hula.

"Turn around," said Chase, his voice a husky murmur beneath the sound of the falling water. "I want your mouth, Pele. Do you want mine?"

Yet even as he spoke, he continued stroking her, making her choose between his caressing hands and the sensual promise of his kiss. She couldn't make the choice because the temptations were too new, too alluring. With a small sound, she tilted her head back against his shoulder, offering her mouth in the only way she could without interrupting the incredibly sweet movements of his hands.

Heat exploded in Chase when Nicole half turned and her hip pressed hotly over his rigid flesh as she came to him. His tongue slid between her lips, filling her with his taste and his heat. She strained toward him, caught in a sensual vise that was tightening with each movement of his palm against her tangled, fiery hair. Chase didn't ask her to choose again. He shifted his hands, turning her, and then he eased his hot, aching flesh between her legs, teaching her that there were many ways for a man to caress a woman.

Chase braced his arms against the wall on either side of Nicole and let her feel him from her mouth to her toes. The coolness of the tiled shower wall against her back was an intense sensual contrast to the textured heat of the male body pressing against her. Recklessly she put her arms around him, running her hungry palms down his back, learning the hard patterns of muscle and bone that had intrigued her since the first moment she had watched him calling elemental rhythms from the drums.

Chase's back rippled powerfully beneath her hands as he twisted very slowly, drawing every bit of pleasure from her touch as his tongue stroked hers, promising her even greater pleasures. The small sound she made as he caught her tongue between his teeth drew a groan of response from him. He thrust deeply into her mouth while he moved slowly against her, caressing her with his whole body.

It wasn't enough. He needed to be inside her. The need was an ache and a wild pressure within him. For an instant he considered taking her in the shower. Then he remembered her hesitations and knew that he had to keep his control for a little bit longer.

"I've had about all the shower I can take," Chase said, biting Nicole's neck not quite gently. "How about you?"

"I've never had so much fun in a shower in my life," said Nicole, her voice catching as she watched him, her eyes wide and catlike in the shower's filtered light.

Chase smiled and moved against her again, drawing out the sensual moment, seeing her eyes half close as pleasure shivered through her. Only the certainty that even greater pleasures awaited them beyond the confines of the shower allowed Chase to turn away from her, shut off the water and step out into the relative coolness of the bathroom.

"Towels?" he asked, looking around, seeing none.

Then he saw her watching him in the mirror. Her expression was more curious than afraid and more appreciative than either.

"Forget the towels," he said thickly. "In this heat we wouldn't stay dry for more than a few seconds anyway."

His hand drew her out of the shower into a hot, slick embrace. She came to him without hesitation, molding herself to his powerful body, clinging to him with her mouth and hands. When he lifted his head, his breathing was quick, strained.

"I'm having a hell of a time keeping my hands off you long enough to get you to bed," he said in a rueful tone, smoothing his fingers restlessly over her body.

"I don't mind," Nicole said honestly as her hands rubbed across the fascinating textures of his chest. She felt the sudden hardening of his nipple beneath her palm and remembered her own pleasure when his lips had caressed her. "I—enjoy it. Do you?"

Chase wondered at the note of surprise in her voice, but the soft, exciting pressure of her mouth against his nipple drove every thought from his mind except that of being held completely within her body. His hands swept down her back, arching her against him, wanting every bit of her softness with a wild, nearly uncontrollable hunger.

Nicole didn't object when he led her to the living room and flipped open the futon, making a resilient mattress for them to lie upon. When he urged her down beside him, she didn't hold back. She would have loved to continue the gentle, exciting caresses they had shared before, but she didn't resent the fact that Chase needed something more. He had already given her greater pleasure than she had ever known; she could hardly deny him his own male release.

The scent of ginger and warm woman flowed over Chase as he pulled Nicole into his arms. Moonlight turned her into quicksilver, giving her a beauty that made his whole body ache. He slid his hand from her breast to the warmth between her thighs, wanting to know if she was as ready for him as he was for her. With barely controlled urgency he tested her softness. The answer to his question was ambivalent. He knew that he wouldn't hurt her if he took her now. He also knew that she was nowhere near the peak of feminine need.

But then, courtesans and other headhunting females are basically cold at heart, he reminded himself. *For them passion is an act. They really don't want any more from a man than a meal ticket.*

When Nicole sensed Chase's hesitation, she kissed his shoulder and the pulse beating heavily at the base of his neck. "It's all right, Chase," she said, urging him closer.

The whispered words were all that he needed, more than he had expected. He took her without hesitation, savoring the sliding, hot instant. She was tight, much tighter than he had expected. For an instant he considered withdrawing, wondering if he was hurting her. Then he felt her breath sigh out, relaxing some of the constriction of her body. She shifted and moved slightly, tugging at him. The last possibility of control fled. Chase groaned and moved within her, letting the welling, bursting pressure of his hunger finally find release.

Nicole held him close, smoothing her hands over his skin, savoring the unique feeling of having pleased a lover and the equally unusual sensation of enjoying the heat and weight of a man's body. When Chase rolled onto his side, withdrawing from her, she made a small sound of protest. She had discovered an unexpected pleasure in being joined with him. Their separation made her feel empty and . . . restless. He hesitated, then pulled her closer and stroked her with slow sweeps of his hand from the moon-bright crown of her head to the alluring curve of hip and thigh. Unconsciously she moved closer, wanting the feel of his skin against hers, hungry for the sweet intimacy he had shown her earlier.

The small movements of Nicole's body as she snuggled into his warmth, fitting herself to him with sensual precision, made Chase's breath shorten all over again. He felt the hot thrill of returning desire, pressure growing with each beat of his heart. He bent over Nicole's breast, kissing her, feeling her tighten beneath his touch. It took only an instant, like the tiny sound she made in her throat when his mouth tugged at her. An instant, and a blaze of hunger returning.

Fire goddess. She'd burn a man alive and never even feel the heat.

When Chase realized that he was on the verge of succumbing again to Nicole's sensual trap, he sat up quickly.

I've done what I had to. Dane's safe from her. Now I'd better get the hell out while I still have the strength to leave. And the desire.

"Chase?"

He looked down at Nicole, his eyes metallic silver in the moonlight. A long tendril of her hair had escaped the coils. It fell between her breasts in a soft ribbon that shimmered with subdued fire. He knew a moment of regret that he hadn't taken down her hair and wrapped it around him, feeling its silken strands binding him to her.

"Don't get up," Chase said. "I'll let myself out."

Nicole blinked, trying to think of something to say. "You—you don't have to leave."

"Lisa is with Janet and Dane. If something happens and they need me, they'll call my cottage, not yours."

It was true as far as it went. And it kept him from saying the rest of the truth. If he stayed, he'd take Nicole again and again, falling deeper and deeper beneath the spell of her cold fire. She hadn't wanted him. Not really. Not completely. Not the way he had wanted her—all the fires of Eden blazing inside him.

The way he still wanted her.

Chase dressed swiftly, wrapping his lavalava into place, going in silence back to the living room. Nicole was up, standing by the door, wearing nothing but moonlight. Without meaning to, Chase found his fingertips tracing the length of the single tendril of hair that fell between her breasts and down over the smooth curves of her body. He lifted his hand, opened the door and stepped through.

Nicole moved aside, holding on to the door with both hands because that was the only way to keep herself from clinging to Chase and asking him to stay and touch her gently for just a few more moments. But she couldn't do that. She knew only too well from her marriage that once a man had what he wanted sexually, he had no further use for the woman.

"Thank you," murmured Nicole, looking down.

Chase paused. "For what?" he asked, his voice almost rough. He knew that there had been no release for her in their lovemaking. She must know it too. She certainly hadn't bothered to hide it.

"For not hurting me."

Her soft words were nearly lost beneath the sound of the latch taking hold as the door shut behind him. For a long moment Chase stood in the silence and shadows, wondering at the sudden uneasiness sweeping through him, as though he stood on the lip of a volcano and sensed the earth shuddering beneath his feet in ominous harmonic tremors.

Something was wrong. Very wrong.

It's called post-coital depression, you jackass, he snarled silently to himself.

There was no answer but a spreading feeling of unease.

With an impatient curse, Chase stalked toward his cottage, concentrating on the only thing that mattered: Dane's marriage was safe from the fiery temptations of Pele.

Chapter 6

Chase's mood was no less savage after a night of broken sleep. He got up early, showered for the second time since he had left Nicole and pulled on a pair of khaki shorts and a frayed white shirt that had been demoted to casual wear. With swift, impatient jerks of his hand, he rolled up the sleeves, wanting only to have the morning over with so that he could get on with his real work in Hawaii—volcano crawling—rather than demonstrating to his younger brother how he had nearly been taken in by a redheaded gold digger.

Too often as he dressed, memories of his own, nearly uncontrollable passion came back to Chase. With them came images of the silk of Nicole's hair, the hesitant sweetness of her mouth, the instant when he had found her breast beneath her protective hand and heard her tiny cry—and the hot, tight, incredibly intense pleasure of sheathing himself within her. He had taken more beautiful women, and certainly more passionate or skilled ones, but Nicole was a fire in his memory and they were not.

She was also a fire in his body. He burned, and he didn't know why.

Disgusted with his uncontrollable male response to even the memory of last night, Chase slammed out of the cottage. As he drove, the Porsche snarled for him, an oddly soothing sound. He pulled into Dane's long driveway and parked at the rear of the old frame house alongside Janet's little car. Bougainvillea overgrew the detached garage and carport, shedding drifts of shocking pink flowers over everything. Chase picked his way through the greenery with respect for its armament. As a recent import to Eden, bougainvillea still had its full complement of inchlong thorns.

The back door to the house was unlocked. Chase knew that the front door was too, but the back was closer. The smell of coffee greeted him as he opened the door, reminding him that he had been in too much of a hurry to make coffee for himself at the cottage. Dane sat alone at the kitchen table, reading the newspaper and sipping coffee. Chase let out a small sigh of relief. He'd just as soon Janet never knew about Nicole and Dane. After all, nothing had happened. And nothing ever would.

Now.

"You're early," said Dane, giving him a shrewd look. "Lisa isn't up yet. Besides, I think this is the morning Nicole gives her drawing lessons." He grimaced. "Damn, there I go again. Give me a bag and a cat and I'll let it out every time. You didn't hear anything about drawing from me. Again."

"I didn't hear anything about drawing," agreed Chase absently, wondering how to broach the subject of the bet he had won and Dane had lost. "Where's Janet?"

"Sleeping. She was up until three polishing the proposal."

"Good," muttered Chase, glad that Janet wouldn't wander downstairs and overhear the brotherly tête-à-tête.

"She'll be sorry you're sorry you missed her," retorted Dane.

Chase shot his brother a hard look and decided that there was no civilized, gentlemanly way to open the conversation. After all, what had been done wasn't very civilized, and as for gentlemanly—Chase's mouth turned down in a grimace of distaste. On the other hand, women like Nicole could hardly expect to find a world full of gentlemen vying to pay their rent.

Radiating barely restrained anger, Chase poured himself a cup of coffee. He sensed Dane watching him.

"I thought after the performance at the club last night, you'd be tired enough to sleep for a week," Dane said blandly, turning to another page in the small newspaper.

Paper rustled loudly in the silence as Dane made a production of folding the sheets just so.

"Were you there?" asked Chase, sipping the scalding coffee. "I didn't see you."

"I came in later," said Dane. Then he looked up at Chase with a mixture of curiosity and amusement. "Must have had ten people tell me about your hot drumming, Nicole's hotter dancing and the magic act."

"Magic?" said Chase, lifting his eyebrows in surprise.

"Yeah," Dane said dryly, bending over the newspaper again. "Now you see them, now you don't."

Chase took a deep breath. "You lost the bet," he said bluntly, his voice rough, wanting to get it over with.

Dane looked up, shock in every line of his face. "What?"

"We went back to Nicole's place. I stayed there long enough to make sure that she'd never go after you again— or if she did, that you wouldn't have her."

"What the hell are you talking about?"

"Screwing," said Chase brutally.

An image of Nicole's softness and beauty rose in his mind. He squelched the memory ruthlessly. He was old enough to know better than to be taken in by appearances. The proof was definitely in the pudding. Or in this case, in the sheets. Nicole had gone to bed with him for reasons other than passion, for she had shown him very little of that.

"You—and Nicole?"

Dane's chair scraped across the floor as he came to his feet with a lurch that sent his empty coffee mug rolling to the floor. It smashed to pieces with a sharp sound that both men ignored. They were too focused in the instant to have attention for anything but each other. They heard nothing except their own words, not even the sound of a soft knock followed by the front door opening.

"Yes," said Chase, his voice rough. "Who else would I be screwing but Nicole? Or is some other gold digger after you, dazzling you with smiles and sweet lies while visions of bank accounts dance in her dear little head?"

There were several moments of stunned silence while Dane tried to take in what his brother was saying. But it didn't make sense. None of it.

"You're crazy!" Dane said, shaking his head as though he couldn't believe what he was hearing.

Nicole stood motionless in the middle of the living room, hearing the male voices erupting from the kitchen, flinching as though splashes of scalding lava were landing all around her. On her. But it wasn't hot. It was cold, freezing cold.

This can't be happening. I'm dreaming. I'll wake up soon and it will be over. Just another bad dream.

The voices came again. It wasn't a dream, and it kept on happening, words burning her until she bit her lip in an effort not to cry out.

"She slept with you?" persisted Dane.

"Yes," said Chase, his voice rough, impatient. "Don't look so surprised, little brother. It happens all the time."

"Not with Nicole!"

"Crap," said Chase in disgust. "She really had you going, didn't she? Well, if it makes you feel better, you didn't miss much. Like a lot of women with a good body, she thinks that it's enough for a man just to be in bed with her."

"What?"

The word wasn't a question so much as a measure of Dane's bafflement. Chase answered anyway. He had come to disabuse his brother of any male fantasies about Nicole, and that was exactly what he would do—even though he'd rather be shoveling out pit toilets at the moment.

"Women like Nicole can't believe that a man wants more than a sexy body in a lover," Chase said coolly. "Most of them substitute skill for passion. Not her. Nicole's about as skillful in bed as a corpse."

"Shut up, damn you!" said Dane in a hoarse voice, suddenly afraid that he understood too much. "I don't want to hear any more!"

"Tough," snarled Chase. His mouth thinned in violent distaste for the whole situation. He was almost finished. He couldn't wait for it to be over with so he could go to the clean slopes of the mountain and study the life that was slowly reclaiming the land born of fire. That was where he belonged. Not here, telling his brother what he should have been able to figure out for himself. "You lost the bet," said Chase heavily, "but that's all you lost. You still have Janet, and she's a better woman than Nicole will ever be."

Nicole tried to turn away, to flee, but her body didn't respond. She swayed slowly, fighting for balance, trying to comprehend what had happened, why it had happened—but the sudden, appalling weakness of her body made both flight and coherent thought impossible. She felt as though her bones had turned to cold sand and were running from her body, leaving her barely able to stand.

The realization that Chase had seduced her as part of a cruel game was devastating. The understanding that she had failed him so completely as a woman was annihilating. It destroyed her in ways she couldn't comprehend.

She felt it all the way to her soul in a single, tearing stroke that took the strength from her.

The room dimmed to gray and started to revolve slowly around her. Instinctively she bent over, letting blood run back into her head before she fainted. She supported herself against a chair, blindly willing her body not to betray her. Only raw desperation kept her on her feet. Inside herself she was screaming *Get out! Get out!* She had to flee before anyone discovered her and knew that she had overheard.

Words kept pouring out of the kitchen, words echoing queasily in Nicole's mind as she fought for control of her body.

"What do you mean, I still have Janet?" retorted Dane.

"Nicole was after you, little brother. Or, to be precise, after marriage and your bank account."

"You're wrong," said Dane flatly. "Dead wrong."

"Don't give me that crap," snarled Chase. "I've seen how you look at her."

"Just like you look at Janet?" suggested Dane, measuring his brother with unflinching eyes. "Just like Janet looks at you?"

There was a moment of electric silence.

"You don't think—" began Chase, shocked.

"No," Dane interrupted, "I don't. I know both of you too well. I know Nicole in the same way. Yes, I care for Nicole a great deal, just as you care for Janet. Nicole is a very appealing woman and not just physically. I'd have to be blind and a liar to say otherwise. But if I'd been so stupid as to make a pass, she would have ducked. She's not like the females you've had since your divorce. And she most definitely is not another home wrecker like Lynnette."

"Oh?" Chase's voice curled upwards sarcastically, then descended into ice. "If Nicole is such a paragon, why did she sleep with me? After all, we'd known each other only a few days. Hardly the act of a virtuous woman, is it? And don't try telling me that she couldn't control her passion for me.'' He laughed curtly, remembering how hesitant Nicole had been. Her relative lack of response still galled him. He had been so hot, nearly wild for her, and she had been controlled down to the last full stop. "She's cold to the core. She doesn't know the meaning of the word *passion*."

A wave of nausea hit Nicole. Icy sweat broke out just as a salty taste filled her mouth. She shoved away from the chair she had clutched for support and bolted toward the downstairs bathroom, heedless of the noise she was making. She barely reached the room in time. She was blindly, wrenchingly sick, as though the convulsions of her body could somehow wipe out the last, terrible minutes when she had overheard herself being dissected and dismissed as a woman by the very man she had trusted herself to, believing he was so right for her.

Both men heard the sudden noise. Chase was the first one to run through the living room to the bathroom near the den. He heard the toilet flush as he reached for the door, then the sound of water running in the sink. He opened the door, expecting to find one of the children in the throes of an attack of flu. What he saw shocked him into silence.

Nicole was as pale as salt. Her hands were shaking so hard that the water she was trying to splash on to her face was pouring all over the front of her bright blue muumuu instead, making it stick to her body in great dark welts of color.

Eyes closed, she bent over the sink. Chase reached past her for a washcloth. He wet it and began to wipe her face as though she were a child.

When the cloth touched Nicole's skin, her eyes opened. Slowly she focused on Chase. She made a low sound and backed away from him so violently that she slammed against the shower door. Chase caught her, steadying her. She trembled convulsively when she felt his hands close around her arms. With an inarticulate sound she turned her face away from him.

"Are you all right?" he asked. "Nicole?" He felt her begin to sag in his arms as though she were going to faint. "Nicole!"

Weakly, futilely, she fought against being touched by Chase, whispering, "no," again and again as though it would make a difference.

"Leave her alone," said Dane, his voice harsh.

"She needs help. She's got the flu so bad she can hardly stand," Chase said tightly, supporting Nicole with one hand and controlling her flailing hands with the other.

Dane muttered a searing obscenity. "Something made her sick, all right, and it wasn't the flu. Let go of her, Chase. Can't you see? She doesn't want you touching her."

The bleakness of Dane's voice shocked Chase. Then he realized what Dane was trying to say.

"How long were you in the living room?" Chase demanded, turning Nicole's chin so that she had to face him. "Look at me! How much did you hear?"

Nicole's eyes opened. She looked through Chase, seeing nothing, wishing she could feel nothing as well. She would have sold her soul for the ability to simply vanish. "Let go of me," she said, her voice thready. "I'm fine. Don't touch me. Don't. Please. I'm fine."

Chase's breath came in with a harsh sound. He looked from Nicole's pale face to the helpless pain on Dane's. "What the hell is going on?" demanded Chase.

"You won the bet," said Dane heavily, "but you lost, brother. You lost big. And so did Nicole. *Shit.*" Dane closed his eyes for a moment. "Let go of her before you make her sick all over again. As a matter of fact, I'm feeling a little queasy myself."

"Nicole?" asked Chase, not wanting to believe Dane's bleak summation of her illness.

Chase looked at the pale, shaking woman he was supporting and felt the uneasiness he had known last night

return in a cold rush. He didn't want to believe that he had
let his own passion and his distrust of women warp his
judgment to the point that he had hurt someone whose
only fault lay in trusting him. There was a better explanation. Flu and eavesdropping. If Nicole had overheard the
conversation, then she had to realize that Dane was out of
reach. A disappointment to be sure, but hardly enough to
literally sicken her. Women who made their living off men
were tougher than that.

"Nicole," said Chase, softly, firmly. "I'm sorry, but it
had to be done. I couldn't stand by and let you break up
my brother's marriage."

There was no answer other than a ragged shudder that
went the full length of Nicole's body.

"If it's money you need, I'll—" began Chase.

"Shut up," hissed Dane, cutting off his brother.
"Christ, what's happened with you and women, Chase?
Can't you see that Nicole didn't want me as anything but
a friend? She wanted you, though, and I'll bet that she
didn't put any conditions on it or ask for any guarantees,
did she?"

Chase closed his eyes, praying that his brother was
wrong—afraid, very afraid, that he was right. *She didn't
ask me for one damn thing. And then she thanked me—
not for the pleasure I gave her, but for the simple lack of
pain.*

He looked at Nicole again. Her eyes were wide, fixed,
and the skin around them looked bruised. He felt a chill
crawl over him.

My God, what have I done?

"Nicole?" he asked softly, stroking her cheek with his
fingertips.

With a small cry, she flinched and swallowed convulsively, answering questions Chase hadn't even asked. She
had overheard enough. Too much. And it had torn her in
a way that he could barely comprehend. He knew one
thing without any doubt, though. She might have wanted

him last night, but she could not bear his touch this morning. It literally nauseated her.

Slowly, very slowly, Chase released Nicole and stepped aside.

"Nicole," murmured Dane, reaching out to give her a comforting hug, as though she were his own child. "It will be all right, honey."

"No. Oh, no." Nicole backed away as far as she could from both men. "Don't touch me," she whispered. "Don't anyone touch me. Not yet, Dane. Maybe tomorrow. Yes. I'll be fine by then. But don't touch me now. Please."

For a long, long moment there was no sound but that of Nicole's ragged breathing as she fought to bring herself under control. The uneasiness that had been with Chase since he had left Nicole last night condensed into an icy certainty. He had been wrong, all the way wrong. She hadn't been after Dane. If she had been hesitant last night, it had been because of something else. Because she had been afraid.

What was she afraid of? My size? But if she was afraid of big men, why had she been attracted to me in the first place?

"Nicole, I didn't mean to—" began Chase.

"That's all right," she said quickly, cutting across his words, staring through him with a ghastly social smile. "I understand. Really I do. You wanted to protect. Your brother." Her eyes focused on Dane. She laughed, a sound that made both men flinch. "I'm sorry. It was just—the idea."

"The idea?" asked Dane softly. "Of what, honey?"

"Of marriage. Of marrying anyone—even you, Dane. Being a man's *thing* again. Legally. Morally. All day. Every day. And the nights." A shudder of revulsion went over Nicole.

For a moment Chase thought he would be as sick as she had been. He finally understood the meaning of her whispered goodbye: *Thank you for not hurting me.*

She had been afraid to come to him because she was afraid of sex.

Yet she had come to him anyway.

"Nicole—" Chase's voice was raw with suppressed emotion, but she was still talking, hearing only her own words, her unfocused eyes seeing things that made Chase ill. He didn't know which was worse, hearing Nicole's shattered voice or hearing the voice in his own mind telling him that he had just made a hideous mistake—and someone else was paying for it, someone who couldn't afford the cost.

Thank you for not hurting me.

Chase began to swear softly, terribly, hating himself and the situation with an intensity that bordered on violence.

"I'm going home," Nicole said to Dane, holding her voice very carefully, trying to sound calm, normal, as though nothing had happened. "Tell Lisa—" Nicole's voice frayed into silence. "Tell her I'll call," she whispered.

"I'll drive you home," said Chase, hearing only that Nicole wanted to leave. "You're in no shape to handle a car."

"I'm fine."

"Like hell you are," he gritted.

"I'll drive her," said Dane, putting a warning hand on Chase when he would have stopped Nicole from easing past him on the way out the bathroom. "You can follow and bring me home."

Chase started to object, then realized it was futile. He hissed a single savage word. Then, much more gently, he said, "We'll talk later, when you feel better."

"No." Her voice was very soft, very final.

"Yes." Chase held out his hand to her, only to have her flinch away again. He ran the hand through his hair in a gesture of barely restrained frustration. "I'm sorry, Nicole. God—I'm sorry. I didn't understand. I really believed that you were trying to break up Dane's marriage. Suddenly every letter was filled with Nicole this and Nicole that, and all Dane had to say about Janet was that she was busy on this or that project. I just assumed that you and he—"

"I understand," Nicole interrupted quickly, her mind working at frantic speed, focusing on a single truth: *I can't hold on any longer. I have to get out of here before I fly apart.* She took a sharp breath, realizing that she had been holding herself frozen too long. "You're right. Dane is funny, warm, intelligent. Gentle." Her voice caught on the edge of breaking. "So gentle. Any woman would want him."

"You left out 'rich,'" said Dane, giving his older brother a slicing sideways glance.

"Rich," repeated Nicole obediently. "Excuse me. I really have to go."

Chase realized that she was hanging on to her control by a shred. "Nicole—" His voice broke. "My God—I never meant—"

"It's all right," she said, talking quickly, never looking at Chase, desperately wanting it to end, all the words, the fears, the feeling of wanting to scream and keep on screaming. "I understand." She gave Dane another ghastly smile. "Sorry I was so obvious about liking you. I hope Janet didn't—"

The thought of Janet wondering if she was after Dane snapped the last of Nicole's control. With no warning, she bolted past Dane and down the hall, catching both of the men flat-footed. She paused only long enough to scoop up the purse that she had dropped in the living room. She heard both men calling her name and knew that they were pursuing her. She fumbled her keys out of her purse, jammed the correct one in the car's ignition and heard the engine roar to life. Leaves and fallen blossoms flew wildly from beneath the spinning tires as she pulled away from the curb, barely keeping the car from fishtailing out of control.

Swearing viciously, Chase spun and headed for his own car. Dane tackled him.

"Forget it," panted Dane, struggling to hold his larger, stronger brother. "By the time you back out, she'll be long gone. No sense in having two emotional wrecks on the road at once. Not a damn thing you could do anyway, even if you did catch her."

"I could see that she gets home safely," Chase snarled. With a quick, violent motion he broke Dane's hold.

"What makes you think she's going home?" asked Dane, circling Chase warily, knowing quite well that his brother would be happy to take out his anger and frustration in a brawl.

"Where else would she go?"

"To the mountain," said Dane simply, gesturing toward Kilauea. "Benny says she always goes there when she gets 'mainland sad.'"

"Benny? Who the hell is he? You said she didn't have any boyfriends."

"Benny Kamehameha," said Dane, watching his brother with narrowed eyes, gauging his mood. He had never seen Chase like this. Raw. Wild. Dangerous. "Bobby's youngest son."

Chase took a deep breath and slowly unclenched his fists. "I see."

"Do you? Nicole likes kids and they like her. Of course," added Dane sarcastically, "she could just be buttering up the kids because they have rich daddies."

"Screw you," snarled Chase, turning on his brother suddenly.

Dane smiled narrowly. "Just wanted to be sure the hair shirt fit, brother. It's so hard to find clothes in your size."

Chase's mouth flattened into a line. "That's the second one," he said softly.

Dane nodded, understanding the old phrase from their childhood. If he needled Chase again, he could expect a fight.

"What is 'mainland sad'?" asked Chase carefully, aching with the effort of controlling himself. But he needed information about Nicole. He needed it with an intensity that he didn't even question. "Is she homesick?"

Dane shook his head slowly. "Nicole loves Hawaii. She was born for this island. It just took her a few years to find her way over here."

"Then what is it?"

"I don't know. I've never asked. She's never offered. I assume it's something to do with men, because she's never dated. Until you. You were different."

Chase closed his eyes, realizing too late the simple truth. "So was she," he said in a low voice as he turned away.

"Where are you going?" asked Dane.

"To the mountain."

"It's a big place. I don't think you'll find her."

"No, but maybe I'll find what she's looking for."

"What's that?"

"Peace."

Chase drove as Nicole had, depending more on reflexes than concentration to keep him on the road. Unlike Nicole, though, he didn't spend the first few miles looking in the rearview mirror. It wasn't until Nicole reached the first sugarcane fields that she began to relax slightly. She had gotten over the worst hurdle. Now all she had to do was hang on long enough to find the tiny kipuka she thought of as her personal sanctuary. There she would be free to do whatever she wanted, cry or scream or ask why until either answers or the peace of emotional exhaustion came to her.

Nicole took the unmarked, rough spur road that dead-ended about two thousand feet up Kilauea's fertile, lava-scarred flank. The road ended in a thick lava flow, one of the many black rivers twisting down from fissures that had opened in the past, gushing incandescent lava from the volcano's flanks as magma shifted and seethed upward in response to unimaginable pressures from below. Each frozen river marked a time of desolation and renewal, of plant life devastated as the land itself was created. Death and ultimate rebirth, the paradox of the burning mountain.

It was both the desolation and the creation that brought Nicole to the volcano. In some way that she couldn't articulate, the land spoke to her, giving silent testimony to the tenacity and endurance and ultimate beauty of life. For each violent moment of new land boiling forth from the earth's molten interior, for each river of fire scoring through green vegetation, there was also a long time of tranquility and renewal. Nor was the devastation ever total. Often kipukas survived, islands of life serving as a core from which plants and animals spread out again, life growing and changing to meet the new conditions of the cooled land, life creating something both soft and vital from the fertile ashes of destruction.

That was what Nicole sought as she stumbled over a track that only she and Benny knew of. She needed to sit in the midst of life that had survived past devastation. She needed to look beyond the kipuka and see the tiny signs of life returning to land that was as hard and sharp as the moment it had cooled years and years ago. What tiny, fragile flowers could do, she could do. Survive.

But first she had to find her own inner islands where emotions had survived the morning's devastation.

And if there were none, then she had to know that, too. Without kipukas it took longer for life to colonize the landscape of volcanic creation, but life did win out. Even islands that had been first covered with, and then surrounded by, half a planet's worth of water ultimately managed to rise above the waves and clothe themselves in ferns and flowers and sweetly singing birds. If Hawaii was possible, anything was possible.

Anything.

The kipuka was small, hardly more than an acre. It was like a lush emerald garden tucked among scrubby plants that struggled to find a foothold in the brilliant black of an old pahoehoe flow. Unlike most kipukas, this one was a hillock rather than a depression around which lava had divided and flowed long ago. The vegetation was lush, almost tangled. Ferns grew in the least fertile parts, and colorful kopiko and ohelo bushes abounded. The familiar ohia tree raised its graceful crown to the sun, silently offering up a future bouquet of tightly furled flowers.

Nicole eased through the thick growth, seeking her favorite spot beneath a many-trunked koa tree. The tree's roots had prevented other woody plants from encroaching, leaving a sun-splashed opening where mixed grasses and small flowering plants like koali morning glories and white strawberries thrived.

With a feeling of relief so great it was almost pain, Nicole sank down onto the grass and leaned against one of the koa's nearly smooth trunks. She sat without moving, letting the peace of the kipuka sink into her like a healing balm. After a while the tiny sounds of the kipuka resumed, a reassuring murmur of pollinating insects and of immigrant songbirds moving like bright, musical shadows just behind curtains of green foliage.

Nicole sat quietly, her eyes closed, becoming part of the timeless kipuka, asking nothing of herself, refusing to let her thoughts go in smaller and smaller circles until her body would become as tightly knotted as her mind. Eventually, when she felt calmer, she allowed herself to think about what she would do when she left the kipuka. The impulse to flee the island was very deep; she had fled a disaster once before, and it had worked.

Had it? Or had it simply set the stage for a bigger disaster? Chase Wilcox.

The thought kept her still for a long time. In the end she set aside the temptation to flee. Flight accomplished nothing. She had fled halfway around the world once before. If she did it again, she would be back where she started. No. She would be even worse off. Hawaii was her home.

And there was the fact that, wherever she went, she would already be there, waiting for herself to arrive. Same woman. Or rather, the same failure as a woman.

She doesn't know the meaning of the word passion. About as skillful as a—

Nicole wrenched her mind away from the harsh words. She would have given anything to doubt their truth. She could not. That was how she had fallen into the sensual trap with Chase. In the deepest level of her mind, she had doubted her husband's assessment of her as a woman, so when something in her had seen Chase and said, *this is the man,* there had been no inner voice to warn her that she was being foolish.

Now there was no doubt. Her husband had been right. She had been wrong. She had made the most excruciating mistake of her life. She had to live with it and finally beyond it, giving whatever islands of life remained within her time to slowly spread out and heal the ravaged landscape of her dreams.

If there was anything left to heal.

Chapter 7

She's not here," answered Bobby, opening a beer and handing it to Chase. The Kipuka Club was empty, chairs tucked under tables, everything suspended, waiting for the Saturday night crowds to arrive. "Benny told me he saw her up on the mountain this afternoon, though."

Chase hadn't thought Nicole would come to the Kipuka Club to dance that night, but it had been his best hope of seeing her. "Was she all right?"

Bobby stopped in the midst of uncapping his own beer and gave Chase a sharp look. "First Dane, now you. What's going on?"

For a moment Chase watched creamy foam climbing the narrow interior of the beer bottle and then sliding down the smooth brown glass. Bubbles caressed his knuckles with tiny, bursting kisses before he bent and licked up the savory froth.

"Thanks for the beer," Chase murmured, looking up and saluting Bobby with the bottle. "Need a drummer tonight?"

The Hawaiian's black eyes narrowed. "I'm beginning to think I might need a dancer named Pele."

Chase nodded slowly. "It wouldn't surprise me."

"So you tell me. Is she all right?"

"If she can climb the mountain, she must be," said Chase, tipping the neck of the bottle to his lips.

Bobby said something in Hawaiian.

Chase met the black glare without flinching.

"Man trouble," said Bobby flatly. "Worse kine trouble. You be dat man?"

Until that moment Chase had thought Bobby's excursions into pidgin both amusing and amazing, given the man's education. Right now it was neither. It was like the harsh rumble just preceding a volcanic eruption.

"Yes-no?" demanded Bobby.

"Yes or no," said Chase softly, "it's none of your damn business. Unless Nicole's your woman?"

"You slower dan aa, haole," Bobby said in sardonic tones. "Dat wahine belong *no* man."

"Ever?"

Bobby lifted his beer bottle and didn't set it down until there was nothing left but a thin interior veneer of foam. In silence he opened another bottle. Only then did he lean against the polished bar and look around the empty club.

"You asking for a special reason?" Bobby said mildly.

"I'm asking."

"I get the feeling that's pretty special for you. Asking."

Chase's head moved slightly. It could have been a nod, or it could simply have been that he had shifted position. He gave away no clues, except perhaps in the very stillness with which he waited for Bobby's answer.

"I don't know how she lived on the mainland," said Bobby. "Don't care. When she came here she looked like hell. Pale. Eyes like bruises. No life in her hair or her walk. Her idea of a smile made you want to cry."

Inwardly, Chase flinched. He had seen that Nicole this morning. The image would haunt him for a long time to come.

"She didn't let anyone close. She got work up on the mountain, did her job and tried like hell to be invisible." Bobby smiled slightly. "Woman like her, that isn't easy. Some of the men gave her a try despite her powerful lack of interest. At first, she just ran."

"And then?" prompted Chase when it became apparent that Bobby was waiting.

"She started turning them down with a quip and a smile. Her skin changed to gold and her smile was the prettiest flower on the island. And her walk..." Bobby's eyes half closed, and his lips curved into a very male smile.

"A man?" asked Chase, the words a bitter taste in his mouth.

"A boy. And a dance."

Chase looked puzzled.

"You see," continued Bobby, "she'd discovered Benny up in a kipuka only God and that kid knew about. She brought Benny home to us. My mother took one long look at Nicole, muttered, 'Pele,' and taught her how to dance." Bobby grinned hugely. "You wouldn't have believed the change in the next year. Nicole laughed. She smiled. She let herself be touched." Bobby saw Chase's subtle flinch. "Not that way. Family touching. Hugs and pats and kisses and kids on your lap smearing you with jam. No lover, though."

"You sound very sure."

"I am."

"Why?"

"I would have been the man," Bobby said simply. "Hazel and I were sleeping separate then, and Nicole was like a little wounded bird to me. I knew I could heal her if she would let me. I wanted to. I used to lie awake nights, thinking of how it would feel to have her sleeping in my arms, that red hair of hers like a cool fire across my chest."

He spun the beer bottle absently on the bar top, watching the color leave Chase's face and then slowly return. "Why does that bother you?" asked Bobby. "It never happened. Now it never will."

"Because you and Hazel are back together?" asked Chase roughly.

Bobby shook his head. "We have an understanding about wounded birds of both sexes."

Chase couldn't completely conceal his surprise.

The big Hawaiian smiled slightly. "It works for us better than being separated did."

"Then what's the problem with you and Nicole?" asked Chase, hearing his own words with another sense of shock. But he had to ask. The memory of Nicole's hesitations with him and her physical ease with Bobby and Dane were part of why Chase had misjudged her so completely.

Bobby sighed. "A while back some mainland scientist did an experiment. He raised kittens in a place that had only horizontal lines. No verticals. After four or six weeks, he put the kittens in a cage with vertical bars. The kittens kept walking into the bars. Couldn't see them. Their eyes only knew how to interpret horizontal lines."

With an oddly graceful motion, Bobby turned his back to the bar, propped both elbows on the polished surface and watched Chase as the words sank in.

"Keep talking," said Chase.

"I thought you were quicker than that, haole."

"Yesterday I thought so, too."

Bobby's eyes narrowed into glittering black lines, but all he said was, "Somebody conditioned Nicole to avoid sex. She literally couldn't see me as a lover, nor any other man. The men who tried to make her see, lost her. I like Nicole too well to lose her just for a romp in the sheets. I want to heal her, not hurt her. She senses that, so she trusts me. But she can't *see* me."

"If I remember that experiment correctly," said Chase, "in time the kittens adjusted to their new reality. They saw both horizontal and vertical lines."

Bobby nodded slowly. "No one tried to find out what would have happened if the kittens had been stuck back in the original cage, though, or in some variation, like a diagonal world. I'll bet it would have paralyzed them. They'd have been afraid to do anything for fear of slamming into more invisible obstacles."

Bobby shifted onto one elbow, making the thick muscles in his upper arm swell with the sheer physical strength that was so much a part of him. "But we're talking about a woman, not kittens. Nicole *saw* you. She took one look and decided that if any healing got done, you'd be the healer, not me." Bobby smiled, but it went no farther than his brilliant white teeth. "You screw it up, brother, and I'll be waiting for you."

For a long moment Chase looked into bottomless black eyes. He didn't blame the big Hawaiian for the threat. If Chase had been in Bobby's shoes, he would have reacted in exactly the same way. No, not quite. He would have tried to break Bobby. He would have tried to break any man who hurt Nicole.

The realization startled Chase, telling him how guilty he felt for misunderstanding Nicole.

"You don't have to wait any longer," he said flatly.

Bobby's breath hissed out in a sibilant curse.

"You see," continued Chase, "kittens aren't the only things that can be conditioned not to see all of reality. Men can, too."

A ripple of simple, physical rage visibly went through Bobby's huge body as he realized what Chase was saying. "Are you seeing all of reality now?" asked Bobby, his voice low, flat.

"I'm working on it."

Bobby's mouth shifted into a smile that was almost cruel. "Then you're figuring out what you lost," he said, flexing his big hands. "I guess that's punishment enough."

"Wrong," said Chase softly. "I haven't lost. Stay away from her. If there's any healing to do, I'll do it. Hear me?"

For a moment it was difficult to tell which man was more surprised by Chase's flat statement. A shadow of amusement crossed Bobby's broad face.

"Would it change your mind to know that I have a black belt in karate?" he asked dryly, looking down at Chase without even having to stand up straight.

"No."

"You think you can beat me?"

"In a fair fight? I doubt it. But I'd beat you, Bobby. One way or another. Count on it."

There was moment of tense silence before Bobby's smile flashed hugely. "It's a good thing I like you, haole. Otherwise we'd trash this club and each other while we sorted things out." He looked around at the tables and chairs and potted flowering plants. "Hell of a waste, too. Just redecorated last fall." Then he turned and pinned Chase with a black glance. "But if she comes to me—"

"She won't."

Chase turned away abruptly and headed for the door with long strides, wishing that he were half as certain as he sounded, wishing he knew why it mattered so much to him that he be the one to heal Nicole's wounds. But he didn't know why. He only knew that the feeling and the need went too deep to be denied or ignored.

He drove quickly to the Kamehameha estate, hoping that Nicole had returned. Her car wasn't parked in front of the path that wound down to her cottage, nor was it parked up on the hill in front of the big house. When he got to his own cottage the phone was ringing. He grabbed the receiver, hoping against all logic that it was Nicole calling him.

"Hello," he said, his voice tight, almost harsh.

"She called Lisa a few minutes ago."

Chase let out a harsh breath as he heard Dane's clipped words. "And?"

"The drawing lesson is on for this evening."

"Where?"

"Here."

"I'm coming to dinner."

"No."

"Look—" began Chase roughly.

"If Nicole sees your car she won't come in," said Dane, overriding Chase's words. "If you arrive after her, she'll leave. You know it. I know it. Do you want the kids to know it, too? Give her some time before you corner her again."

Chase hissed a pungent word as he realized that he wouldn't have a chance to drum for Pele that night. He wouldn't have a chance to talk to Nicole at all, and if he tried to force the issue he would just make things worse.

If that was possible.

"When should I pick up Lisa?" asked Chase, accepting the inevitable.

"No rush. You can worry about moving her into the cottage when you're here for more than a few weeks at a time."

"That could be Christmas," said Chase, thinking of all the loose ends that needed tying up on the Mount Saint Helens project. "I'm going to be commuting back and forth to the mainland for quite awhile."

"And you're going to be spending most of the next few weeks hiking all over the island. Why not leave Lisa here? We love having her around. She has the sweetest little smile."

"I know," said Chase. "I missed her like hell after the divorce."

Dane hesitated, then said bluntly, "Lynnette damn near ruined Lisa. She needs a home, Chase. A real one. You can't give her that right now. Janet and I can."

"So can I."

"Can you?" Dane drew a deep breath. "I realized this morning that a lot has happened to you that I didn't know about. Lynnette . . . changed you."

Chase's hand tightened around the phone until his knuckles ached. "I won't argue that," he said carefully, remembering all too clearly what he had done to Nicole because he couldn't believe that she wasn't another Lynnette, out to wreck homes and lives for no better reason than pure selfishness. "But Lisa is my daughter. I love her and she loves me. Don't fight me on this, Dane. You'll lose. I don't want it that way. There's been too much hurting already, too much losing. It ends now. Here."

There was a long silence on the other end of the line, followed by a sigh.

"Sorry," muttered Dane. "My protective instincts are in overdrive. I'll call you after Nicole goes home. You can pick up Lisa tonight. I know you wouldn't do anything to hurt her. It's just—damn it, Chase!"

"I know," he said, his voice aching with the effort of speaking calmly. "I'm sorry I hurt Nicole. I don't want to corner her. I just have to make her understand that it was my mistake, not hers."

"She'd rather be left alone."

"Scars aren't the same as healing," said Chase. "I learned that this morning when I realized how badly Lynnette had scarred me. I thought I was whole again. I wasn't. I don't want Nicole to 'heal' the same way I did. I couldn't live with that."

There was another long silence. When Dane spoke again, his voice was warm, affectionate, full of memories. "That sounds more like the older brother I used to worship. You always were a rough son of a bitch, but you were also the one who taught me the meaning of the word decency."

Chase's laugh was short, almost sad. "Pull the other one, brother. You fought me tooth and nail over the damnedest things."

"Like I said, full hero worship. I had to keep testing myself against you to find out how much I'd grown."

"Now you know," said Chase, his voice ambivalent, layered with emotions.

"What?"

"You outgrew me."

Very gently, Chase hung up. He went to the living room and sat by the wall of windows overlooking the garden. The path to Nicole's cottage was an elusive, flower-lined thread winding through the trees. He wanted to walk down it, sit on her doorstep and wait for her to return. He wanted to make her understand. His mistake, not hers. He had to make it right again, somehow. Only then would he be able to look in the mirror without a grimace of disgust.

Once, when he had been studying an erupting volcano, the wind had shifted, wrapping him in corrosive gases and an erratic rain of hot cinders. No matter which way he turned, he had been seared. It was that way now. Impressions of the morning kept erupting without warning, burning him: Nicole's pale face and wounded eyes; the clear knowledge that she would have walked through fire to avoid him; a humiliation so deep that it had literally sickened her.

Thank you for not hurting me.

Grimly Chase stared into the night, his jaw clenched until the pain of it shot through him. He had not felt such helpless rage and disgust since the day he had stood in court and listened as his daughter was handed over to a woman who shouldn't have had custody of a potted plant. There had been nothing he could do then. But there was something he could do now. He could talk to Nicole.

Corner her.

The thought made uneasiness spread through Chase, the kind of uneasiness he had felt and dismissed last night.

Tonight he didn't dismiss what his instincts were telling him. Dane was right. Nicole wasn't ready to talk with the man who had cut her up so badly, so mistakenly.

Yet Chase had to talk to her. He wanted it so violently that he got back in his car and drove beneath the rising moon to the Kipuka Club, putting temptation beyond his reach.

The moon was well above the trees when Nicole's car pulled to a stop in front of the path to her house. Although she had told herself that she would be able to handle the inevitable moment when she confronted Chase again, she was so relieved that her hands shook when she saw that his car wasn't parked in its usual place. She hurried down the path, not stopping as she normally did to touch the cool, fragrant petals of the night-blooming flowers.

For an instant the memory of Chase delicately tasting a hibiscus flashed into Nicole's mind, shaking her. She shoved the thought aside, unable to deal with it. She knew he was a sensual man. She didn't need to be reminded of it, for then her own failure as a woman simply loomed larger.

Like a corpse.

She flung her purse onto a chair as she shut the door behind her. The cottage was stifling. She pushed open the windows, then the French doors which led into the garden. Filmy curtains began to lift and turn on the breeze like streamers of fog.

Nicole knew that she should shower and eat and go to work on her ideas for *Islands of Life*. But the instant the thought came, she rejected it. Chase was a part of that project. It was up to him to tell her what to draw, when to draw it, where to draw it. She had already settled that in her mind while she'd been sitting in her tiny, hidden kipuka.

Enter a new world of ROMANCE...FREE PRIZES...
No purchase necessary to enter and win!

4 FIRST PRIZES
Pearls from the Orient. Win a strand of the world's most beautiful treasures—earrings to match.

10 SECOND PRIZES
Bask in the Bermuda Sun. Take a long, romantic weekend for 2.

25 THIRD PRIZES
5-Piece Luggage Set. Lightweight and durable for stylish adventures—anywhere!

200 FOURTH PRIZES
$25.00 Cash. Buy yourself a gift in any store in the country—on us!

SILHOUETTE SPECIAL INTRODUCTORY OFFER

4 SILHOUETTE INTIMATE MOMENTS novels FREE, a $10.00 value. Satisfy your cravings for romantic fantasies, intense sensuality, stirring passion.

FREE FOLDING UMBRELLA, just for accepting 4 FREE BOOKS with this introductory offer.

FREE EXTRAS: Our monthly Silhouette Books Newsletter... a Mystery Gift Bonus.

SAVE 10%. We'll then send 4 brand-new books each month, as soon as they are published to examine FREE for 15 days. Pay just $9.00 ($10.00 value)—that's it. No shipping, handling or any other charge. Cancel anytime you wish. The 4 FREE BOOKS AND UMBRELLA are yours to keep.

She wasn't going to leave Hawaii. She wasn't going to leave any part of the life that she had found for herself here, either. She would continue to dance at the Kipuka Club. She would work at the observatory. She would illustrate *Islands of Life*. She would take Chase's daughter on picnics.

Nothing would change.

Nicole's glance skimmed over the futon. It was still open, the sheets still tangled. The memory of those few instants when she had felt hot and wild and had shivered at Chase's touch raced through her, tightening her body. The sensations were new, all but unbearable. She had no defense against them. With a choked sound she looked away. For an instant she swayed almost dizzily, wanting desperately to be capable of the kind of sensual response that would hold a man like Chase.

But she wasn't. Nothing had changed. Nothing would change. Nothing *could* change.

She had to remember that. She wouldn't survive another mistake like the one she had made with Chase. She wasn't even sure how she was going to survive that one. The aftershocks of it kept ripping through her unexpectedly, shaking what little calm she had managed to find.

After a few minutes of pacing the cottage, Nicole knew she had to do something or she would be in worse shape than she had been when she fled to the kipuka that morning. Automatically she reached for a record, put it on the turntable and waited for the sound of Tahitian drums to beat within the aching silence that was herself.

At first Nicole only listened, letting the primal rhythms sweep through her, driving everything else from her mind. But it wasn't enough just to listen. The drums called to her in a way that she had never really understood. She simply accepted it. She had accepted it from the first moment Grandmother Kamehameha had held out her hand, said, "Come," and taught Nicole's body the dances that had always lived in her soul.

Nicole threw aside the entangling folds of her muu-muu, shook out her hair and gave herself to the elemental rhythms. She danced until the record stopped and began all over again, and then again. And yet again. She danced until her body gleamed like molten gold and her hair was wild around her. She danced until she could remember nothing that had come before the endless moment of the drum's rolling thunder and could imagine nothing be-yond that moment. She danced until she was a flame burning in the midst of midnight, and she and the drums were one, indivisible, perfect.

Finally, exhausted, she slept.

The next morning she woke to the sound of someone knocking lightly at her door. For a moment she froze, afraid to move, terrified that Chase had finally caught up with her.

"Nicole?" called Lisa softly. "Are you awake?"

Nicole's hammering heart settled into more even rhythms. *What on earth makes you think that Chase would come after you?* she asked herself silently. There was no answer but the same inner certainty that had once told her that Chase was the man she had been looking for all her life without knowing it.

Well, you found him, she told herself grimly. *Lucky you.*

"Nicole?"

Hastily Nicole reached out and pulled on the muumuu she had tossed away last night. "Come in, Lisa."

The door opened hesitantly.

Nicole sat cross-legged on the futon, stretched and held out her hand to the little girl. "Where's Janet?" asked Nicole, yawning. "Or did Dane bring you?"

"No, Daddy did."

The last bit of sleepiness fled Nicole. She came to her feet in a single rapid movement, as though she expected Chase to be right behind his daughter.

"Where is he?" asked Nicole carefully.

"Asleep. When I woke him up he said the drums kept him awake until nearly dawn."

"The drums?"

"Your drums."

The thought of Chase staying awake, listening to the drums as she danced, sent unfamiliar sensations sliding through Nicole. "Sorry," she said tightly. "Next time I'll turn down the sound."

"Oh, don't, please. It was fun. I sat in Daddy's lap and we watched the moon and listened." She smiled shyly. "I wanted to come to your cottage and see you dance, but he wouldn't let me. He said that if you'd wanted an audience, you would have gone to the Kipuka Club."

The evidence of Chase's thoughtfulness was as unexpected as his attack on her yesterday morning had been. Nicole made a small, helpless gesture, then smiled with more determination than cheerfulness.

"Are you staying with your father all day?"

"I'm staying with him until he has to go back to the mainland."

Nicole knew that Lisa's presence would make it very hard for her to avoid Chase. She also knew how much it meant to Lisa to be wanted by her father after being rejected by her mother.

"I'm glad for you, honey," Nicole said in a husky voice. "I know that you've missed him." For an instant Nicole was tempted to send Lisa back home for fear that Chase would wake up, miss her and come looking. Abruptly Nicole realized that she was trying to hide again, and this time Lisa would be the one hurt. The little girl was hypersensitive to adult rejection. "Have you had breakfast?" asked Nicole.

Lisa shook her head.

"Good. We can have it together. Just give me time to shower, okay?"

"Should I get Daddy up, so he can—"

"No," said Nicole quickly. "Let him sleep. Why don't you try drawing the garden path while I shower? Remember what I told you about shadows all coming from the same direction and how things get smaller the farther they are away from you?"

Lisa nodded, her gray eyes serious. Nicole smiled and went to the shower, wishing every step of the way that she could get her hands on the female who had made a seven-year-old child as serious as an adult. Lisa didn't smile enough and rarely laughed. Also she simply vanished at the first sign of disapproval, as though she had no defenses, no sense of her own worth. Nicole knew how painful and destructive it was to feel that kind of personal failure. It enraged her that a child as gentle, bright and potentially loving as Lisa had been driven so far into a protective shell by a woman who wasn't worthy of the name.

Nicole dressed, returned to the living room and bent over Lisa's shoulder. The little girl was looking skeptically at the lines she had drawn and the pencil in her hand. Nicole knew that Lisa didn't have a tenth the natural talent that Benny had, but that didn't prevent Lisa from enjoying drawing.

"I like that," said Nicole, stroking Lisa's dark hair. The braids were shiny but rather mussed, as though she had slept in them and had not combed them out since. "I can feel the coolness of the shadows."

Lisa looked over her shoulder, smiled shyly and returned to her drawing with renewed confidence.

As Nicole sliced fresh fruit for breakfast, Benny materialized at the garden doors.

"Eat?"

"Sure, Benny. If you want eggs, though, you'll have to beg them from your mother. I'm out."

"Fruit," he said, managing to get a world of approval into the single word.

Benny stepped into the room, limping slightly, yet graceful and sure despite that. He spotted Lisa and broke into a beguiling smile. "Li-sa," he said, accenting her name oddly, musically.

Lisa's smile came and went so quickly that it was like a shadow of light chasing across her serious face. The two children had met on one of Nicole's picnics a few weeks before. Benny had been fascinated by the fragile little girl. It was a fascination she returned in full.

"Hi," said Lisa. "How did you get here?"

"Home," he said, gesturing with his hand toward the big house on top of the hill.

Lisa's smile came again, and stayed. "Yours?"

Benny nodded.

"The garden, too?"

He nodded again.

"And the beach?"

This time he smiled and held out his hand in a gesture that reminded Nicole of the time his grandmother had extended her hand and had drawn Nicole into another world.

"Share all with you, Li-sa," said Benny. "Come."

Lisa jumped to her feet, forgetting about her drawing. Nicole was too startled at hearing six consecutive words out of Benny to object as the two children ran through the French doors and into the beckoning Eden.

"No swimming until I get there!" called Nicole hastily.

Benny's answer was a wave that somehow managed to tell Nicole that she was being foolish—he would never do anything that might hurt the delicate, gray-eyed little girl.

Nicole packed fruit and honey muffins into a wicker basket, changed into her bathing suit and gathered up her sketchbook and a handful of towels. As she stepped into the garden, she hesitated, wondering if she should try to get a bathing suit for Lisa. The thought of waking up Chase made her decide that Lisa could swim quite well in the cotton shorts and tank top she was wearing. As for Benny, he usually swam in whatever he happened to be wearing when the mood took him.

Although it was early, the black sand was already warm. It was a warmth that varied only a few degrees throughout the year. One of the hardest things for Nicole to get used to in Hawaii had been not only the lack of seasons, but the absence of any real change in the weather at all from sunrise to midnight. The Hawaiians didn't even have a word for weather. The closest they came was a word describing the rare days when the trade winds died and the southern winds blew, bringing a muggy, stifling heat to the islands. Then natives spoke of "volcano weather," and left Pele offerings of food and fiery drink on Kilauea's brooding rim.

Nicole glanced up toward the place where she knew Kilauea rose, looking for signs of an eruption with the same casual eye that mainlanders use to measure thunderheads for their storm potential. There were no visible signals of the magma seething beneath the island's black skin. Nor did the surface of the land shift restlessly, reflecting the rhythmic quivering of molten stone as it tested the hardened lava relentlessly, seeking the fractures and channels and fissures through which to give birth to yet more land. Despite its long period of quiet, Kilauea showed no signs of revving up for a big show.

Looks like the hotshot pool is going for a record, thought Nicole as she settled cross-legged onto a towel.

Rumors of an impending eruption had been going through the observatory for several weeks, but other than the patterns of tremors that the scientists argued about every night in the Kipuka Club, nothing had happened. Nicole knew that an eruption wasn't imminent because none of the active rift zones had been closed to tourists. Nor had the road up to Kilauea become lined with cars driven by expectant natives and tourists. On Hawaii, volcanic eruptions were usually predictable, mannerly and awesomely beautiful. As a spectator sport, they were without peer.

"Niiicolllle!"

She glanced up from her idle sketch pad in time to see Benny and Lisa burst from a clump of coconut palms and pelt over the sand toward her. Benny had a huge green nut in his hands. Despite his limp, he shinnied up and down coconut trees with the ease of a cat. The first few times she had watched, Nicole had held her breath. Now she merely licked her lips in anticipation of the fruit.

Benny pulled out his pocketknife and went to work on his prize. The three of them ate in a companionable silence punctuated by giggles from Lisa as various kinds of fruit juices trickled between her fingers and down her arms. Nicole had the distinct feeling that getting grubby was a relatively new delight to the child.

"C'mon," said Nicole as they finished the snack. She held out her hand. "Time to wash up."

Disappointment clouded Lisa's transparent features as she looked at the path leading back to the cottages.

"No. This way," Nicole corrected, pointing toward the turquoise sea. "Don't you know how to swim?"

Lisa shook her head.

"Do you want to learn?"

Dubiously, Lisa nodded. "It looks awful big."

"That doesn't matter," Nicole said reassuringly. "You're in only one part of it at a time."

The sudden sound of male laughter froze Nicole in place. She looked over her shoulder and saw Chase standing in the shadow of a coconut palm, almost close enough to touch. He wore black swim trunks, an aura of potent masculinity and a smile. The sight of him was like a blow. She nearly went down beneath a sensual tide of memories as she realized that she had touched the rippling male power of this man, held him, felt him move inside her—

And failed to please him in any way at all.

Nicole felt herself flush, then go pale, and prayed that she was the only one to notice. She looked around almost frantically, seeking a way to escape.

Chase's gray eyes admired the braided fire of Nicole's hair, the golden skin, the black two-piece suit, which was modest by Hawaiian standards yet nonetheless revealed an enticing amount of womanly curves. He had seen the instant of sensual awareness and approval in her eyes when she'd looked at him.

And he had seen the humiliated retreat as she searched for a way to avoid him.

"Daddy!" said Lisa, throwing herself into Chase's arms. Then her smile faded. "Oh. I'm dirty." She pushed away from his chest and looked at him with wide eyes, obviously expecting to be punished.

"Are you? Where?" he asked, ignoring the liberal smears of sand and juice and the less definable stains that had come from racing through Eden down an overgrown path. He smiled and kissed Lisa's sticky cheek. "Mmmmm," he said, licking his lips. "Got any more of that coconut for me?"

Lisa giggled and snuggled against her father's furry chest, confident again. "Mother always got mad at me if I was dirty."

"Your mother worried about a lot of things that weren't important," said Chase calmly, despite the hot lick of anger that went through him at the reminder of Lynnette's treatment of Lisa.

Over his daughter's shoulder, Chase watched as Nicole knelt and began gathering up the remains of breakfast, tucking them blindly into the wicker basket. As she stood and shook out the towel, it became obvious that Nicole was leaving.

"Aren't you going to teach me how to swim, Nicole?" Lisa asked plaintively, unwrapping her arms from around Chase.

Nicole forced a smile. "That's what fathers are for."

"Me," said Benny, stepping close, indicating that he, too, would help Lisa learn to swim.

"You couldn't have a better teacher than Benny," said Nicole, easing back toward the path up the hill, smiling brightly. "He taught every fish in the lagoon how to swim."

Lisa's eyes widened as she looked into Benny's bright black gaze. "Is that true?"

He smiled and wisely said nothing.

Chase bent over, set Lisa on her feet and said to Benny, "Take her down and get her feet wet. Just her feet. I'll be right with you."

Chase straightened and turned toward Nicole, wanting to get those first, awkward words behind them, to tell her again that there had been nothing wrong with her. He had been the one at fault. Wholly.

There was no one there when Chase turned, only an empty garden path and palm trees swaying beneath the caressing wind.

Chapter 8

Are you going to run forever?'' asked Chase quietly.

Nicole turned around so fast that she almost lost her balance. For an instant she was afraid she wouldn't be able to breathe. Air returned in a rush, and with it came a surge of color that she was helpless to control. She sensed the lull as people in the Kipuka Club turned speculatively toward her. Word had gotten around that something had happened between the untouchable redhead and the mainland lady killer.

Rumors linking Nicole to a newcomer had been spread before, and she had been able to squelch them with a quip and a shrug. She hadn't been able to this time. She knew she looked as pale and tense as she felt.

"Exercise is good for you," she said, shrugging, avoiding Chase's eyes, refusing to really look at him.

"Then let's exercise together," he retorted.

Nicole paled.

"On the mountain," said Chase grimly, hating the flinching away from him that had become reflexive for

Nicole since the disastrous morning at Dane's house. After nearly a week of stalking her only to have her slide like fire through his fingers, his temper was more than a little savage. "Illustrations, remember? Or have you decided to give up on the *Islands of Life* project?"

"No," she said, her voice strained.

But she wished that she had. She hadn't known how difficult it would be to see Chase, to never know when she would turn around and find him watching her with his bleak gray eyes, to be forced to exchange meaningless pleasantries with him while humiliation twisted through her.

And to endure it all under the very interested eyes of her coworkers. They knew. All of them. She might as well have hung signs from every one of the Kipuka Club's ceiling beams.

"Then let's get cracking," said Chase. "I've got a tentative list worked out, starting with the fire pit and going all the way to the sea. I figure it will take at least two weeks just to visit each area and select the various microenvironments that should be dealt with in detail."

Nicole nodded stiffly.

"With luck, we'll find everything we need on Kilauea," continued Chase. "Otherwise, we'll have to shift to Mauna Loa. That means overnight camping." His eyes narrowed at the appalled look that came to Nicole's face. "Yes, I thought you'd feel like that," he said, leaning toward her, his voice so soft that only she could hear. "Nicole, don't you know that the last thing I'd do is touch you again?"

She went white, and her eyes dilated with helpless pain. She hadn't thought he would be so cruel as to bring up her inadequacy again.

Chase saw her lips go pale, heard the echo of his own words and realized that she had taken them wrong. His hand went out to touch her. "I didn't mean— Damn it, there's nothing wrong with you as a woman," he said bluntly. "All I meant was—"

She turned away, cutting off his words.

"Nicole."

As she stopped and turned around slowly, Chase sensed the curious stares of the people in the club. It had been like that since Monday—as if they were living on center stage. The difference was palpable. What bothered him was that Nicole was bearing the brunt of it. Before, she had joked with the people she'd met, turning aside any too-evident male pursuit with a quip and a smile. From her friends— men and women alike—she had received welcoming smiles, a friendly pat, even a quick hug if she hadn't seen a person for a while.

It was different now. Every man who had been to the Kipuka Club seemed to know that Nicole had joined the pool of sexually available women. To most men it made little difference beyond a certain speculative quality in their look, as though they were rearranging their mental land- scape, putting her in a new category and then forgetting about it. To some of the men, though, it was as though she had been stripped naked and thrown into an invisible sex- ual arena. They pursued her with every expectation of eventual success.

Chase understood exactly what had happened. When the men had been sure that Nicole slept with no one, they had accepted the fact that she turned down their tentative or overt advances. Now the men knew otherwise. Chas- tity and humor had been her shield and her weapon. Chase had stripped them from her, leaving her defenseless. What had once been joking advances had become anything but a joke. The knowledge enraged Chase, but there was nothing he could do about it, no way he could protect Ni- cole.

Chase didn't know which he felt worse about—the men who pursued her or the male friends whose touch she would no longer permit. There were no more friendly pats, no exchanges of small talk, no sense of camaraderie re- turned. He didn't know whether it was that she couldn't bear being touched or that she was terrified of appearing to encourage more than friendship. It didn't really matter. In the end, the result was the same. She had cut herself off from the very people who might have held the more predatory men in check.

The thought did nothing to ease Chase's guilt. Or his temper. The longer Chase spent stalking Nicole, the more deeply he understood the enormity of his misjudgment of her.

"Draw up a list of plants you want illustrated and in which stages of development," she said tonelessly. "Tell me when and where you need me. I'll be there."

"Here. Now. We have to talk, Nicole. This can't go on any longer."

For the first time Nicole met Chase's eyes. They were bleak, implacable.

"Hey, babe," said Fred cheerfully, coming up behind her and slipping an arm around her waist. "I've been looking for you."

Nicole tried to step beyond Fred's reach. His arm tightened, holding her in place.

"When are you going to teach me how to dance sexy?" he asked, bumping his hip against hers several times.

"On the thirtieth of February, just like I promised," said Nicole, hoping that she was the only one who heard the desperation in her voice.

Once, Fred would have let go of her with a laugh and a shake of his head. Now he simply smiled and bumped intimately against her again. Discreetly Nicole struggled against the arm clamped to her waist.

"Babe, the moves I've got in me can't wait that long," drawled Fred.

Nicole sensed the instantaneous tension in Chase's body as though her nerves were connected to his. Suddenly she felt trapped, cornered, half-wild. She couldn't bear being touched by the overconfident, overeager scientist any longer.

"Joke's over," she hissed between her teeth. "Let go!"

"Do I look crazy? The fun's just beginning," Fred said, running his hand from her waist to her ribs and back again. "I'm going to teach you a few horizontal moves that will blow your—"

The words stopped in a gasp of surprise and pain as Chase's hand shot out. He peeled the intrusive fingers from Nicole's waist with a ruthless twisting motion that stopped just short of breaking bones. When she was free, Chase smiled unpleasantly and stepped up the pressure of his large hand until Fred's face was more pale than Nicole's had been.

"You know," said Chase conversationally, looking at Fred with frankly lethal intent, "in the last few days I've gotten a gutfull of your comedy routine. Clean up your act or I'll put it on the hospital charity circuit."

Fred's breath came out in a rush as his fingers were released. He stepped back and looked warily from Chase to Nicole. "I thought you were through with her," he muttered.

"You thought wrong," Chase said softly, his voice vibrating with anger. "Any man who wants to touch her better wait for an engraved invitation. From her. Pass the word, pal, or there's going to be a rash of broken hands on the mountain."

Fred hesitated, flexed his hand tentatively, then shrugged. "February thirtieth it is, babe," he said, glancing at Nicole.

"Sure," she said, her voice faint. As he turned away, she shuddered, unable to control her emotions any longer.

"Are you all right?" asked Chase tightly.

"I'm fine," she said, the words too quick, too brittle. Then she whispered helplessly, "Oh God, I hate being a *thing*!"

Chase remembered what she had said about marriage, about being a man's *thing*. "Let's get out of here," he said, his mouth grim. "You look like you could use some air."

Nicole stumbled as she turned toward the door, her normal grace deserting her.

"I'm going to put my arm around you," warned Chase.

"I—" She stumbled again.

Chase's arm caught Nicole, supporting her. He saw Dr. Vic close in from across the room.

"Nicole?" asked Dr. Vic. "Are you all right?"

She forced a smile onto her face. "Just a little tired."

The scientist gave Chase a hard look. Chase gave it right back, too angry to be politic with the elderly professor. "Excuse us, sir. I thought some fresh air would help Nicole. The club is a little close tonight."

"Hmmm, yes. Fred can be a little, er, cloying. I'll have to speak to him about it."

"Do that," said Chase. "There are a few more you might put on your list, too," he added, thinking of two other men he had seen at the observatory hotly pursuing Nicole despite her manifest lack of interest.

"Who?"

"Oh, you'll recognize them," Chase assured him grimly. "They'll be the ones with broken hands."

Chase led Nicole toward the club's side door. His grip on her was gentle but implacable. He had waited as long as he was going to wait before he talked to her. Running wasn't helping her—and it sure as hell wasn't doing him any good, either.

In silence they stood just beyond the partially open side door of the club. They were in a small fenced yard that ended at the alley. There was little chance that they would be bothered; it was a private, rather than a public, entrance to the club. As they stood there, a curtain of mist lowered from the clouds and swept across the tiny yard. Nicole felt the rain as though at a distance, a coolness more sensed that experienced. She felt no need to go back inside, preferring the damp but private shelter to the communal dryness of the club.

Chase unzipped the windbreaker he had worn and slipped it over Nicole's shoulders. She looked at him, surprise showing clearly in her pale brown eyes.

"That isn't necessary," she said quietly. "I'm used to the rain. Hawaiian rains are like sunshine. Warm."

"Wear it," he said tersely.

He heard the anger seething just beneath the surface of his voice like magma seething below the black lid of Kilauea's caldera. He cursed quietly and ran a hand through his hair, wondering how to start. Now that he had her alone, he didn't know where to begin.

How do you ask a woman why the hell she slept with you?

The answer when it came was quite simple.

"Why the hell did you sleep with me?" demanded Chase.

Nicole turned her face up to the rain, accepting it, just as she accepted the fact that she had run as far as she could and that now there was no place to hide.

"It seemed like a good idea at the time," she said finally, her mouth turning down in a bitter smile at her own expense.

"That's no answer," he said roughly.

"Why do you care?" she asked in a tired voice. "It's not going to happen again. Is that what's worrying you? That I might expect something from you? I don't. All I want is to be left alone."

"Nicole—"

She lifted her hand suddenly, cutting off Chase's words. "You thought I was after Dane. I wasn't. You apologized. I accepted. That's the end of it."

Slowly Chase shook his head. "But it hasn't ended," he said, his voice dark, strained. "I hurt you badly. You're still hurting. I want to—heal you."

Nicole closed her golden eyes and tried to think of nothing at all. "That isn't possible," she whispered. "You can't heal a corpse."

"What?" asked Chase, shaken.

"You're the one who pointed out that that's what I was like in bed. A corpse. You don't heal a corpse. You bury it and walk away." Nicole fixed him with eyes that were like tarnished gold. "So walk away, Dr. Wilcox. The autopsy is over, the dirge has been sung, the grave is sealed."

Chase's hands closed swiftly over Nicole's shoulders. "Stop it," he said harshly.

With an effort, Nicole halted the scalding flow of words. She took a deep, shaking breath and wrapped her arms around herself as though she were cold. Chase watched her through narrowed eyes, hearing her words echo, trying to make them fit with the hesitant lover who had thanked him for not hurting her.

"What the hell happened to you before you came to Hawaii?" he whispered hoarsely.

Nicole closed her eyes and shook her head, saying nothing. Beneath his hands her whole body radiated rejection and refusal.

"You haven't dated, you weren't after Dane, and you were more frightened than passionate with me." Chase's hands tightened on her shoulders. "Why did you do it, Nicole? Why did you sleep with me?"

"Chalk it up to loose morals. I'm a slut."

"That's crap and you know it."

"But that's what you saw when you looked at me. That's what I proved when I went to bed with a man I hadn't known a week. After all, what 'paragon of virtue' would—"

"Don't do it," Chase interrupted, his voice low, warning.

"What?"

"Use my words like weapons against yourself."

"But they work so well," she said. "Truth is like that. A weapon."

"Then use it on me," said Chase, closing his eyes, feeling tired and angry at everyone and everything, but most of all at himself. "I made the mistake, not you. You're the furthest thing from a slut that I've ever met."

"You thought I was as hot as my hair," said Nicole, her mouth turning down again as she remembered another man's words, another man's weapons. *The only thing hot about you is your hair.*

"I thought you were after Dane," began Chase, his voice both gritty and patient as he tried to make Nicole understand that it had been his fault, not hers. There was no need for her to look so stricken, so fearful, as though she were waiting to be hurt again.

"I wasn't after Dane," she said quickly. "I wasn't after anyone before you came."

"I believe you." Chase saw the faint surprise on Nicole's face as his words finally sank in. "I've watched you since—that morning. I've seen how it really is for you."

Numbly Nicole turned her face up to the rain again and waited to be told about her failures as a woman.

"At the observatory, you clown with the single men, ignore or top their double entendres, and don't give an inch otherwise. But you used to allow the married men to touch you. A hug here, a pat on the arm there, a slap on the shoulder and a smile. Why?"

"They're married. They're—safe."

Chase thought of Bobby Kamehameha and smiled grimly. "Not always, Nicole. Not always."

"They are to me! I would never—"

Nicole's voice broke beneath the tension that was making her body like carved stone. Suddenly the need to flee was so great that it was like a craving for oxygen after spending too long underwater. She knew that Chase was going to make her admit that she had wanted him, and then the depth of her failure as a woman would be even more humiliating. She didn't know if she could endure hearing about it from his lips again.

Suddenly she knew that she could not endure it. Yet she could not flee, for his hands had slid from her shoulders to her wrists, and he was gently unwrapping her arms from their defensive position around her waist. If she tried to move away from him, the strong fingers would close, holding her in place.

Trapped.

"And the single men?" Chase asked softly, trying to understand Nicole because he had learned how very painful misunderstanding could be. He did not want to hurt her again. He didn't think she could take that. He didn't think he could, either. "Do you avoid them because they aren't 'safe'?"

Nicole's dismissive shrug was jerky, harsh. Adrenaline flooded through her, yet she couldn't run, couldn't hide. Almost frantically she cast about in her mind for weapons, reasons, something, anything that would make him leave her alone. Suddenly it came to her. Words were weapons. And the most lethal weapon of all was truth.

She should know. The truth of her own failure had destroyed her like a river of molten rock, burning alive everything in its path, covering everything in a mantle of cooling stone. She had survived, though. She had even conquered the rock enough to grow again, putting out tentative leaves and flowers of friendship, soaking up the affection that came in return like a plant soaking up warm rain and warmer sunshine.

"As far as I can tell," Chase continued gently, relentlessly, "you haven't slept with any other man in the whole state of Hawaii, *so why did you sleep with me?*"

Nicole shuddered and turned her face away from him to look at the tiny, enclosed garden. "I've asked myself that at least a hundred times a day," she whispered, telling him as much of the truth as she knew.

"And?"

"I have a real talent for trusting bastards. You're my second, you see."

Chase's breath came in sharply. Eyes the color of summer rain probed Nicole's pale face and saw pain accentuate her cheekbones and darken her eyes. He leaned toward her. Her lips were moving again, but she was speaking so softly that he could barely hear.

"No, that's not quite true," she murmured, listening to her own thoughts, learning from them even as she spoke. And it was anger she was learning. She had been wrong to trust Chase, but that didn't give him the right to destroy her. "You're different from my former husband. Next to you, Ted was a legitimate son of gentle society. He was merely impatient with me and unkind about my shortcomings as a woman. You have a cruelty in you that cuts all the way to my soul." She looked at Chase again, her face as calm as her words were bitter. "I hope that cruelty cuts both ways."

"Nicole," he whispered, understanding only her pain and the knowledge that being his lover had cost her more than she could afford to pay. Unconsciously he caressed the softness of her inner arm, wanting to soothe and pleasure her.

"Let go of me," Nicole hissed, her body suddenly alive with the sensual knowledge of Chase's heat so close to her, burning her. His hand was strong and hard but gentle with her flesh in spite of the intensity with which his eyes were searching hers. "Don't tease me with what I can't deliver. Despite my past performances," she continued, her voice shaking with emotion, "I've just discovered I'm not a masochist."

"I know," Chase said softly. "You were made for pleasure, not pain."

As Chase spoke, he slowly stroked the length of Nicole's arm again. He saw her eyes widen in shock and felt the ripple of response racing through her as though it were going through his own body rather than hers. *She's turned away all men for years, yet she shivers at my touch.*

The thought sent a shock wave of desire through Chase. The force of it surprised him. He had felt nothing like it until the night he had been driven by his need to take her too hastily, before he knew her. He wouldn't make that mistake again. She had been hurt too many times; and against all odds, all experience, she had turned to him for healing. He wouldn't hurt her again. It was too much like hurting himself. When he held her in his arms next time, it would be a healing thing.

For both of them.

Slowly Chase bent his head and lifted Nicole's fragrant wrist to his mouth. He kissed the frantic pulse beating just beneath her skin, touched his tongue to her softness and closed his teeth over her inner wrist as delicately as though she were a flower brought to his lips for a taste of honey.

Caught between the conflicting needs to flee his sensual danger and to drink as deeply of his sensuality as she could, Nicole stood without moving but for the shiver of her flesh at each caress.

"I'll be good to you this time when we make love," he said huskily.

Desire and fear warred for control of Nicole's responses. She tried to jerk her wrist from Chase's grasp. He was too quick, too strong.

"Make love?" she said in disbelief, her voice shaking.

"You weren't wrong to trust me," he said, caressing the shadow network of her veins with the tip of his tongue, licking up raindrops and the indefinable taste of woman. "Give me another chance, sweet dancer. There's so much that we can give each other."

"I don't have anything to give a man. Ask my ex-husband. Oh God, why bother? Ask yourself!"

Nicole wrenched free and bolted back into the club.

Chase could have stopped her, but he was too shocked by what she had said: *I don't have anything to give a man. Ask my ex-husband. Ask yourself!*

For long minutes Chase stood motionlessly, oblivious to the rain pressing his shirt against his chest and making his lavalava cling wetly to his hips, remembering his harsh summary of Nicole as a lover. If she had been a courtesan, the summary would have been as true as it was brutal. But she wasn't. She was a woman who had been taught to believe that she had nothing to offer a man. Given that, her responses were generous and sweet and shivering with potential for intense sensuality. A potential he had first ignored, then scorned. A potential he would kill to have offered to him again.

Bobby stood in the doorway, a wet windbreaker in his huge hand, watching while pain pulled Chase's face into forbidding lines.

"She dropped this," Bobby said laconically.

Automatically Chase reached for the jacket. Bobby moved his hand suddenly, keeping the windbreaker beyond reach.

"Stay away from her," said Bobby flatly.

"No." Then, his voice harsh, Chase added, "I can't."

He pushed past Bobby into the club's dimly lit interior. The room was full of Friday-night refugees from the university and observatory. Chase nodded to the people he knew but stopped to talk with no one. Nicole had already slipped behind the stage curtain. Quickly he unbuttoned his dripping shirt, hung it over the back of a chair and went backstage to the drums. He took his position and waited motionlessly, his mind churning.

She's afraid of men, afraid of sex, yet she slept with me before we'd known each other a week. Why? Why did she trust me?

Even as he began to drum, the question ate at Chase, giving a hard edge to his drumming as the students stepped onto the stage to dance. Nicole wasn't with them. No glorious flame burned at the back of the stage. Her absence went into him like a knife, making him want to cry out at the futility of the hurt he had given in place of the pleasure she deserved.

Why didn't I trust her?

No answer came, only the memory of a snapshot of Nicole standing on a black sand beach, her hair a glorious swirl of fire around her, and Lisa laughing among the flames. He had held that snapshot in his hand and stared at it until he ached with hunger. He had wanted Nicole before he even knew her name. He had wanted her before he had ever seen her sensual body. He had wanted her before he had ever seen her fiery dance. A single look at a snapshot and he had wrapped up his Mount Saint Helens project in a fury of work and flown to Hawaii.

Was that how it was with her? Did she look at me and want me enough to forget her fear?

There was no answer but the primal sound of the drums speaking darkly beneath his hands.

I was so certain that Dane was in danger. Why?

That answer was simple. Chase had believed that no man could look at Nicole and not want her enough to throw over everything to have her. Perhaps he had known intellectually that wasn't true for every man, but emotionally he had been utterly convinced.

It had been that way with him. One look.

The rhythms of the dance radiated from the drums, but beneath the complex beats, Chase's barely restrained savagery prowled throughout the darkened room. He had been in such a rush to taste the honey that he had crushed the blossom and, in the end, had tasted only bitterness, given only injury.

Christ, if only I'd known . . . !

Sound poured out of the drums in a rolling thunder that resonated through the night, calling up a darkness that had nothing to do with the absence of light. The students could not keep to the furious rhythms. One by one they dropped to the stage floor, spent. Nor did they try to chant encouragement to the remaining dancers, for they had neither words nor legends to equal the drums' raging soliloquy of injury and regret.

Nicole watched from the wings, her heart beating as wildly as the drums. Before Chase had begun to drum, she had told Bobby that she had decided not to dance, that she was going home. Then the drums had spoken to her from the darkness, telling her things for which she had no words, emotions resonating. She hadn't been able to refuse the seething rhythms of anger and isolation and regret. They spoke to her so exactly, so perfectly. She could no more turn away from their dark, syncopated violence than Kilauea could turn away from its own searing fountains of molten stone.

With quick motions of her hands, Nicole took down her hair and stepped onto the stage. A murmuring went through the room, a low wave of sound that was her other name.

Pele.

From the first step, the first thud of bare heel on wooden floor, the dance was different. There were no flashing smiles, no teasing, flirting hips, no graceful fingers describing languid invitations. Tonight Pele's body described an anger that equalled the drums' wild discontent. She was no longer a laughing girl dancing her suitors into the ground. She was a goddess scorned, and every quick movement she made proclaimed her seething emotion. Graceful, dangerous, untamed, as all fire is untamed, Pele claimed the stage, burning amid the drums' violent laments.

Neither drummer nor dancer noticed when the last student abandoned the stage. Nor did they notice that Bobby had lifted his pipes to his lips once, then put the instrument away before a single note had come. The two people on the stage had attention for nothing but each other—though Nicole refused to look at Chase, had refused since the first instant of the dance. She didn't have to look at him. He was in the center of her soul. He was the blood beating wildly in her veins. He was the heat turning her body to shimmering gold.

Chase sensed the transformation from wounded Nicole to angry Pele. As he watched her, his gray eyes reflected both the raging regret of the drums and the fiery accusations of the woman who called to him with every movement of her body. He had wanted her, had taken her, had lost her. He knew it, all of it, and that knowledge was a river of molten stone pouring through his soul. Emotions he had no words to describe beat wildly within him, tearing at him, seeking a release that had no name, finding that release in the sweet violence of the drums and the dancer burning just beyond his reach.

The dance went on without pause, rhythms increasing and then increasing again, separate pulses and movements compressed into impossibly small intervals of time. Distantly Chase realized that his hands had gone from aching to numbness to sudden, flashing pain. He knew that he should stop beating the drums, knew that with the next impact, or the next, his skin would give way beneath the relentless demands. He kept drumming, ignoring the pain. He wanted to give something to the woman from whom he had taken too much, and he knew that this was her dance, her moment, her time to burn.

Deliberately Chase stepped up the rhythm yet again, building thunder into a wild, beating crescendo, knowing that Nicole was capable of meeting the elemental challenge. Yet even knowing it, he was nearly stunned by the unleashed fury of her dance. He held the violent drumroll as long as he could, then threw up his hands with a cry.

In the instant before the lights went out, Nicole saw blood bright on Chase's hands, on the drums, blood welling in silent apology between her and the man who had hurt her as no other man had, not even her husband.

"Chase."

The single, involuntary cry was buried beneath an eruption of sound from the audience. Nicole shuddered in the darkness and let go of the last of the dance's hypnotic fascination. For a long moment she waited to feel Chase's arms coming around her, his mouth claiming her, the hot, powerful length of him pressing against her until she arched like a drawn bow. She didn't know whether she feared or wanted him—she only knew that she was trembling like the mountain just before all the fires of Eden were unleashed, destroying and creating in the same instant.

The lights came on with a blinding rush, revealing a stage empty but for a woman with fiery hair and dazed golden eyes.

Chapter 9

Watch it!''

The warning was barely out of Nicole's mouth before Mark Wilcox grabbed the tottering jar of pickles and put it back onto the counter without a drop being spilled.

"Nice catch," said Nicole, sighing. "Thanks. I don't know what I'd do without you."

Mark gave her a quick, pleased smile. At fourteen, Mark was already taller than Nicole, although he hadn't begun to fill out. He had a long way to go to equal his father's muscular build, much less the even more powerful physique of his uncle.

"Hey, shorty," Mark said to his sister. "You going to use that peanut butter or just torture it to death?"

Sandi grimaced at her brother before passing the jar. Serenely Mark built himself a gooey sandwich consisting of peanut butter, pickles and mayonnaise. Sandi made retching sounds, which sent her friend Judy off into a gale of giggles. No sooner had she settled down than Benny came pelting through the garden. Normally he would have been followed by anywhere between two and ten of his cousins and siblings, but today the rest of the family was off to Oahu. Knowing that a kipuka picnic was scheduled, Benny had stayed home. Mark's best friend, Tim, was missing from the expedition due to a sore throat and a mother who couldn't be persuaded that her son's hoarse voice was the inevitable result of shouting during a baseball game. Steve, the other third of the traumatic teenage trio, was running late as usual. They would meet him at the bus stop.

"Ponchos?" asked Nicole.

A ragged chorus of affirmatives answered her query.

"Canteens? Bus fare?"

Another ragged chorus.

"Okay. Pack up your lunches."

"Li-sa?" asked Benny plaintively.

Nicole couldn't think of Lisa without also thinking of Chase. Her fingers suddenly clenched the material of her small knapsack, then moved on with only a slight tremor to mark the sudden hammering of her heart. The image of Chase's bleeding hands had haunted her in the long hours before she fell asleep the night before. The knowledge that he was in a cottage only a few hundred feet from hers was a slow fire burning in the silences of her mind.

"Lisa is living with her father now," said Nicole carefully. "He may not want her to come with us today."

Benny said nothing, but his disappointment tugged at Nicole's heart. She bent over and hugged him.

"Go ahead, honey," she said, smiling into Benny's black eyes. "Run up and ask if it's okay for Lisa to come with us."

"It's fine for her to come," said Chase from just beyond the open garden door. "As long as I'm invited, too."

"Hi, Uncle Chase," said Mark, obviously delighted by his uncle's unexpected appearance. "Want a P.B.P. and mayo to go?"

"Do I have a choice?" he said dryly, but his eyes were only for Nicole, who stood stricken in the center of her small kitchen. "May I come along?" he asked.

There was no way Nicole could refuse. "Of course," she said, turning away, stuffing her sandwich into a backpack.

"Hold the mayo," Chase said to Mark. He looked down at his daughter. "You didn't tell me we should bring lunch."

"Don't have to," she said, smiling. "Benny's here."

Benny smiled and held out a sack lunch that was big enough to feed four. "Share."

Chase opened the bag and saw fried chicken and fresh fruit, scones and raw vegetables. "Hold the P.B.P.," he said thankfully, looking up with a smile. He turned to Nicole. "We're ready when you are."

Nicole didn't say anything. She couldn't. She was still caught in the moment when Chase had reached toward the lunch and revealed fingers that were bandaged and palms that showed shadow bruises beneath a pattern of calluses.

"Golly, Uncle Chase," said Sandi. "What did you do to your hands?"

"Played with fire," he said, smiling crookedly.

"You get burned?"

"All the way to the bone."

Sandi's blue eyes widened. "That musta hurt."

"Yes." Then he added softly, "But I hurt the fire more."

Only Nicole and Lisa heard the words. Only Nicole understood them. She looked away from the rain-clear depths of Chase's eyes to his taped fingers. Her hands trembled as she picked up the knapsack.

"Okay, gang," she said, holding her voice even, with an effort. "Which kipuka?"

"Kamehameha Iki," said everyone instantly, voting for a lush, hidden kipuka more than halfway up Kilauea's slope. They had named the kipuka "Little Kamehameha" for Benny, who had led them to it.

"How about it, Lisa?" asked Nicole. "You feeling up to that kind of a scramble?"

"I'll help her," said Mark. "Right, squirt?"

"Me," insisted Benny.

"Me, too," said Chase. Then he added, "Is that in one of Kilauea's active rift zones?"

"No. Why?" asked Nicole.

"Bells went off on the rim this morning."

Instantly the children came to attention. They knew that there were alarms wired to the seismographs at the volcano observatory. Whenever harmonic tremors lasted for more than ten minutes, the alarms went off, telling resident scientists that magma was approaching the surface of Kilauea. But since 1975, when a big earthquake hit the mountain, the pattern had changed. The mountain had shifted, closing off old avenues for the release of magma and not opening any significant new ones. Before there had been four spectacular surface eruptions for every invisible intrusion beneath the surface of the land. Now the ratio was reversed.

Land was still being born, but silently, almost painfully, as though the mountain and the molten rock struggled against invisible bonds. As a result, Kilauea was far less predictable now that it lay in its self-made chains. One day those bonds would be thrown off, for nothing could stand for long against the enormous forces at work beneath the green Eden of the land. Then the fires of creation would leap freely again, and fountains of incandescent rock would shoot a thousand feet high.

"When? Where?" demanded the children, wanting to get a front row seat for the next eruption, if and when it came.

"It already was. Don't worry," Chase added as he saw the disappointment on their faces. "It was an intrusion rather than an eruption." To Lisa he said, "That means that the liquid rock never made it to the surface. It just sort of squeezed between the cracks of solid rocks down below.''

Mark made a disgusted sound. "Another sleeper. Boy, I'm gonna be old and gray before I see a real eruption."

Chase laughed. "I doubt it. The hotshot pool will be claimed within a few weeks. Bet on it."

"I tried," he said indignantly. "Dad wouldn't let me!"

Mark's friend caught up with them at a bus stop along the island highway. As the children paired off in the seats, Nicole found herself left to sit with Chase. The children spent the bus ride betting pickles against peanut butter on just when and where the mountain would blow. They peered out the windows, hoping for some sign. As usual, the top of Kilauea was swathed in clouds and rainbows, telling the children what they already knew—it was going to rain. It rained almost every day, but only for a short time. They accepted it the way mainland kids accept sunshine or snow.

Nicole spent the ride wishing fervently that she weren't so aware of Chase beside her, of his leg resting against hers for an instant whenever the bus rounded a right-hand turn. The first time she felt the heat of his skin against hers, she flinched as though she had touched molten stone. The second time it happened, she flinched, but not as much. By the fifth time, she had subdued her reaction to a slight tremor when she felt his hair-roughened thigh touch hers.

The bus made an unscheduled stop for Nicole and the kids just over halfway up Kilauea's flank. There was a trail that led to a popular island picnic spot. With Benny in the lead, they followed the trail until it frayed into ferns, shrubs and towering ohia trees. Like a well-drilled team, everyone shifted into hiking formation. Mark moved up to third place, behind Lisa. The other girls followed Mark, and Steve closed ranks after them, ready to help if needed. Nicole brought up the rear to keep an eye on everything.

But this time Chase walked behind her. She tried not to think of him as she struggled through some of the overgrown passages or scrambled down and up a steep ravine. Even though there was no real trail, no one was worried about being lost. Benny had an uncanny sense of place, a kind of three-dimensional memory that allowed him to see and retain forest landmarks that were invisible or unremarkable to others.

As Chase walked behind Nicole, he admired the grace of her long legs, remembering what it had been like to feel that smooth golden flesh alongside his own darker skin. The memory was so vivid that he was almost grateful when his thoughts were interrupted by Mark's cheerful voice.

"Let's hear it for ocean jokes," called Mark.

The kids all groaned in anticipation: punning had begun.

"Do you know where fish come from?" Steve called out over the girls' heads.

"No. Where?" they chorused.

"Finland."

There were groans all around, then a pause.

"Why can't a shark sing 'do re mi'?" asked Sandi.

"Don't know," said Lisa. "Why?"

"Cuz it doesn't have any scales!"

"Drown her," yelled Steve, laughing in spite of himself.

"Was there a porpoise to that joke?" asked Mark slyly. He smiled and bowed, acknowledging the round of boos that was his reward. There was a long pause. "*Fin*ished?" he asked. "Maybe we should move on to bird jokes."

"You mean like the one about the owl that was so lazy he didn't give a hoot?" asked Chase, smiling innocently beneath the midnight slash of his mustache.

Nicole groaned.

"Is that a sketch?" asked Lisa eagerly, turning to look at Nicole for an instant before giving her attention again to the uncertain ground beneath her feet.

Before Nicole could answer, Mark asked, "If a hummingbird does in his brother, it's fratricide. If it's his father, it's patricide. What is it if a hummingbird does in a stranger?" He waited for a long moment of silence before he said triumphantly, "Humicide!"

Chase stopped walking, threw back his head and laughed without restraint, enjoying his nephew's agile mind. The sound of Chase's laughter rippled over Nicole like an invisible net, wrapping around her, tugging her closer to him with each instant.

"Sketch!" demanded all the children except Mark, who waited modestly for Nicole's decision.

"Sketch," she agreed. "I've been *pun*ished enough for one day."

As everyone groaned, she pulled out her sketchbook and pencil. With a few quick strokes, she captured Mark's face as he enjoyed the applause of his friends. She also captured something beyond the moment, the quality of his intensity and his unfolding strength, the man growing beneath the boy's handsome, smiling surface. The sketch didn't flatter Mark; it appreciated what he was and what he would become.

Chase saw Mark's pleased grin as he watched the sketch forming and the quick, shyly admiring look he gave Nicole. The look told Chase that his nephew had more than a little bit of a crush on her. He doubted that Mark was even aware of it. And then Chase wondered if Nicole knew.

Nicole added a bloodthirsty hummingbird diving at Mark's ear. The boy laughed with delight and took the sketch to show everyone else. As Chase watched, he realized that Nicole knew about Mark's fragile, inchoate feelings toward her. The sketch had told Mark that she approved of him, while the maniacal bird had channeled the boy's response into laughter. Deftly, gently, Nicole had ensured that Mark would have no reason to be embarrassed by his adolescent awareness of her as a woman.

Chase appreciated Nicole's tact, and at the same time he wished that she would show half as much gentleness to him. Surely she knew that he regretted what he had done. But even as the thought came, Chase dismissed it sardonically. He might want her consideration, but he himself had shown damn little gentleness to her.

Benny led them out of the forest and across a lava flow that had only isolated streaks of vegetation on it. It took the rain, sun and wind a long time to erode the pahoehoe's glassy surface, allowing purchase for dust and seeds. Chase wondered how long ago the lava had flowed. Relative dating was easy enough—the older lava was usually underneath, and the newer was on top. But whether an eruption was one thousand, or seven thousand, years old was a matter of opinion. Even the kipukas were hard to date. In the tropics, trees didn't have well-defined seasonal growth rings, for the simple reason that there were no well-defined growing seasons.

Pahoehoe gave way to the much rougher, aa type of lava. Ferns, shrubs and grass appeared, and with them the lovely ohia tree. Within a few hundred feet the forest resumed as though the molten river of stone had never flowed and solidified, burning away the old and creating the new.

Overhead, clouds bent low, trailing streamers of warm rain over the land. The rain came down hard, passed quickly and left every little crease and crevice of the land alive with water. Rills and waterfalls appeared, enjoying their brief life before they sank into the porous lava and vanished. Some water would reappear as springs and streams farther down the mountain. Most of it would simply disappear, returning to the ocean through seeps far beneath the breaking waves.

The land got rougher, as though barely cooled lava had been churned with a huge stick and then left to harden. The children scrambled forward with the assurance of hikers who had been there before. They helped each other over the worst spots and went on eagerly. Chase noticed that Mark waited to see if Nicole needed help, only to be sent on with a wave of her hand. She went up the lava jumble gracefully, hesitating only once, when her foot slipped on the rain-slick leaves of a plant. Instantly Chase moved to her side, catching her arm, supporting her until she could regain her balance.

The feel of Chase's fingers on her upper arm made Nicole's heart lurch. Heat washed over her, followed by an instant of weakness. She was aware of the differing textures of his skin and of the tape that protected his sore fingers. She breathed in sharply and was surrounded by the hot male scent of him. She looked at him and saw his pupils widening in primitive response to her. For an instant she saw again his face above hers, his eyes dark with passion as he covered her body with his own.

"Nicole?" asked Chase quietly, "Are you all right?"

She closed her eyes, but that only increased her awareness of the man standing so close to her. Her eyes flew open. "Yes. You—startled me. I'm not used to—"

When Nicole abruptly stopped speaking, Chase finished the sentence for her.

"—being touched by a man who isn't 'safe.'" His eyes searched hers. "It's all right," he said gently. "You know that I won't hurt you." Then Chase heard his own words and his mouth turned down. He had hurt her very badly, and he hadn't even touched her while he was doing it. "Not like that, anyway. Physically. You can trust me that far, can't you?"

Numbly Nicole nodded, for it was the truth. Even when Chase had believed her to be a gold-digging little tart, he hadn't hurt her. His hands had been careful rather than harsh on her body. He had made her feel—good.

"Nicole," said Chase, his voice low, "let me make it up to you."

"There's no need." Then, quickly, before the objections she saw tightening his lips could be spoken, Nicole said, "You were better to me than my husband ever was, and he never felt guilty. Why should you?"

Chase heard the confusion in Nicole's voice and remembered the instant when he had undressed her and she had covered her breasts defensively. "Did he hurt you in bed? Is that why—"

"Uncle Chase!" called Mark from the top of the lava flow. "Is everything all right?"

Relief washed through Nicole as she registered Mark's presence. Now the uncomfortable conversation would have to end. Eagerly she turned toward the boy, but before she could speak, Chase did.

"Everything's fine, Mark. Nicole has a pebble caught in her shoe. Go on ahead. We'll catch up in a minute."

Mark hesitated until Chase turned around to face him fully. Even twenty feet away it was impossible to miss the command in Chase's gray eyes. Mark waved, turned and scrambled to catch up with the other hikers.

"Answer me," said Chase, but his voice and his touch were far more gentle than his words.

"He didn't beat me, if that's what you mean."

"That isn't what I asked."

Suddenly Nicole wanted to scream at Chase's lack of perception. Couldn't he see that she didn't want to think about it, to talk about it, to remember? In her anger at Chase's insensitivity she forgot to retreat, forgot to be humiliated by her own lack of response as a woman.

"You went to bed with me," Nicole retorted. "Can't you imagine why a man would get impatient and—careless? A corpse doesn't have any feelings to—"

Chase said a single, searing word. Nicole's own words stopped as Chase's mouth covered hers and his tongue thrust between her teeth. After the first overwhelming instant, the kiss changed. His tongue touched hers slowly; he sipped from her mouth as though she were a flower. Although the caress itself was very gentle, she couldn't have retreated if she had tried. His arms held her with a certainty that made her feel both fragile and, oddly, safe. He wouldn't hurt her physically. She knew it. In that, at least, she had been right to trust herself to him.

The knowledge made heat swirl in tenuous currents throughout Nicole's body. The currents softened her, changed her, made her breath into a sound wedged deep in her throat. The small cry shuddered through Chase. He lifted his mouth and looked down into Nicole's face, wanting to tell her how very much he regretted the cruel remarks he had made in the hope of thoroughly discouraging Dane.

The sight of Nicole's reddened lips made Chase forget everything but how good it had felt to join her mouth to his. With the same ravishing delicacy he had used on the flower, he caught her lower lip between his teeth. She felt each serration of his teeth as a separate caress, felt his tongue tasting and stroking her captive flesh, felt the tiny, sensual shocks as he tugged softly on her lip.

"You are a woman," he murmured, "not a corpse." He groaned and dipped his tongue between her softened, parted lips. "All woman. And if I don't let go of you," he added huskily, "I'm going to embarrass the hell out of those kids."

But instead of releasing Nicole, Chase kissed her again, slowly, deeply. When he lifted his head he saw desire in her eyes, and fear.

"Don't be afraid of me," said Chase, his voice aching.

Nicole shook her head. "It's not that," she said. The words were tight, as flat as the line of her lips. She tried to step back away from him but could not. He held her too closely, too powerfully, too carefully.

"Then what is it?" he asked.

"Let go of me. Please, Chase," she said desperately. "It —hurts."

"But I'm not holding you hard enough to hurt," he said, releasing her despite his words.

"That's not what I meant."

"What hurts, sweet dancer?" he asked, stroking her cheek with the back of his fingers.

She took a deep, broken breath. "Knowing that I'm only half a woman—hurts. When I'm around you, it hurts even more. You make me want things that are just—impossible."

"What things," he said coaxingly, touching the full curve of her lower lip with the callused pad of his finger, wanting to feel her softness between his teeth again. "What do I make you want?"

"To be woman enough to please you in bed," she said starkly. As shock widened Chase's gray eyes, she almost smiled. Almost. But it hurt too much to be alive just then. Smiling was out of the question. "Yeah," she said huskily, looking at Chase's dark expression. "Some joke, right? Go ahead and laugh. Don't wait for me. I'll laugh tomorrow, or the day after. Or—" She shrugged, running out of flippant words.

Chase stared, stunned, as Nicole turned away. "For the love of God," he said in disbelief. His hand shot out, wrapping around her wrist, holding her without hurting her. "Did it ever occur to you that I didn't please *you* in bed?" he asked bluntly. "It sure as hell occurred to me!"

"But you did," she said in a dull voice. "You pleased me more than my husband ever did. And I pleased you much less than a real woman would."

Chase shook his head, hardly able to believe what he was hearing. Then, from the corner of his eye, he saw a movement along the top of the lava flow. Someone was coming back to check on them. With a sliding pressure of his fingers, Chase released Nicole's wrist.

"We'll talk later," he said flatly. "In private."

"There's nothing left to talk about," said Nicole, her expression as weary as her voice. "You felt guilty for hurting me. Well, it wasn't your fault, so you can stop worrying about making it right. It was the truth that hurt me. I'm not much of a woman in bed, and you're all man. Talking won't change that. Nothing will.''

"Nicole?" called Benny from above their heads. "Path?"

"No thanks," she called back, understanding Benny's one-word question. "You don't need to find another way up for me. There's nothing wrong with this path that walking on it won't cure."

Chase watched Nicole disappear over the top of the lava flow, moving cleanly, gracefully. He followed in a coordinated rush, using strength where she had used finesse, wishing urgently that they were alone. Her words echoed in his head with each step, each rough caress of stone beneath his palm.

I'm not much of a woman in bed, and you're all man.

You're half-wrong, Nicole, he retorted silently. *I can't wait until we're alone, and I can show you which half!*

The tantalizing thought recurred to Chase more than once during the rest of the hike. He had no opportunity to talk to her about it or even to touch her for the sheer pleasure of feeling her tremble with the sensual response she had categorically denied being capable of. Nicole gave him no chance to get close to her. When they rested along the trail, she either had her sketchbook out or Lisa on her lap or both. Chase was relieved that fear no longer darkened Nicole's eyes when he talked to her, but neither did any other emotion appear. In some elusive manner, she avoided him while looking straight in his eyes.

The third time it happened, Chase had to overcome a desire to shake Nicole until she looked—really looked—at him.

Great, he told himself sardonically. *Shaking her until her teeth rattle is a hell of a way to impress her with how gentle and understanding you are. You might try remembering, hotshot, that a frontal assault on the defense is the least likely way to move a football, much less a woman.*

The next time everyone stopped, it was in the center of Kamehameha Iki. The kipuka was at least several hundred years old, for huge ohia and koa trees grew there. A deep, clear spring welled up in the north end of the kipuka, giving rise to a pool where scarlet blossoms were reflected along with the changing, rainbow-hung sky. Lush plant life cushioned the ground in shades of green punctuated by splashes of color from flowers.

The kids lost no time in peeling down to their swimsuits and washing off the heat and the dust of the hike. Nicole posted herself on a fern-covered outcrop and watched the swimmers, making sure that Lisa didn't get lost in the shuffle. Soon Benny signaled Lisa, and the two of them stole off into a quiet corner of the kipuka. Nicole noted their leaving and returned to her sketch.

Chase made no effort to sit next to Nicole. Instead, he got out his own notebook and began doing what he should have been doing all along, which was taking notes on the type of flora growing on lava of differing ages and compositions. He looked up from time to time, assuring himself that the remaining kids weren't getting too enthusiastic in their game of water tag. Satisfied, he returned his attention to his notes.

Without seeming to, Nicole watched Chase's growing concentration on the land around him. She was relieved that he no longer sought her out with rain-colored eyes and stormy urgency. She told herself that it was good that she had finally made Chase understand that he shouldn't feel guilty for what had happened. It wasn't his fault that she couldn't respond to a man. Perhaps it wasn't even her fault. Perhaps it was simply a fact, like the hardened lava twisting over the land. Just a fact.

But it would have been so nice to be able to stand within Chase's arms again, to know the shimmering sweetness of his tongue sliding over hers, to feel his heat and strength radiating through her. Even the thought was enough to send delicate currents through her body. The memory of his mouth caressing her breasts made her nipples rise and tighten, adding more currents to the restlessness deep inside her.

It won't happen again, so quit torturing yourself. That kind of touching doesn't please a man, not really. A man wants more. Chase knows he isn't going to get it. Not from me. I can't give it to him. So why should he waste his time petting me and frustrating himself?

The answer was simple. He shouldn't. And he wouldn't.

"Sad?" Benny whispered, appearing from nowhere to stand next to Nicole.

Nicole forced a smile onto her face, wishing silently that Benny's emotional radar were less acute. "Where's Lisa?"

"Hunting."

Nicole blinked, startled, then remembered what Benny had taught the little girl. "Syrup?"

Benny nodded. "Sketch?"

"You mean she caught one?" asked Nicole, scrambling to her feet and reaching for her pad.

"Big-big," Benny said, nodding, his smile lighting up his face.

Nicole gave a quick look around. The older children had exhausted themselves for the moment and were lying on the ground making up awful puns. Nicole tiptoed after Benny. She twisted and turned through the sometimes clinging greenery, envying Benny's ease and silence. As soon as he slowed down, she did. When he stopped, she crept up behind him and looked over his shoulder.

There in the middle of a small, flower-strewn clearing was Lisa, still wearing her scarlet bathing suit. She was sitting cross-legged, with the backs of her gently curled hands supported on her knees. Three huge butterflies rested on the edge of her left hand, drinking from the tiny pool of sugar syrup cupped within her palm. Each butterfly was as big as her hand, with velvety black wings set off by splashes of orange and white.

Lisa sat entranced, a look of breathless pleasure on her face. Nicole memorized everything about the glade and the girl and the moment, afraid that if she lifted her sketchbook, she would startle the butterflies into flight.

Suddenly Nicole sensed a presence behind her. She didn't need to turn around to know that Chase was standing there, close enough for her to feel his heat and hear the intake of his breath when he saw his daughter sitting in the sunlight with a handful of bright velvet butterflies.

For long minutes no one moved or spoke. The breeze shifted, sending a flurry of shadows over the seated girl. The butterflies on her hand lifted with the new currents and chased one another in wild spirals that took them out of sight among the trees.

Nicole let out a long breath. "Thank you, Benny. That was beautiful."

Benny gestured toward the little girl, then toward himself and said proudly, "Kamehameha," as he set off across the clearing toward Lisa.

"The butterflies are named after the Kamehamehas, the last Hawaiian royal family," said Nicole softly, knowing that Chase would hear.

"So Benny is descended from kings," murmured Chase. "And Bobby, too."

"Perhaps." Nicole smiled. "I don't know of a native on the islands who doesn't boast direct descent. But Bobby has one thing going for his claim."

"Oh?"

"Size," said Nicole succinctly. "The Hawaiian kings and queens were huge. Seven feet was not uncommon for male royalty. A woman under six feet was a shrimp," she added in an unconsciously wistful tone. "They were big eaters, too. A few centuries ago, Bobby would have weighed at least a hundred pounds more than he does today. That's why the butterflies are called Kamehameha."

"A four-hundred-pound butterfly?" asked Chase, his voice teasing.

Nicole smiled. "No. Just giants among their own kind. A four-inch wingspan."

"Daddy," called Lisa excitedly, looking beyond Benny to the underbrush where the two adults were hidden. "Did you see me? Three butterflies! Benny says I must be related to the old kings to be such a good hunter."

"How did he say all that in one word?" asked Chase beneath his breath.

"Princess," retorted Nicole softly.

She sensed, as much as heard, the laughter rising within his chest.

"I saw you," said Chase to his daughter as he stepped out into the clearing. "You were very good. Do you think Benny can teach me to hunt butterflies as well as you do?"

"We don't really hunt," said Lisa. "I mean, we sort of catch butterflies, but we don't hurt them or anything."

The voices of father and daughter floated back through the sun-dappled clearing to the place where Nicole stood concealed in the shadows.

"I know that, honey," said Chase, scooping up his daughter and settling her in the crook of his arm. "Otherwise it wouldn't be any fun for the butterflies, would it? Or for me." With his free hand he reached down and ruffled Benny's thick hair affectionately. "What about it? Can the descendant of Hawaiian kings be bothered to teach a mere haole the secrets of butterfly hunting?"

Benny laughed. "Sure-sure."

Nicole watched as the three of them sat cross-legged in the tiny, warm clearing. Benny's voice had the clarity of a silver bell as he told Chase how to sit, how to rest his hands palm up on his knees, how to breathe quietly and slowly.

And all in four words.

Benny squeezed a clear, viscous pool of sugar syrup into Chase's palm, stepped back and said, "Wait."

"That's all there is to it?" asked Chase.

"Sure," said Lisa. She pointed toward a velvet-winged butterfly settling onto a flower a few feet away. "She knows you're here. If she's hungry, she'll come to you."

"She?" asked Chase.

"Uh huh. All butterflies are girls. Like me."

Chase smiled and said nothing. "What if it, er, *she* doesn't come to me? Do I chase her?"

"No," said Lisa. "You're too big. You might hurt her. You don't want to do that, do you?"

"No," said Chase quietly. "I don't want to hurt anything that beautiful."

Lisa settled into place and waited as Benny applied the potent sugar solution to her hand. Silence and utter stillness reigned in the clearing. Nicole watched, almost afraid to breathe, as various butterflies skimmed and swirled over the clearing's flowers.

Finally a huge Kamehameha butterfly hovered around Chase's hand in a slowly closing spiral. The butterfly settled, fled, settled and fled again. Chase didn't move at all, not even to present his lure more openly. He waited motionlessly while the velvet wings fluttered closer and closer. Finally the butterfly rested completely, safely, in the palm of his hand, drinking deeply of the sweetness that he offered.

Nicole knew the exact instant the butterfly trustingly drank—that was when Chase's gray eyes looked up and found Nicole hidden among the green shadows, watching a butterfly cherished within the hard curve of his hand.

Chapter 10

The image of those delicate velvet wings and the restrained power of Chase's hand haunted Nicole as she waited for him to join her on Kilauea's rugged rim. Because the volcano observatory was across the caldera from the Hawaii Volcanoes National Park buildings, there were usually fewer tourists underfoot on the observatory side of the rim. Both a narrow road and a foot trail circled the caldera, but the path was quite rough in places. That and the fact that today Kilauea was about to receive part of its annual ninety-five inches of rainfall combined to give the caldera rim a privacy that Nicole wasn't sure she wanted.

Although Chase hadn't attempted to be alone with her as they organized their calendar for the *Islands of Life* project, his very presence had made Nicole restless. Like the butterfly spiraling down in the sun-dappled clearing, Nicole sensed the sweetness waiting for her if she would only alight within the reach of his leashed male power. All she had to do was trust him not to close his fingers while she drank, crushing her.

Nicole closed her eyes and inhaled deeply. Trust. That's all it took. Such a simple thing.

And so impossible. She knew that Chase wanted her. He made no effort to disguise it in the lingering of his hand when he brushed against her in passing. He made no effort to conceal his naked emotions as he watched her— sadness and anger, passion and regret. The same emotions gripped her when she listened to him talk about the earth and the places he had seen or wanted to see, heard him laugh with unrestrained pleasure, heard the sensuous promises his hands made upon the drums.

She knew that Chase was capable of great gentleness and sensuality. She knew that she wanted to be held by him, touched by him, and she wanted to hold and touch him in return. Yet she could not bring herself to light trustingly within his grasp again. It was not Chase she feared. It was herself. If she gave herself to him once more, and disappointed him once more, she knew she wouldn't have the nerve or the strength to pull her life together afterward. There was nowhere left to flee, no place remaining to hide, nothing but the restless currents inside her, pressing for release.

Trusting Chase was frighteningly simple. She had done it at first glance. Trusting herself was—impossible.

Nicole stood and brooded over the rain-swept rim of Kilauea's caldera, every sense alert for the sound of Chase's footsteps coming up behind her. In front of her, the cliff fell away to the flat caldera floor. Nothing but hardy ferns and a few straggling weeds grew on the rim. Only steam moved below. The landscape was both desolate and magnificent, a bold statement of the power seething deep within the earth.

There were only two significant interruptions in the caldera floor's level surface. The first was Kilauea Iki. Little Kilauea, the cone of a new volcano that was growing from the larger volcano. The second break in the floor was Halemaumau, the fire pit, the traditional home of Pele. Once it had been a fiery, liquid lake of lava that seethed and bubbled and occasionally burst into a display of burning fountains hundreds of feet high. A major earthquake in the first quarter of the twentieth century had changed all that. The incandescent lake had vanished, never to appear again. The fountains had vanished also, but they reappeared occasionally along the flanks of the mountain, a searing, dancing reminder of the continuing power of Pele.

"Penny?" asked Chase, his voice a laconic imitation of Benny's.

Nicole realized that she should have been startled by Chase's sudden presence, but she wasn't. Even though she had been lost in thought, somehow she had known that Chase had come up to stand silently beside her.

"I was just thinking that volcanoes test your faith," she said. "Intellectually I know that all this—" her hand swept out, describing desolation in a single arc, "—is necessary. Without it, Hawaii wouldn't exist."

"But?" he said, reading the objection buried beneath her quiet words.

"But it's hard to believe that anything good could ever come of this—this wounding," said Nicole, choosing her words as though it mattered very much that Chase understood. "The land looks not only bleak, but unalterably sterile, as though nothing could ever find a foothold for survival, much less for growth."

"Volcanic soil is among the most fertile on earth," said Chase quietly.

"Not at first."

"No," agreed Chase. "At first, it's exactly as you described it. A wounding. Only later does the rest of the truth show through—the ferns and the waterfalls and the flowers blooming in a midnight garden."

Nicole's golden eyes broodingly measured the caldera, seeing through the solid rock to the torrential, incandescent power beneath. "On Hawaii, we're all butterflies drinking out of a god's cupped hand," she murmured. "And the god's name is fire."

"Does the idea frighten you?" asked Chase. He remembered the instant when he had looked across the clearing, sensing Nicole's presence. She had watched his delicate care of the butterfly with an intensity and hunger that had made him curse the men who had hurt her—and himself most of all.

"Yes, it frightens me," she admitted. Then, quickly added, "No. That's not true." Nicole made a frustrated sound. "I don't know how to describe it."

Chase's laughter ruffled across her nerves. "Exciting?" he offered softly. "Do you feel more alive knowing that the earth beneath your feet is alive, too? That it has heat and rhythmic movements, that it is more powerful than you will ever be, more enduring, more incredible—and that without you to understand it, the earth is just one more piece of cooling stone circling a cooling, dying star in a universe that is also dying."

He turned and looked directly into her eyes. "But in that vastness your life is all that matters, all that makes a difference. Being alive to all the possibilities, accepting them, turning and sharing them with other lives in every way you can. Living always as though you were dancing and I were drumming. *Alive.*"

Nicole felt the intensity in Chase like a caress luring her closer, stroking her, promising her things for which she had no words, simply yearnings.

"Chase—" Her voice broke. "I can't!"

"Can't dance?" he asked, deliberately misunderstanding her. "You sure as hell could have fooled me, Pele, along with the entire population of Hilo."

Nicole's laugh was as frayed as her voice. "I can't—share."

"But you already have."

She looked up at him, confusion clear in her amber eyes.

"Just because I was too stupid to appreciate the gift," said Chase quietly, "don't think that you can't share. If you don't believe me, ask Lisa."

"Lisa?"

"Yes, Lisa—the little girl who heard herself belittled and then rejected by her own mother; the little girl who didn't believe she was worth—"

Nicole heard the break in Chase's voice, saw the pain in his eyes and knew that it was very difficult for him to talk about his former wife and his daughter's pain.

"The little girl," continued Chase, "who was so certain she was worthless that she rarely spoke above a whisper and never laughed. Lisa, who watches you with worshipful gray eyes whenever you walk into a room. You taught her more than drawing. You taught her how to laugh and play and look in the mirror without wincing. You shared yourself with her in a way her own mother never had, never would. You taught Lisa how to be alive."

"Janet—" began Nicole.

"Janet is a warm, loving person," interrupted Chase, "but she hasn't been hurt enough to recognize how deeply Lisa was wounded. You've been hurt like that." Chase closed his eyes, thinking of Bobby and wounded birds and healing. And hurting. "I guess it takes a wounded bird to help one. You've helped Lisa a lot. Thank you for that. Having to leave Lisa with Lynnette, making my own daughter pay for my stupidity in choosing a wife—that was the worst thing that had ever happened to me until I hurt you, making you pay for my mistake."

Abruptly his voice stopped, then resumed. "It was the same with Benny, wasn't it?" asked Chase. "Bobby told me about it. You found Benny when he was hurting, and you helped him to heal."

"Anyone would have done the same," said Nicole. "Benny is very special."

"I'm told some of his teachers have thought he was so 'special' that they wanted to use him as shark bait," Chase said dryly.

She smiled a bit, knowing how maddening Benny could be when he felt like it. "Well, I didn't say he was perfect, just very special."

"Like you," murmured Chase, wishing he could hold Nicole, heal her, feel her laughter against his skin.

Nicole looked up into his rain-colored eyes and forgot to breathe. She was afraid that he was going to touch her.

And she was afraid that he was not.

Chase saw both the fear and the yearning, and remembered vividly the velvet flutter of wings as a butterfly hovered and fled only to approach once more. Patience had lured the butterfly. Patience and gentleness.

Deliberately he turned away and looked at the caldera spread out beneath his feet. "You said that we should start at Kilauea's rim," Chase said. "We're here. Now where do we go?"

Nicole drew in an uneven breath, disappointed, relieved, restless. "I thought we could start here, work our way down to the fissure zone and go from there to the sea. Not all in one day. Parts of the trail are really rough. But you should get a good idea of the rate that life's establishing itself on the lava."

"And?" he prompted, sensing there was something more beneath Nicole's request. To his surprise, he saw red staining her cheeks.

"I thought you could answer my questions about volcanoes at the same time," she admitted. "I've tried asking some of the other vulcanologists, but their specialties are so narrow it's like they speak another language."

"Told you more than you wanted to know?" guessed Chase.

Nicole smiled, grateful that he understood. "A lot more," she said fervently. "I'm sure that the fractionalization—if that's the word!—of magma is fascinating."

"To someone else?"

"Anyone else," she groaned. "Dr. Vic gave me a post-graduate course in it the last time I asked him why some rocks were heavy and some weren't and they all came out of the same spout."

"Dr. Vic is a very, er, enthusiastic man," agreed Chase, hiding a smile beneath his midnight mustache.

"Then I tried to get some answers out of the textbooks that are always lying around the observatory," admitted Nicole.

Chase's mustache shifted as he gave up and smiled openly, revealing the cleanly curving line of his lips. "Problems?"

"Nothing that a graduate degree in physical chemistry wouldn't cure," Nicole said wryly.

"What kinds of things do you want to know?" asked Chase, truly curious.

She hesitated. There was no easy answer to that question, and no quick explanation. "It's not so much facts, it's feelings. You understand. You have a feeling for the land that comes from both knowledge and experience. It shows when you talk about the planet as though it were alive."

"It is. It just lives in a different time frame from us."

Chase could see the words sink into Nicole, rippling through her, giving her a pleasure that had nothing to do with her body and everything to do with her mind.

"That's what I mean," she said, her voice husky. "You see things in ways other people don't, and can share what you see. The instant I stepped off the plane from the mainland, I sensed what you just said about the land being alive. But I couldn't express it. I didn't know the why or the how of it. I simply knew it *was*. That's what drew me to the volcano observatory. I thought that I would learn facts and words to describe what I had sensed."

"And?"

"The first time I saw the harmonic tremors on the seismograms, I felt—" Nicole stopped, trying to find the words.

"As though you were eavesdropping on God?" suggested Chase, his voice soft.

Again, Chase saw his words sink into Nicole, saw pleasure in her sudden smile. He smiled in return, finding a unique enjoyment in being able to touch Nicole's mind. He had long since given up expecting, or even hoping, to find a woman who shared his wonder at the great natural processes of the earth. To discover Nicole's curious, receptive mind was both surprising and exciting.

The thought came to him that it would be an extraordinary pleasure to talk to a woman as well as to simply take her to bed.

"That's just how I felt," said Nicole, excitement in her voice. "Seeing all those lines reflecting the invisible movements of magma was eerie and wonderful and frightening and grand and—" She made a frustrated sound and laughed wryly at herself. "It's a good thing you're doing the words for the *Islands of Life* project. I'd sound like a high school sophomore writing home to her best friend."

Chase shook his head in silent disagreement. "But it's a good thing that you're doing the illustrations. Your *Volcano Portfolio* captured the emotional truth, as well as the physical reality of the islands. That's a gift I'd love to have." He smiled crookedly and admitted, "You see, I can't draw worth a damn."

"Did you ever want to?" asked Nicole, even more curious about Chase than she was about the hidden life of the earth.

"Many, many times. There's a sensual beauty to natural processes that words just can't recreate."

Nicole thought of wild rivers of molten stone and of jacaranda buds swelling toward the instant when they would come unwrapped in the sun. "Yes," she breathed. "There is so much to see, to feel, to know, to share."

Chase closed his eyes and looked away from Nicole, not trusting himself to keep from pulling her into his arms and holding her gently, inescapably. Being with her, talking to her, knowing her—these things were teaching him how empty his life had become of feeling and sharing. He remembered Dane's words, *Lynnette changed you,* and realized how right his brother had been.

But the change had happened so gradually, so casually, that Chase hadn't even realized what he had lost until it was too late.

Silently Chase turned toward a trail that led across the caldera to Halemaumau. The way was marked by cairns. The path wasn't difficult, although the land itself was tortured, telling of its past violent birth and equally violent future.

"I've spent a lot of time around active volcanoes," Chase said, his gray eyes searching the contorted land beneath his feet, "but I have to admit that the idea of walking across a lid of stone covering a seething cauldron of liquid rock is both exhilarating and—unnerving. A bit like helicoptering into Mount Saint Helens's crater to run some tests after the first big blow. We knew that another eruption could come at any moment, but probably wouldn't. Probably."

Nicole shivered at the thought of Chase doing field work on a volcano whose violence had already killed many people.

"That's the appealing thing about Hawaii's volcanoes," continued Chase. "All things considered, they're remarkably safe. Or, to be more precise, predictable."

"Don't tell the folks at the hotshot pool," said Nicole wryly. "They'll cut you out of the action."

"Well, not *that* predictable," admitted Chase. "Especially since 1974. That earthquake really rearranged Kilauea's interior plumbing." He gestured toward the southwest rift zone of Kilauea. "This hasn't gone since 1971. Magma still moves beneath, still swells the land, but no eruptions."

"Do you think Kilauea is dying, like Mauna Loa?"

"Don't count Mauna Loa out of the game," said Chase. "That mountain could bubble over at any time. It's not so far away from the hot spot yet that it's lost touch with the central mass of magma."

Nicole looked up at Chase for an instant, wanting to ask a question. She stumbled on the uneven land. Chase's arms swept out and steadied her. He wanted very much to keep his hands on Nicole's warm skin, but he didn't want to make her retreat. Reluctantly he released her, letting his hands slide down to her slender wrist bones.

"Okay?" he asked.

Wordlessly Nicole nodded and drew back, not trusting her voice. Chase's touch both lured and frightened her. The more she was with him, the greater the lure. And the greater the fear. Without looking back, Nicole hurried on to her destination. From the fire pit's three thousand foot width, vapors arose in twisting veils, telling of the molten rock seething not far below. When both she and Chase were overlooking the crater from a safe spot, she turned back to Chase.

"What did you mean by 'hot spot'?" she asked.

Chase hesitated, wondering how to explain. "We think of the ocean bottoms and the continents we live on as fixed. They aren't. They're like rafts floating on the molten rock deep beneath the outer, cool skin of the earth. The raft we're on is moving very slowly northwest. As it slides over the area beneath the central Pacific, the raft comes into contact with a very special feature of the earth, a place where magma wells up continuously, endlessly. We don't know why it wells up there," he said, forestalling the question he saw as Nicole turned toward him, "but it happens. There's a chain of volcanic islands, atolls, reefs and the like stretching from here damn near to the Aleutian Islands to prove it.''

Chase sensed the question before it came to Nicole's lips. "How did they grow?'' he asked for her. "Give me your hand.''

Nicole did as he asked without hesitation. He flattened out her fingers and held her hand, palm down, over his own hand.

"This,'' he said, gesturing to his own hand, "is the hot spot. It doesn't move. The raft—your hand—does.'' He began moving her hand slowly across the tip of his little finger. As her hand moved, he prodded the juncture of her palm and her little finger. "The magma that's welling up is irresistible. It either finds, or creates, a weakness in the moving raft. When the raft is pierced—'' he slid his little finger between two of hers "—magma pours out. Since the raft moves very slowly, there's plenty of time for the upwelling magma to build an island on top of the raft.'' He wriggled his little finger, now caught between two of hers, until the tip poked above her hand. "See? An island.''

Nicole looked into Chase's clear gray eyes and tried not to feel his touch expanding through every cell of her body. It was impossible.

"Chase—''

"Listen up,'' he said, smiling down into her eyes. "We've got a long way to go yet.''

Leaving his finger caught between hers, he moved her hand very, very slowly across the sensitive pad of his ring finger until it was beneath the solid flesh of her matching finger. "Guess what happens now?''

Nicole tried to speak, swallowed and shook her head.

"The island that the magma built—'' he wiggled his captive little finger again "—has drifted too far from the source of its molten rock, the hot spot. The raft is more or less northbound and the hot spot is stationary. But the magma—'' he tapped lightly with the pad of his ring finger against her hand "—has to be released. So a new split

in the surface of the raft is made." The tip of his finger slid
into place between her ring and middle fingers. "A new
island is formed, which becomes part of the raft. The raft
keeps moving, slowly taking the first two islands away
from the hot spot that created them."

Chase's middle finger prodded gently against Nicole's,
seeking a place to slide along the sensitive skin to the
opening that had to be there. "A third island forms," he
said softly, shifting his hand, sliding again between her
fingers. "And in time, a fourth. And a fifth." Now he held
her hand completely captive, his fingers threaded deeply
through hers. "Care to go for ten?" he asked, his voice low
and faintly husky.

Nicole's golden eyes widened. She started to pull her
hand away, only to find that she couldn't.

"That's all right," continued Chase, his voice normal
again. "You can learn just as much from five. Look."

Automatically she glanced back down at their joined
hands. As she watched, his little finger began to withdraw.

"Without the constant eruptions to bring new lava to the
surface, the sea and wind and rain wear away the island
until there is nothing left but a few rocks on their way to
becoming a coral-covered reef."

"Like Pearl and Hermes reefs?" she asked, referring to
two of the northernmost islands in the Hawaiian arc.

He nodded. "Millions of years ago those reefs were islands like Hawaii or Maui or Oahu," he said, slowly sliding his fingers in sequence from between hers, and letting
them settle like lost islands beneath the surface of her
hand, leaving nothing behind. "The reefs are Hawaii's
future."

Nicole's hand felt empty, almost cold. "All of the islands—gone?" she asked, knowing that it was true and
wanting to hear that it was not.

Chase nodded again. "All of them. Gone. But there will
be new islands to take their place. Only the skin of the

planet moves. The hot spot remains in place, welling over with new land, new possibilities for life. Mauna Loa gives way to Kilauea, Kilauea to Mauna Ulu, Mauna Ulu to an unnamed fissure on the ocean floor southeast of here. The hot spot endures, creating new volcanoes, new islands. Life colonizes the new islands from the old before they sink beneath the waves. Nothing is lost, not really. It just seems like it to us because our lives are less than a flicker of lightning against the vast endurance of the planet.''

Chase took Nicóle's hand again and stroked her sensitive palm with his fingertips, wanting to do more, much more. "But it's a very special lightning," he said huskily. "I wouldn't trade it for all the millions of years in an island's life."

Before Nicole could pull away, Chase released her. She stood motionlessly, feeling that she had lived for a moment in another time, another place. She looked at him as though she had never seen him before, wanting to thank him and not knowing how. Without thinking, she lifted her fingertips to his cheek, remembering only that his gentle touch had pleased her, hoping that hers would please him in return.

"Thank you," she whispered.

She saw the instant of surprise on his face, felt the sudden, silky brush of his mustache against her palm as he turned his lips into her hand. For a moment she thought that he would do more, that his arms would close around her, and he would pull her against his hard body, changing the moment of touching from gentleness to something else, something that she feared.

Chase brushed his lips across her palm again and smiled so tenderly that Nicole caught her breath. "You're more than welcome," he said, looking into her golden eyes as she quickly pulled her hand away. "Don't worry," he said, his eyes as clear and sad as rain. "I'm not cruel or stupid enough to crush a butterfly twice."

Nicole went white as she remembered listening to Chase talk to Dane, words tearing her apart until she'd fled. And then Chase had found her huddled wretchedly in the bathroom—She made a small sound and shuddered with the aftershocks of that awful moment.

"Don't," he whispered, seeing Nicole's memories in her suddenly dilated eyes. "Knowing what I did to you is like a knife twisting in my guts. I deserve the pain, but you don't. Don't think about it, butterfly. Please. It was my mistake, not yours."

"Is that why—" began Nicole. Then her voice broke, and for a time there was only the sound of the volcano breathing steam into the air.

"Is that why—?" encouraged Chase, aching with the need to put color back into her skin and voice.

"Is that why you're gentle now, because you feel guilty? You don't have to be. You were trying to—to protect someone you loved. You had no way of knowing that Dane was in no danger from me. I can't—" Her voice broke again. She closed her eyes and continued, determined to have it over with once and for all. "I can't respond to a man. I'm not a sensual woman. You didn't create the problem, Chase. You simply described it. Brutally, yes, but accurately. Don't be gentle to me now because you're feeling guilty about telling the truth. That isn't fair to either one of us."

"Nicole," said Chase carefully, "whatever gave you the idea that you couldn't respond to a man?"

"Experience," she answered, her voice bleak.

He hesitated, not wanting to hurt her more, yet knowing he had to be very certain that he didn't misjudge her again. He had to understand what had made her fear men. "Was your husband your first lover?"

An odd sound escaped Nicole's lips. "Lover. Oh God, if only!" She shuddered. "Yes. Yes, he was the first man to discover what a loss I am as a woman."

Anger narrowed Chase's gray eyes. "Don't. You're only hurting yourself. And it's a lie. You're very much a woman." Before Nicole could give words to her objections, he continued, "Did you want him?"

Nicole made a tight, restless movement that could have been a shrug. "Once I would have said yes." She took a deep breath and let the scalding truth pour out. *Chase had to understand. He had to know how useless his guilt and desire were.* "But then I heard you play the drums, and it was—different. Immediate. I wanted you, for all the good it did either one of us." She forced herself to shrug in a travesty of carelessness. "At any rate, that night taught me that I hadn't ever wanted my husband."

Chase looked down into her haunted eyes and remembered her defensiveness, her hesitations, and felt the knife turning deeply inside him. "Did he hurt you?"

Her lips turned down in a sad smile. "Do you know, I thought it was supposed to hurt, until you. It felt so good, so warm, to have you close like that." She took a shaky breath. "So you see, you have nothing to feel guilty about. You taught me a lot." She saw the pain twisting across Chase's features and said urgently, "I didn't mean it the way you took it. Truly, Chase."

"I know," he said, his eyes narrowed against the pain that she had known, the pain that he was sharing now. "That's why it hurts," he said simply. "I taught you just enough that you now believe you can't find pleasure in the act of love. You—"

"I can live with that," she interrupted quickly, her words tumbling out in an effort to make him understand. "It's knowing that I can't please a man that—"

Nicole's courage and her voice failed her at the same time. She looked helplessly up at the only man she had ever wanted, but not enough. Not enough to please him.

"My husband was right. The only thing hot about me is the color of my hair. Please, don't want me. Please. Leave me with some pride, some illusions. Because I still want you. I enjoyed being held and touched by you so much that there are times when I can't sleep for remembering. No,'' she said when he would have interrupted. "Let me finish while I still have the nerve.''

Nicole closed her eyes and took a ragged breath, wishing there were any other way to make Chase understand besides this upwelling of searing, burning truth from her vulnerable core. "But the kind of gentle touching I enjoy isn't enough for a man and I—I just don't have anything else to offer. So don't want me, Chase. Don't try to seduce me. *Don't make me fail both of us again.* I couldn't survive that.''

Experience told Nicole that denying men what they wanted made them angry or cold or cruel. She kept her eyes closed, not wanting to see the contempt she was sure would be on Chase's face. She expected him to turn away and leave her alone in the center of the seething caldera, to go and seek his pleasure somewhere else without a word of farewell.

She didn't expect to hear her name whispered in a raw, aching rush of breath, to feel herself gently enveloped in his arms and rocked slowly against his chest. For an instant she stiffened in despair, wondering if Chase had heard anything she had said at such costs to herself.

"I'll never hurt you like that again,'' promised Chase, his voice husky.

Relief and disappointment warred for control of Nicole's emotions. The relief she understood, for she was free of the threat of seduction. The disappointment she ignored, too exhausted to cope with anything more. She sagged against Chase, letting his strength support her, savoring every instant of being close to him without having to fear his making a sexual demand and her subsequent failure to satisfy him. She didn't hesitate to stay within his arms now, for she had no doubt that it would be the last time she would know the exquisite sweetness of his embrace. No man would waste time simply holding a woman he wasn't going to take to bed.

That certainty gave Nicole the courage to put her arms around Chase and hold him as he was holding her, gently, with no demands beyond the warmth of holding and being held. She put her cheek against his chest and let herself absorb him in the same way that she absorbed the perfection of a moonlit garden, every sense alive, wholly caught up in the moment. With a sigh, she let her senses drown in the sharp male scent of his skin, the heat of his body, the vaguely rough texture of his cheek against her forehead, the soothing, sliding pressure of his hands stroking her back.

Nicole had no idea how much time had passed when she realized that Chase had made no move to end the embrace. Even knowing that she wasn't going to bed with him, he stood holding her as though he were enjoying it as much as she was. Gently, slowly, reluctant to disturb the embrace, she tilted her head back until she could see his face. His eyes were closed and there was an expression of intense pleasure on his face. Nicole let out a breath she hadn't been aware of holding and smoothed her cheek over his chest again.

"Chase?" she whispered.

His answer was a low murmur against her temple and a tightening of his arms as though he were refusing to let her go.

"Do men like being held, too?" asked Nicole softly. "Even if—"

Her hesitant question went through Chase like a shock wave, rearranging his understanding of her yet again, telling him how little she expected from a man in terms of sensuality, much less simple affection.

"I don't know about men in general," said Chase, rubbing his cheek slowly over the braided softness of Nicole's hair, "but I've discovered that I love being held. By you. No ifs, ands, buts, or evens about it."

He hesitated, afraid to disturb the fragile communication they were sharing. But he had to know. "You touched me as little as possible the night we were together," he said softly. "Why? Is there something about touching me that you dislike?"

Chase felt the sudden stiffness of Nicole's body. He murmured low reassurances and stroked her with long, soothing motions of his hands. "It's all right, butterfly. Whatever you say, I won't get angry. If I did something that night that you didn't like, I want to know, that's all."

He felt the warmth of Nicole's long sigh against his chest. Her arms tightened around him. Her tension fairly vibrated against him as she spoke.

"The only part of sex that I liked at all with my husband was before he was violently aroused. Then he might hold me, pet me a little—" Nicole waited for her voice to come back. All that gave her the courage to continue was the gentleness of Chase's hands stroking her back and the knowledge that even when he had been fully aroused he hadn't hurt her. "If I touched him in return, he just—" Her voice frayed into silence.

"Lost control?" suggested Chase quietly.

"Then the hurting would begin," she whispered. "So I learned not to touch. That made him mad, too. He had a high sex drive. He wanted it all the time. Having a frigid wife must have been awful for him, even though he always had women on the side."

Chase closed his eyes and wished to the soles of his feet that he could have a few minutes alone with Nicole's former husband. Just a few. Just long enough to discover what the bastard's neck would feel like between his hands.

"Why did you marry him?" asked Chase. His voice was too rough, but he couldn't control it. His rage was too great.

Nicole made a sound that could have been a sob or a laugh. "That's the really funny part of it all. Since the change, Ted was the first man I'd ever gone out with who didn't make a grab for me. I thought I'd finally found a man who saw past the body to—me.''

"Since the 'change'?" asked Chase, not understanding.

For a time there was no answer. Chase continued stroking Nicole reassuringly, despite the fine tremors of rage that rippled through him at the thought of her being at the mercy of a man who had neither respect nor gentleness in him. With a feeling of cold horror, Chase finally understood Nicole's reaction to the idea of marriage: *Being a man's thing. Legally. Morally. All day. Every day. And the nights.*

Nicole's breath came out in a long, aching sigh. She spoke again, telling Chase things she had told no one else, things she hated to confront even in the privacy of her own mind. But the gentleness and heat and strength of him were too great a lure to turn away from, and his hands smoothing her back gave her a sense of safety.

"I was one of those tall, gawky girls they call late bloomers," said Nicole. "A redheaded clown on stilts. Boys either ignored me or made fun of me. Until I was seventeen. Then I changed so quickly that I was buying new bras every month. And then—" She drew in a short breath.

"And then the boys started lining up," finished Chase, remembering all too well the average teenage male's response to a pair of well-developed breasts.

"And grabbing. They didn't even care about me as a person. They just wanted to get their hands on me. Ted was different." Nicole's voice changed, revealing some of the bitterness, as well as the humiliation. "He wanted my family's money. He never pushed at all, sexually, until we were married. When Dad went bankrupt, Ted walked out on me. Then he told—he told—"

Chase felt Nicole trembling and regretted asking about her husband. "It's all right, Nicole," he said gently, kissing her temple and cheek, smoothing his hands down her back. "You don't have to tell me if it hurts you."

Nicole took a deep breath and realized that she wanted Chase to know. "Ted told all our friends he left me because I was a closet lesbian. And they—they believed him because I'd never gone to bed with any other man." She looked up at Chase with tears overflowing her wide golden eyes. "I've never wanted to touch a woman," she said starkly. "But I wanted to touch you. I was just—afraid. Do you believe me?"

"Yes," he murmured, brushing his lips over her eyelashes, tasting her tears. "Yes, I believe you."

Nicole's arms tightened around Chase, and she held him as though she would never let go.

Chapter 11

Chase helped Nicole down a very rough portion of the path, silently congratulating himself on his choice of trail. The worse the trail, the more he got to touch her. Casually, of course. He had no intention of making her examine the promise he had made to her a week ago: *I'll never hurt you like that again.* It was the exact truth. But not the whole truth. He meant to seduce her, but this time there would be pleasure, not pain.

Nicole had taken his promise to mean that he would never attempt to seduce her again. Chase understood that. He also understood what she did not: that it was impossible for him to walk away from her. He wanted her more with each day, each smile, each thought that they shared with one another. But he had been very careful not to let her know the depth of his desire.

Chase was hoping that Nicole would come to him, like the butterfly in the glen. He sensed that she wanted him more with each touch, each companionable silence, each conversation, each moment they spent together. He saw it

in the way her eyes followed his every move, in the softening of her mouth when she watched him, in the visible
shivers that sometimes moved over her golden skin when
he touched her.

It was slowly driving him crazy. All that kept his desire
for her in check was his even greater desire not to hurt her
again. Ever. If that meant never making love to her, so be
it. Somehow he would find a way to live without having
her in his bed.

And each day he lived, he would curse himself for the
unspeakable fool he had been weeks ago, when he had
closed his hand and crushed the fragile beginnings of her
trust in him.

Yesterday he and Nicole had hiked from Kilauea's caldera past Kilauea Iki, where in 1959, fountains of lava
nearly two thousand feet high had showered ash, pumice
and globs of cooling stone over an ohia forest. The trees
had lost their leaves and bark, but hadn't burned completely. Their graceful skeletons lingered on, rising from
the black, devastated land like ghosts of a greener yesterday frozen in time.

Chase felt the same way. Frozen in time. He could control the physical ache of wanting Nicole. He could not
control the agony of having had her and then losing her,
leaving behind him a mental landscape more bleak than
any volcanic devastation he had ever seen.

"You're sure there's a kipuka between here and the
ocean?" asked Chase, his rain-colored eyes measuring the
dark rivers of lava twisting down to the turquoise sea.

Nicole looked guilty for an instant. "It's not a true kipuka," she admitted. "But it's very special. It's the only
place I've seen on this lava flow where anything more than
Hawaiian snow grows."

Chase smiled crookedly. "Hawaiian snow," he murmured, shaking his head at her reference to the plant life
that was always the first to colonize cooled lava flows.
"White lichen."

"Hey, when you're hungry for a white Christmas, you take what you can get," she pointed out reasonably. "Besides, from a distance the stuff really does look like snow."

Tactfully Chase held his tongue. He thought the lichen looked like milk that had been spilled and left to curdle in the sun.

He scrambled down a particularly rugged stretch of aa lava, cursing as pieces crumbled and broke off beneath his feet, leaving sharp edges that abraded his hiking boots. When he had found secure footing, he turned and held out his arms. Nicole came into them without hesitation, enjoying his strength and the tingling currents that spread through her when she was held against his body. He set her gently on her feet but didn't release her.

"Pay the toll," he murmured, gathering Nicole even closer, savoring the supple, feminine curves pressed against him.

What had begun a few days before as a joke had become the highlight of the hikes for Chase—and the reason that he chose the most rugged trails he could find. With each rough spot on the trail Nicole was becoming more accustomed to his touch, to the feel of his body close to hers, to being held and holding him in return. She no longer flinched at his touch. It was a small thing, perhaps, but it was balm for both their wounds.

Nicole laughed softly and hugged Chase, savoring the care with which he arranged her length along his body, matching curve to hollow, strength to softness. After a few moments she knew that she should pull away and continue the hike as she had done just a few minutes back up the trail. But she did not. As soon as she had seen the rugged spot coming, shivers of anticipation had gone through her. She'd known that soon Chase would turn to her and hold her, that soon she would feel the hard muscles of his body shift and move beneath her hands as though he were savoring every bit of her touch. She felt the same about touching him. Now she turned her head slowly, unconsciously nuzzling aside the open collar of his shirt, wanting to feel her cheek against his skin.

For an instant Chase was afraid that the sudden hammering of his heart would alarm Nicole. When she didn't withdraw, he let out a long breath. His fingers spread until they all but spanned her back. Then he gently shifted her from side to side, slowly rubbing her breasts across his chest. He felt an instant of stiffening in her before she softened in his hands and let him hold her in an embrace that was more than a friendly hug.

Nicole closed her eyes and floated on the sensations Chase was creating with the slow, slow stroking of her body. Her breasts began to tighten, sending currents of fire radiating through her. Vividly she remembered the feel of his mouth on her swollen nipples, and the sweet, rhythmic tugging that had made currents of fire spiral through her.

"Chase?"

The catch in Nicole's voice was as exciting to him as the feel of her nipples hardening beneath her flowered halter. "Yes?" he murmured, keeping his voice normal with an effort.

"I don't think this is a good idea."

"Why? I thought you liked being held."

"I do. It's just—" Her voice caught again as his hands shifted, somehow increasing the sweet friction on her breasts. "This is different."

"How?"

Nicole tried to think of a way of explaining that avoided raising the subject of sex.

There was a long silence.

"You can touch me if you like," said Chase huskily, twisting slightly, subtly against her. "I'm not like your husband was. I won't fall on you like a starving dog on a tenderloin."

She made a choked sound that could have been a gasp of surprise or laughter or both together. She didn't withdraw, though. In the past week she had become accustomed to more than Chase's touch; she had also become accustomed to his unexpected, sometimes outrageous, always reassuring, conversations about her past.

"Don't you believe me?" murmured Chase. "Even when I didn't know how badly you had been hurt, I still didn't attack you when you touched me. Remember?"

Nicole remembered how much she had wanted to touch him that night in the shower. Even her husband's harsh teachings hadn't entirely kept her from touching Chase's chest with its fascinating patterns of hair, and muscles that shifted and slid so intriguingly beneath his skin. His eyes had changed at her touch, becoming smoky rather than clear, dark rather than light. But he hadn't dragged her out of the shower and taken her on the bathroom floor, which her husband had done once when he had come home early and found her in the shower.

"Yes," she murmured, nuzzling again at the V of skin revealed by Chase's unbuttoned shirt. "I remember."

Chase waited, holding her so skillfully that every way she turned increased the sensual pressure. He shifted his stance slightly, savoring the delicious hardness of her nipples moving against him.

"Are you afraid that if you touch me, the holding will stop and the sex will begin?" he asked, his voice as gentle as the hands holding her close.

Nicole lifted her head enough to look at the unforgiving lava heaped around them. She smiled crookedly. "Despite all the unlikely positions detailed in the books my husband gave me—no. We'd bleed to death long before anything else happened."

Wisely Chase refrained from telling Nicole that if she were willing, he could lift her, wrap her legs around him and take her right here, right now, with never a scratch on her golden skin. All it took was unusual strength and a hunger to match.

He had both, in abundance.

"Then you're safe," said Chase, smiling. "So how would you like to touch me?"

"But—"

He waited, watching the rise of color in her cheeks.

"Wouldn't that—? That wouldn't be—" Nicole made a frustrated sound.

"Say it," he encouraged, moving against her again, tensing the muscles of his chest, increasing the pressure on her breasts.

"Won't that be hard on you?" asked Nicole. Then she heard her own words and blushed to the roots of her hair.

Amusement flickered in Chase's clear eyes as he smiled down at Nicole. "No matter what your husband might have told you, it's not a fatal condition."

Nicole's flush deepened even as she returned Chase's teasing smile. "Lucky for you, huh?"

"Damned lucky," he agreed. "Think about it, butterfly. I'm yours to touch any way you want."

Chase released her slowly and turned away while he could still control his desire to caress the sweet curves and hard peaks of her breasts. "C'mon," he said without looking back. "The beach can't be that far away. I'm ready for a swim."

Nicole closed her eyes and tried to control the hammering of her heart. She felt on fire. Never before had a man held her, sweetly teased her until she ached, then smiled gently and turned away. She made a small sound and opened her eyes, watching almost helplessly as Chase descended the steep trail with both power and grace. Being touched by him was a temptation nearly beyond her power to resist. The thought of touching him, of perhaps being able to find out *how* to touch him, how to please him— that thought was definitely beyond her power to resist.

"Chase?" she called, her voice ragged.

He turned and looked back up at her. "Need help?"

"If I—if I touch you, will you tell me if I please you?" Nicole asked in a rush, afraid she would lose her courage and with it the chance to touch him.

For a moment Chase thought Nicole was joking; there was no way she could touch him and not please him. Then he saw the tension in her body as she walked toward him, waiting for his answer. She wasn't joking. She really didn't understand how even her most casual touch gave him pleasure.

"Yes," said Chase simply as she came to stand next to him. "I'll tell you. Will you do the same for me?"

"What?"

"Tell me if I please you."

He saw the look of surprise on Nicole's face.

"Don't you know?" she asked. "Your touch has always pleased me."

Chase's smile was both sad and regretful as he remembered how he had taken her. "There's more to touching than not being hurt."

Nicole's breath caught. "I know," she said in a throaty voice. Her hand came up and her fingertips brushed across his mustache as lightly as a butterfly's wing. "You taught me that."

"And that," said Chase, moving his head slightly, increasing the pressure of her touch, "pleases me more than I can say."

Her eyes widened in surprise until they looked like pools of molten gold.

"Didn't you know?" whispered Chase huskily, turning her face up to his with a gentle touch of his hand. "Your pleasure is also mine." He smiled crookedly. "Of course, I'm not a saint. If you'd like to make me feel even better by kissing me I wouldn't object."

"You wouldn't?" she asked, her eyes lighting with both laughter and anticipation.

He shook his head.

Nicole braced her hands on Chase's shoulders and stood on tiptoe. Even so, he had to bend down to bring his lips close to hers.

"It's the oddest feeling," she whispered.

"What?"

"You make me feel small, feminine, sleek. All the things I'm not."

"You're all of those things to me," he said, testing the resilience of her waist with his hands. "Or are you trying to say tactfully that I'm a little, er, oversized?"

Nicole smiled and brushed her lips against Chase's jawline. "Bobby's even bigger, and he doesn't make me feel this way. Small maybe, but not—delicious."

"Thank God," muttered Chase. "The day he makes you feel edible, tell me. Then we'll see who dines on whom."

Chase smiled as he felt Nicole's body move with silent laughter. Then her lips touched his, and all thought of laughter fled. Remembering the fragile, trusting butterfly, Chase held himself still except for the sensual tightening of his body as her tongue touched his and her breath sighed into his mouth, filling him with her sweetness.

"I like that," he whispered, lifting his head slightly as she withdrew.

"What?"

"Tasting you."

"Do you? Do you really?"

"Shall we try again?" he suggested softly, brushing his lips over hers. "I might have been mistaken."

Nicole's lips parted even more. With a feeling of luxuriousness, she fitted her mouth to his and permitted herself the undiluted pleasure of kissing him without being afraid that the action would escalate into sexual demands that she wouldn't be able to meet. As delicately as Chase had once tasted the flower, she tasted him. The tip of her tongue found his, caressed gently, retreated and then returned. She sensed the quiver of response in the taut male muscles beneath her hands and hesitated, fearful of arousing him too much and having to end the intimacy far too soon.

"It's all right, butterfly," he said quietly. "Take as much or as little of the sweetness as you want. I won't hurt you or ask for more than you want to give."

She looked up into Chase's clear gray eyes and saw that he meant every word. "Does that mean I can kiss you again?" she asked, her voice both husky and hopeful.

"Please," he murmured. "I love the taste of you."

With a sigh, Nicole stretched up on tiptoe again and threaded her fingers into Chase's thick black hair. This time when she fitted her mouth to his, there was no hesitation. Suddenly she was hungry to know again the heat and textures of his kiss, to feel the delicious velvet roughness of his tongue sliding over hers. This time when she felt the tremor of his response, it set off tiny shock waves of pleasure in her. She was pleasing him. She knew it as surely as she knew that he was pleasing her.

Unconsciously Nicole deepened the kiss, wanting more of him. Chase felt the change in her, and his blood began gathering heavily. He tried to subdue the depth of his response, but it was impossible. So he simply accepted it, as he accepted that he would not have the release his body was demanding with every rapid heartbeat. He had had release before. He wanted more this time. Much more. He wanted Nicole. For that, he would have to be patient.

Very slowly, Chase shifted Nicole's body with his hands, rubbing her breasts against his chest. The tiny intake of her breath as her nipples became more sensitive, more responsive, told him that she was forgetting her fear and drinking more deeply of the sweetness he was offering. He told himself that it was sneaky and unfair to use such tricks on her, to turn her own awakening sensuality against her, to seduce her. She had never known pleasure with a man, so she had no defenses against it.

And in that lay his best hope of having her again.

Nicole didn't know how long she had stood on tiptoe kissing Chase. She only knew that at some point her bones had turned to honey and his arms had come more firmly around her to support her. When she finally surfaced from the slow mating of tongues, she could barely breathe. She opened her eyes, wanting to see Chase, wanting to know if he had enjoyed the kiss as much as she had.

"Yes," he said, seeing the question in her eyes. "Oh God, yes!"

Nicole smiled almost shyly, her teeth white against her reddened lips. She touched Chase's full lower lip with her finger, loving the sensual heat and resilience of his flesh. His tongue flicked out and curled around her fingertip as it had once curled around her nipple. He pulled her finger into his mouth and stroked it with his tongue. Her breath caught.

"I like that," she said in a husky voice. "But it makes me—restless."

Slowly she withdrew her finger, wondering at the very hot, very male smile on Chase's face.

"Then maybe we'd better get down to the beach," he suggested. "You can work off some of your restlessness in the water."

"I didn't bring a swimming suit."

"That's okay," said Chase casually as he set off down the hard lava river again. "There's nobody around to see you."

"Funny," she said to his broad, retreating back. "You look like somebody to me."

"Ah, but I've already seen you." He turned around and looked at her with undisguised approval. "And I liked everything I saw. Does that embarrass you?"

Nicole opened her mouth to say yes, then realized that it wasn't true. "It's difficult for me to be naked with a man," she admitted finally. "Except for the time with you, the memories I have of it aren't very good at all."

Chase closed his eyes and tried not to think of all the ways a man could demean a woman. "Did I hurt you?" he asked, suddenly needing reassurance. "That night—did I?"

"No," she said quickly, seeing a hunger in him that had nothing to do with sexuality. "I meant what I said. I never enjoyed sex before that night."

Chase's breath came out with a ragged sound. Not trusting himself any further, he turned and picked his way down the jumbled, dark river of lava. Nicole followed, feeling unsettled in a new and intriguing way. The lava flow went all the way to the water. They stood on a cliff, looking at the black tongue of stone licking out into the yielding sea.

"That must have been one hell of an explosion," said Chase.

"I thought lava flows, especially pahoehoe, were quiet, not explosive."

"You ever throw a few drops of water on a hot griddle?" he asked, smiling.

"Every time I make pancakes."

"Well, that lava was once hell's own griddle with a whole ocean pouring over it. I'll bet water and stone vaporized with a sound like cannon going off. It was like that at Surtsey—a river of molten stone running down to a cold sea." He looked off to the left at the black sand beach and the fringe of graceful coconut palms that had recolonized the strand after the violence. "That's how you get black sand. Some of it comes from the wearing away of old lava. A lot of it comes from the instant when incandescent stone and water explode on contact."

Nicole looked at the peaceful sand curving out to embrace the sea. "I'm glad everything has cooled off."

Not quite everything, thought Chase ruefully, feeling the heaviness of his sex with every heartbeat. *But there's no danger of an explosion, either.*

I hope.

Together they left behind the chaotic jumble where Kilauea had met the sea. They walked to a grove of palms. Chase sat down, leaned against the smooth trunk of a fallen palm and began taking off his hiking shoes.

"There are three ways we can do this," he said matter-of-factly, tucking a sock into his shoe.

"Do what?"

"Go swimming nude. We can pretend we aren't—" he began.

Nicole made a strangled sound and tried not to laugh out loud.

"Yeah, my feelings exactly," said Chase wryly. "Or we can sneak sideways looks and trip all over our own feet in the process."

Nicole couldn't help laughing. "What's the third way?"

With a smooth, powerful motion Chase came to his feet and began pulling off his shirt. "We can just take a good look and get used to it." He peeled off his shorts and underwear and stood before her. "Of course, a man is at a distinct disadvantage in this situation."

"He is?" said Nicole in an odd voice as her glance traveled helplessly down Chase's hard male body. Very male. Very hard. "Oh," she said, understanding.

"Yeah. 'Oh.' I want you, and there's no damn way on earth I can disguise it when I'm naked. But I'm a man, not a child. I don't expect to get everything I want the instant I want it." He waited until her golden eyes came up to meet his. "Don't be frightened, butterfly," he said, his voice deep and very gentle. "This is just my body's way of saying that, as a woman, you please me very much. Is that so bad?"

Nicole let out the breath she hadn't been aware of holding. She waited for fear to come. She was still waiting several breaths later, when she realized that the thought of pleasing Chase as a woman was not frightening in the least.

"No," she said huskily, trying to be as honest with him as he was being with her. "It's good. I like the idea of—exciting you."

"Do you?" he murmured, smiling slowly.

Nicole closed her eyes. "You won't be angry with me?" she asked painfully. "Ted always was. He expected me to want him instantly, constantly. I'm not like that."

"Neither am I. I don't walk around ready to rut on anything that will hold still for it."

Her eyes flew open at his bluntness.

"I know that might be hard for you to believe," he said ruefully, "considering the evidence to the contrary. But it's true all the same. You have a potent effect on me. I want *you*, not just sex. Hell, if it was just sex, I'd be in town right now, screwing some faceless body."

Chase turned and walked into the waves, leaving Nicole to admire the fact that his tan was the same even shade of brown all over. She realized that she was staring and flushed—and kept staring. Despite his size, his body wasn't bulky. He was simply powerful, coordinated, and very, very male.

With fingers that trembled, Nicole went to work on her shoes. A few minutes later she gathered her courage in both hands and walked into the water. Chase stood waist deep in the jeweled blue sea. So did Nicole, but she was still half-naked.

"Women," said Nicole, her voice desperately normal, "are at a disadvantage in this case."

He turned and looked at her amber eyes and the slanting line of her cheekbones, which were stained with red. Her neck was long, elegant, as smooth as the shadow in the hollow of her throat. Her nipples were taut and deep pink and her breasts were the same golden brown as her arms.

"I see you don't like bathing suits any better than I do," said Chase.

"I hate them," said Nicole. "I like—" She swallowed and admitted, "I like to feel the sun on my breasts, and the breeze and the warm rain everywhere."

Her words undid whatever dampening effects the ocean had had on Chase's desire.

"Someday you'll feel me like that," he said, running his fingertips from Nicole's forehead to her thigh, which was concealed beneath a bright surge of water. "I'll be all over you like a warm rain. I won't even take you. I'll just pleasure you." His wet fingertip touched first one nipple, then the other, leaving a diamond drop of water behind. "Think about it, butterfly. All you have to do is ask."

The thought sent currents of heat through Nicole that made her nipples tighten even more. Chase saw, and cursed silently. He wished with wild urgency that he could seize the initiative and seduce her. But he knew that it couldn't be that way. If she became fearful at the last moment and withdrew, she would blame herself, not him. It would hurt her more than anything he had done to her.

He had to be as he had been in the clearing, motionless, offering himself while she spiraled closer and closer to him on velvet wings. She had to come and drink the sweetness from him. Only then would she lose her fear of being crushed and thrown aside.

Even knowing that, Chase couldn't stop himself from bending down and licking the drop of seawater from one nipple.

"Salt is bad for the skin," he said huskily. "And you have such beautiful skin."

Nicole watched with a shivering feeling of inevitability as his head moved to her other breast and his tongue flicked out, touching her far too briefly.

"Chase," she said, her voice ragged.

He straightened, expecting her to retreat. "Yes?" he asked.

"I like that. Would you . . . do it again?"

Slowly Chase touched each nipple with a wet fingertip, leaving behind a drop of glittering water. This time, he removed the drop with utmost care before he took the taut peak into his mouth and tugged at it, making currents of fire gather and run through her body. Long before he turned to the other breast, Nicole's hands were clinging to him for support. His mustache stroked her like a silk brush before he drew her deeply into his mouth. She made a tiny sound in the back of her throat and arched her back instinctively, offering herself to him as she never had to any man.

By the time Chase finally released Nicole, she was trembling and breathing unevenly. Resolutely he closed his eyes and held her in his arms, letting the warm surge and retreat of the water bring her to him and then take her away. After a few minutes of holding her quietly, he trusted himself not to lift her and fit her intimately over his body as he knew again the satin heat and tightness of her surrounding him.

When Chase felt Nicole stir in his arms he reluctantly loosened his hold. Her cheek rubbed against his chest. Slowly she turned her head from side to side, plainly enjoying his male textures.

"If I touched you the same way," asked Nicole softly, "would you enjoy it?"

"Yes," said Chase, "but you don't have to. I don't expect—"

The rest of his words were lost in the sharp intake of his breath as Nicole's tongue found his nipple beneath the curling midnight hair on his chest. She felt the tightening of his whole body as she transformed his flat nipple into a tiny, hard nub. The knowledge that she could please Chase was intoxicating. So was his taste, his scent, and the heat of his body radiating beneath her hands. She discovered how sensitive her tongue could be to textures as well as tastes, how good it felt to twist her body slowly against his, to pleasure him as thoroughly as he had pleasured her.

Finally Nicole lifted her mouth, only to return again and then again in sensual forays, as though she couldn't bear to be separated from him. Beneath her chin she felt his hard fingers, tilting her head back. When she started to ask what was wrong, his mouth claimed hers deeply, leaving no room for anything except the hot, sweet completion of his kiss.

A larger wave came, washing them in a warm surge of water that went up to Nicole's collarbone and threatened to pull her from Chase's arms. Smoothly he lifted her beyond the reach of the wave.

"One of us," he said against her mouth, "has to watch for the big ones." Smiling, he turned her in his arms until she faced toward the sea. Slowly he pulled her back against his chest, fitting her hips into the cradle of his thighs. "I nominate you as watcher."

"But now I can't touch you," protested Nicole, looking at him over her shoulder.

"Then I'll just have to touch you, won't I?" asked Chase reasonably. Silently he admitted to himself that it was just as well he was out of reach of Nicole's mouth for the moment. The obvious pleasure she had taken in his body was dangerously exciting. "Come here, butterfly," he said, snuggling her even closer with one hand between her breasts and the other flattened just above her thighs. "Tell me what you like," he murmured, nuzzling her ear, then tracing it with the tip of his tongue. "This?" he asked, thrusting slowly into her ear, withdrawing, thrusting again.

Nicole's breath stopped.

He nibbled delicately around the rim until he felt her arch into the caress. He smiled and continued along her hairline to the nape of her neck. There he stopped. With exquisite gentleness, he used his teeth on the sensitive nerves.

The currents of heat that had been gathering in Nicole suddenly radiated through her with a force that made her weak. She trembled and leaned against him.

"Yes?" asked Chase, repeating the caress, feeling her body soften in his arms.

"Yes," she said, her voice catching.

Chase bent over Nicole's nape again, feeling her response in the trembling of her body. His hands found the smooth weight of her breasts, caught the hard peaks between his fingers and caressed the nipples as his teeth closed on her nape. She made a small sound as her whole body tightened. He caressed her until she was crying softly with each breath and her hips were moving in slow, instinctive rhythms, seeking an embrace more satisfying than that of the surging water.

One of Chase's hands slid down Nicole's body into the warm sea, wanting to discover the even warmer woman. He caressed the smooth skin of her thighs and the tangled silk of her red hair as his teeth closed not quite gently on her nape. The combination of sensations made her gasp and press against him, wanting more. His hand moved between her thighs, holding her in a sensual vise whose pressure increased with each small, involuntary movement of her hips. Slowly, languidly, his fingertips found and stroked her softness.

"Yes?" Chase murmured.

Nicole's answer was a moan and a slow, rhythmic movement of her body, as though the smooth thunder of the breaking waves was the drumbeat of a stately dance. As her hips moved against Chase, his whole body clenched with a desire that was more fierce than any he had ever known.

Pele—God, she'll burn us both to ash!

With an inarticulate sound, Chase closed his teeth on Nicole's nape as he slid deeply into her softness. She cried out and shivered helplessly against his hand. He caressed her repeatedly, inflamed by her clinging satin body. He felt the shivering take her again, felt her heat flowing over him and groaned as desire ripped through him, tearing away his control, making him shake with the force of his need.

Another large wave came, pressing Nicole against Chase in a warm surge of power. Without warning, he turned her in his arms and lifted her. "Wrap your legs around me," he said, his voice husky, urgent.

Chase's strength and the sudden change of position caught Nicole by surprise. She stiffened in his arms, feeling almost dizzy. He felt the change and realized what he had almost done. He had almost taken her rather than waiting for her to come to him. Instantly he released her.

"I'm sorry, butterfly," Chase said, letting Nicole slide back down his body into the warm sea. "It won't happen again." Gently he turned her and pushed her toward the black sand crescent and the fringe of palms. "Go back up on the beach. No problem with sudden waves there."

When she found herself alone on the beach, Nicole felt empty, dazed, lost. She turned to see where Chase was. The sea was empty.

"Chase?" she asked, looking around wildly.

There was no answer.

A few moments later a dark body broke the surface of the ocean out where the waves were coming apart. Chase swam smoothly, powerfully, spearing beneath the white combers and reappearing on their far side. Nicole watched with an aching in her throat that she didn't understand. It seemed like forever before he turned and began swimming back to her, riding the wild whiteness of breaking waves.

It won't happen again.

Nicole trembled and felt tears flowing hotly down her cheeks, and didn't know why.

Chapter 12

Nicole sat cross-legged on the oversized chaise, trying to concentrate on the jacaranda trees arching overhead as they lifted a mass of lavender flowers in silent offering to the sun. Thousands upon thousands of blossoms shivered as the breeze slid caressingly over their soft surfaces. Some of the blooms came undone in the gentle tugging and were swept away on currents of air. Flowers floated to the ground to lie heaped in sweet windrows that swirled with each new touch of the breeze.

Normally Nicole loved these days when the jacaranda bloom was at its peak and blossoms showered the land in a fragile lavender rain. But for the last week she had done little more than sketch unhappily during the day and pace her cottage during the night. When she slept, it was badly, and she awoke to a body quickened by sensations that made her breath wedge in her throat and stay there until the dawn came.

Just the thought of the time she'd spent in Chase's arms was more than enough to send heat lancing through her, tightening her until she wanted to scream. She had talked to him once since the day he had taken her into the sea and taught her that he knew far more about her body than she did. The next morning he had called and told her he had to go back to Mount Saint Helens. She had been so disappointed that she had barely responded to his words. He had been due back yesterday. She had waited with an anticipation that had made her tremble like a wire strung too tightly. She didn't know why. She only knew that she trembled.

He hadn't come.

Maybe today. Or tomorrow, she thought, doodling on the edges of a failed sketch.

She ached to return with him to the warm, wild sea. She wanted him to miss her the way she missed him, to be awake nights and distracted days, to not take three breaths without thinking of her.

So you pleased him a little, she told herself grimly. *So what? The world is full of women who can please him a lot.*

She tried not to think about it. It was impossible. With a silent curse she threw down her pencil and stopped pretending to be sketching the jacaranda trees.

"Bad day?"

Nicole spun around so quickly at the sound of Chase's voice that the sketchbook went flying. Without stopping to think, she jumped up off the chaise and into his arms and held on to him as though she expected him to be torn away from her.

Chase held her in the same way. "Miss me?" he asked.

Her answer was a shudder and an incoherent sound.

"That's the way I missed you," he said hoarsely, burying his face in the fragrance of her braided hair. "God, I thought that if I couldn't see you or touch you, I wouldn't want you so much that I felt like I was breathing molten lava." His laugh was short, harsh. "I was wrong. I keep being wrong about you, Nicole."

He picked her up in a surge of power, held her against the length of his body and let her presence in his arms flood through him. All that he had been thinking and feeling since the moment he realized just how badly he had misjudged her came pouring out in a torrent of words. He knew that it was too soon to say such things, but his own exhaustion and her uninhibited greeting had eroded his control.

"I kept thinking about how Lisa smiles when she sees you coming up the path," said Chase. "Then I'd remember your laughter at one of Mark's awful puns and the way you listen, really *listen*, when I talk about the islands." Chase found Nicole's lips and kissed her deeply, fiercely, shuddering at her sudden, wild response. "I remembered that, too—the taste and the heat of you. Marry me, Nicole. Be with me all the time. Let me—"

Nicole drew back in shock. "Marriage?" she repeated, her voice breaking, her eyes wide.

Even before she spoke, Chase felt the stiffness of her body. Too late he remembered: *Being a man's thing. All day. Every day. And the nights.*

He closed his eyes and silently, savagely cursed his foolish dream. Just because Nicole jumped up and threw herself into his arms didn't mean that she was ready to risk belonging to him in any meaningful way. He had shown her just a little of the fire buried within her body, let her taste just a bit of the wild honey. Naturally she had missed him. She didn't know that any man could kindle the flames and drink the sweetness of mutual sensuality with her.

"Sorry," Chase said, releasing Nicole. "I should never have asked. Blame it on jet lag and the heat of the moment. Like I said, you keep taking me by surprise. You make me respond at every level. I make you respond, somewhat, at one." He smiled crookedly and touched the tip of her nose. "But then, nobody ever said that life was fair."

Nicole tried to hold onto her spinning thoughts long enough to make a coherent statement. "Chase, I didn't mean—It's just that I hadn't thought about—After Ted, I promised myself that I would never, ever—"

Chase kissed her lips gently, stopping the chaotic words. "Hush, butterfly," he murmured. "I understand. You have no reason to trust me with your life and a lot of reasons not to."

He let go of her and backed up several steps until she was out of reach, cursing himself for jamming three weeks of work into one just to rush back and ruin everything.

"Chase, please—" said Nicole, her voice raw. "Don't feel guilty about that morning at Dane's house. I know you'd never hurt me."

"But the absence of pain isn't enough," Chase said bleakly. "Not for love, and certainly not for an enduring marriage. Mind. Body. Soul. That's the way it has to be. I didn't realize that the first time around, and Lisa paid the price for my foolishness. But I know now. All, or nothing at all."

"Does that mean you won't—that we can't—" Nicole closed her eyes and clenched her hands together fiercely. "Oh Chase," she whispered, "please don't go away from me. You make me feel so many things that I didn't even think were possible."

"Any man could do the same."

Her eyes flew open. "That isn't true!" she said, her voice shaking.

"It is true," Chase countered softly. His mouth turned down in a sad smile as he measured her disbelief.

"But it's only with you—"

"I just happened to be the man you saw when you were starting to split the past's painful cocoon. For you, I'm a stage that will pass." Chase looked at the tears brightening Nicole's eyes and realized that she didn't believe him. "Don't look so sad, butterfly. You can respond to other men. But I won't leave you until you know that's true." He held out his cupped hand as he had in the forest glen. "The honey will be here until you open those velvet wings and fly away."

Nicole blinked against the tears that had come in response to Chase's sad voice. With a choked sound she went back into his arms and held him fiercely, shaking with emotions and thoughts that were too new to deal with.

"What's this I hear about a big luau?" asked Chase, his voice matter-of-fact despite the darkness of his eyes and the taut lines on either side of his mouth.

Nicole drew in a deep, broken breath and accepted the emotionally neutral topic. "It's the annual Kamehameha bash. Pig in a pit, fires on the beach, dancing all night—everything."

"Where?"

She pulled away just enough to point to the tangle of greenery leading from the high ground where they stood to the center of the beach below. "Down there."

"Will you dance?"

"If you'll play the drums for me."

"You've got a deal, Pele," Chase said, stroking her hair lightly and then releasing her. "When?"

"Tomorrow night."

"That soon? Good."

Something about Chase's voice made Nicole hesitate. "You're going back to the mainland again, aren't you?"

Chase nodded.

"When?"

"Soon." Silently he added, *A lot sooner than I'd hoped. But it's the only way, butterfly. I can't trust myself around you. I almost took you in the ocean, and I want you far more right now than I did then.*

Nicole watched Chase undo his tie with a few quick jerks. For the first time it registered on her that he must have come straight from the plane, not even stopping long enough to pick up Lisa or to change out of his mainland business clothes. Her throat tightened as she saw the line of strain beneath his exterior calm.

"You must be exhausted," she said quietly.

"I've been up most of the last three nights," he admitted. The tie hissed out from beneath his collar. He unbuttoned more buttons, took a deep breath and let it out in a sigh. "Have any sketches for me to look at?"

"None that I like."

"Do you ever like them?" he asked, the corner of his mouth curling up slightly.

"Not very often," she admitted.

"Good thing I have the final say, then. I'd hate for my words to have to carry the whole *Islands of Life* project." He unbuttoned his shirtsleeves, rolled up the cuffs and started back up the trail. "Can you meet me at my cottage in about an hour? That will give me time to clean up and eat before we look at the sketches."

"Eat?"

"Dinner. My stomach is still on mainland time."

"I'll make you something," she called after his retreating form.

"That's all right, butterfly. I've been cooking for myself for years. I'm getting pretty good at it."

Nicole watched Chase vanish into the tangled garden trail and wondered why she couldn't stop crying.

Her throat was still aching when the moon rose, filling her cottage with a silent silver tide of light. She threw aside the sheet with an impatient movement and began to pace the room as she had every night since Chase had left.

But he's back. So why are you pacing again?

There was no answer except the seething, volatile currents deep within her, as though she were Kilauea, racked by tiny, secret tremors.

The sketches spread out across the table caught her restless eye. Chase had praised all of them, but only one had truly riveted him. Nicole went to the table and saw the sketch lying in a pool of moonlight. The drawing was almost stark in its simplicity, a single jacaranda bud at the tip of a supple twig. The bud was swollen to bursting, but there was neither color nor the softness of bloom showing anywhere.

As she touched the sketch, she remembered Chase looking at the bud for a long, long time and then setting it aside, saying, *On the verge of sweet becoming... but it never will bloom for us, will it? Caught forever between all and nothing at all. A brilliant drawing, Nicole. I don't know when I've ever seen anything quite so beautiful or half so sad.*

The bud blurred and ran beneath the tears that Nicole could no longer hold back.

He hadn't touched her that night. Not even once. She had waited and waited, her heart a wild thing caught within her body; and then she had realized that if she wanted him, she would have to come to him like the butterfly in the forest. The sweetness was there, waiting for her. All she had to do was light within his hand and drink.

"Oh Chase," she whispered, putting her face in her hands. "You want too much from me. You're too much man. I'm too little woman. I'll disappoint you and destroy myself."

All or nothing at all.

And like the bud in the sketch, she was imprisoned between.

By the time morning came Nicole was as restless as the melted rock seething beneath Kilauea's black shield. She had nearly gone to Chase's cottage many times during the long hours of darkness, wanting—

What? she asked herself impatiently. *What do you want?*

There had been no answer in the moon-silvered night, just a mixture of fear and restlessness, loneliness and longing. There was no answer in the rising sun or in the dazzling rainbows arching down from the clouds. There was no answer in the blazing glory of sunset or the excited speculations of the scientists at the luau about Kilauea's latest harmonic stirrings. There was no answer in any of the familiar faces gathered around the three luau fires on the beach or in the conversations of friends. There was no man with rain-colored eyes and midnight hair and a bittersweet smile to break her heart. There was nothing for Nicole but the feeling of being frozen between past and future, pain and pleasure, nothing and everything.

And then the drums began to beat.

Nicole turned away from Bobby in midword, leaving him to watch her retreating back with rueful understanding. She didn't notice. She had room for nothing but the elemental summons of the drums.

Come to me.

Barefoot, her hair tumbling freely to her hips, Nicole came to stand in front of Chase. She wasn't aware of the applause or the sudden end to conversations around her. Nothing existed for her but the drums and the man who made them speak to her soul.

His hands moved quickly, and the drums called out to her in complex, driving rhythms.

Dance for me. Dance. For me. Dance.

Nicole shook back her hair and let the rhythms take her body, giving it to the drums, to Chase. Her hips moved sinuously beneath the fiery curtain of her hair. Firelight gleamed on her skin, giving it a deep gold cast. The lava-lava she wore low on her hips was the same golden-red as her hair, making her seem wrapped in fire. She moved elegantly, sensually, letting her body speak, dancing for the only person in the world besides herself. Chase.

He watched her through narrowed silver eyes as his hands moved skillfully, relentlessly, demanding everything from himself and the drums and the dancer.

Burn for me, Pele. Burn. For me!

And she did. For long, long minutes she danced out at the edge of her control, giving herself to the wild, sweet violence of the drums. Finally her body could no longer sustain the blazing demands. With a cry she threw up her arms, ceding the night to the intricate thunder of the drums.

But they had stopped in the same instant she had, leaving only the bonfires to burn among the stately rhythms of the breaking waves.

Chase stood and smiled in acknowledgment of the applause, then stepped back into the shadows of the palms and disappeared. Nicole watched in disbelief. She called out to him but the sound of clapping hands drowned her words. She started after him, only to be cut off by the enthusiasm of her friends. She put them off with a smile and raced to catch up with Chase.

There was no one waiting for her on the moonlit path. There was no one waiting for her in her cottage. No one waiting in his.

Wearily Nicole returned to her own cottage. She waited. Nothing came to her except the sounds of laughter floating up from the beach. She stood for a long time in the shower, wishing she could wash away memories as easily as tears. When she could stand the sultry confinement of the shower no longer, she pulled on a black silk blouse and an ankle-length lavalava. As she anchored her hair in place, using the ivory chopsticks with tassels of chiming bells, she realized that she didn't want to go back to the luau.

She didn't want to stay in the cottage, either.

Slowly she walked back out into the garden and down the twisting, overgrown, all but hidden path to her jacaranda grove. In the moonlight the blossoms were shimmering silver clouds crowning midnight branches. Petals lay in drifts and shifted in pale streamers over the ground. With each sigh of wind, more flowers floated down, falling soundlessly to the warm earth.

Nicole stretched out on the oversized chaise, feeling the smooth coolness of petals against her skin. Others drifted down, settling over her body as softly as a kiss. For a long time she lay without moving, letting the silent, fragrant cascade of blossoms swirl around her, trying very hard to think of nothing at all. Finally she slept.

Only then did Chase step out of the shadows and come to stand by Nicole, watching her sleep in the moonlight, all her fires banked. As he looked down at her, he told himself how many kinds of fool he was. He should have kept walking along the beach, counting the thundering waves. He shouldn't be here, counting the silent flowers drifting down to rest on skin that was softer and more fragrant than any blossom.

She wanted him, but not enough. He wanted her.

Too much.

The way he had hurt her weeks ago. Too much. Nothing he did could take back that morning, those cruel words, the harsh destruction. In those few scalding minutes he had lost her. All that remained of what might have been was her own buried sensuality. He could release that, giving it to her and to himself, burning gift and epitaph to what might have been. Making love would free her from the cruel past.

And enslave him to a cruel future.

He knew it as surely as he knew that there was nothing else he could give to her but the velvet wings of her own sensuality and the freedom to fly. There had been no one for him like the woman sleeping amidst a gentle storm of falling blossoms. She had shown him how wrong he had been about women and love. She had healed the black scars that life had left on him, and scarred herself in turn on the uncooled fires of his rage at women.

He could heal some of Nicole's scars. And if it hurt him in return...

Chase smiled sadly as he sat next to Nicole. She stirred, turning toward his warmth. Gold bells sang, their tiny notes unexpected, sweet, piercing. Gently Chase slid the ivory chopsticks from the piled coils of her hair, letting it spill like cool fire over his hands. Ivory and gold gleamed in the moonlight as he set the ornaments aside and bent over Nicole.

He kissed the moonshadow of her eyelashes, which lay like black lace along her skin. He kissed the delicate warmth of her eyelids, the smooth hollow of her cheek, the sensitive inward spiral of her ear, the sensual curve of her lips. He felt her come alive at his touch, felt her lips opening to him, and her breath washing sweetly over him.

"Chase?" asked Nicole, her voice husky, dreamy, neither fully awake nor asleep. "I looked for you. I wanted to drink the sweetness from your hand." Her breath came out in a broken sigh. "You were gone."

His hands tightened in her hair. "I know," he murmured, sipping gently at her lips. "I'm here now, butterfly."

"Don't leave me," she said, threading her fingers deeply into the rough silk of his hair.

"Not until you know that you can fly," he promised softly.

Chase took Nicole's mouth before she could ask what he meant. Any thought of questions vanished as his tongue caressed her, showing her again how complex a simple kiss could be. She made a soft, broken sound and kissed him in return, feeling the first currents of fire stir deep within her body.

Nicole's hands trembled as they slid from Chase's hair to the flexed power of his shoulders and back. Her fingers dipped into the open collar of his shirt, tracing lines of sinew and muscle, tangling in the curling midnight hair of his chest. She tried to search lower, wanting to know the delicious power of teasing his nipples into hardness. The buttoned shirt was a barrier stopping her sensual foray. She made a frustrated sound.

"Tell me what you want," said Chase, biting Nicole's lower lip with exquisite precision, wordlessly showing her how gentle he would be.

"You," she whispered, opening her eyes, seeing him looming over her in the moon-silvered darkness. She had no fear of his strength or his size, nothing but anticipation of his caresses. "I want to touch you like I did before. And then I want you to teach me other ways to touch you."

Chase's breath came in swiftly, hotly. With slow movements he eased his hands from the silky bonds of her hair. Watching her eyes, kissing her between heartbeats, he unbuttoned his shirt and let it slide to the ground as he lay down beside her on the chaise.

"Better?" he asked softly.

"You're so beautiful," she breathed, then smiled as she saw his expression. "I know, men aren't beautiful. But if something as powerful and wild as a volcanic eruption can be called beautiful, why can't you?"

Chase laughed, not knowing that his laughter sent more currents of fire through Nicole. But when he felt the heat of her mouth tracing a path across his chest, laughter wedged in his throat. She gently scraped her teeth over first one nipple, then the other. When she felt the sensual tightening take him, she smiled against his skin.

"I like that," Nicole murmured, tugging lightly at the tiny, hard nub she had called from his flesh.

"That definitely makes two of us," he said, torn between a smile and the almost painful flare of desire that came in response to her caress.

When Nicole began to nibble lower, following the dark path of hair, Chase's breath came in and stayed. With loving deliberation, her hands and mouth traced every line and ridge of muscle, every hollow, every shift in the pattern of dense hair. After a few minutes of that unexpected, shimmering torture, Chase buried his hands in her long hair and slid down to capture her mouth with his own.

"Come here, Pele," he said huskily. "Give me that sweet, teasing tongue."

His words licked through Nicole like fire, telling her that she had pleased him. She opened her lips eagerly, anticipating the hot instant when his tongue would thrust inside. He paused, knowing that she was waiting for him, wanting her to wait, knowing it would be all the sweeter for the tiny disappointment.

"Chase," she whispered, "why—"

The question became a moan of satisfaction as she felt his tongue stab deeply, claiming her softness. It was a kiss unlike any she had ever known, taking everything, giving everything, calling to the untamed currents of fire swirling deep inside her. She shivered as her whole body tightened in response. She kissed him as wildly as he was kissing her, arching against him, instinctively wanting more of him, wanting to be closer still.

Chase's hands rubbed over the silk of her blouse, soothing and inciting her with the same long strokes of his palm. Nicole's breathing quickened as her eyes closed and she twisted slowly beneath his touch, for her breasts ached with the need to be caressed. He touched her everywhere else, running his warm hands over her face and shoulders and hips, her arms and her thighs and her stomach, teasing her relentlessly, smiling as he watched her body shimmer and twist, seeking the caress that always eluded it.

"Don't you want to touch me?" she finally asked, her voice as ragged as her breathing.

The answer was a soft, broken laugh and his hands held in a pool of moonlight so that she could see their trembling.

"Then why?" she asked, only to gasp as his fingertips brushed over her silk-sheathed nipple and fire burst through her.

"That's why," said Chase, his voice husky. "And this."

He captured her suddenly taut nipple between his thumb and forefinger and squeezed not quite gently. She gave a wild little cry and arched helplessly, feeling only pleasure lancing through her in sharp, hot currents. He released her and brushed his fingers teasingly over her again and again, rewarded by the fierce rise of her nipples beneath the black silk.

"Chase," she moaned. "You don't know what you're doing to me!"

His smile flashed in white contradiction before he caught the hard peak of her breast between his teeth. The thin silk served only to heighten the damp velvet caress of his tongue and the sudden heat of his mouth on her aching breast. She made a soft sound of pleasure and held him against her, knowing only that she needed the sweet, tugging heat of his mouth more than she had ever needed anything. When he turned his head away she cried out in disappointment.

He pulled her mouth to his, drinking deeply, stilling her cry. His fingers moved over her ankle-length skirt, finding and unwrapping its secrets until black silk slid open, revealing the golden warmth of the woman beneath. He began to undo the blouse's tiny buttons, not stopping until he spread his hands apart and silk fell away, leaving her naked in the moonlight.

Slowly Nicole's hands came up, shielding her breasts from his touch.

"I won't hurt you, butterfly," said Chase, his voice aching. "Don't you know that yet?"

"Yes," she murmured. "I know."

Chase looked at Nicole's sweet smile and felt both relief and blinding desire burst in him as he remembered the tantalizing version of a child's game they had once played in her shower. Slowly, gently, he traced the length of Nicole's body as he had while she was clothed, teasing her despite the fact that his hands were shaking. She didn't know what that smile had done to him.

But she would.

"So you like to play, do you?" he murmured, bending down until he could tease the fingers shielding her breasts.

Nicole felt the warmth of his breath and the damp, resilient tip of his tongue. He traced each finger as though he were memorizing it, nibbling on fingertips, making no attempt to slide his tongue between her fingers to the sensitive breast beneath.

When Chase began the same tender tracing of her other hand, Nicole trembled and gave a soft sigh. His teeth tugged at her little finger in response. He pulled it into his mouth, then released the warm flesh with a slowness that was another kind of caress. Her hand loosened, offering the taut peak of her breast to his mouth. Chase made a deep sound of pleasure as he accepted the gift. Her response was a shudder and a tiny cry that ripped through him. His mouth changed, less gentle now, more urgent.

"Yes," she said, twisting slowly against him, wanting more. "Harder," she whispered, not even knowing that she spoke, not realizing that her words and her nails flexing into the muscles of Chase's back were like fire burning through him.

He put his palms beneath her shoulder blades and arched her supple body to meet his hungry caress. With barely controlled power he took her into his mouth, tugging on her deeply. She made a broken sound and clung to him, knowing nothing but the currents of fire lancing through her, fire called forth by the man who held her imprisoned between his hands and his mouth, freeing her from years of sensual restrictions.

When his hands finally slid from her back to her hips, kneading slowly, Nicole moved in unconscious response, seeking another kind of caress. With languid, teasing strokes, Chase smoothed her taut hips and resilient thighs. His mouth followed his hands, biting gently down the length of her body until she shivered and called his name.

"Do you like that?" he asked, kissing the silky flesh of her inner thigh.

Her answer was a broken laugh and then a sudden gasp as his mouth moved higher, caressing her with an intimacy that shocked her. Reflexively her hands moved to shield her softness.

"Hide-and-seek," he said huskily. "I'm glad that you like to play the same games I do, Pele."

Nicole tried to speak, to explain, but the words caught in her throat at the first caressing touch of his tongue between her fingers. He nuzzled and bit delicately on her fingers, silently proving how very gentle he could be. After a while, shivers of desire coursed through her continuously, telling of the fires gathering inside her, waiting for release.

"Come to me, Pele," Chase murmured, tugging at her finger with his teeth. "Dance for me."

Long before her hands gave up the sensual contest, her hips were moving in slow, sinuous rhythms. His hands caressed her in the same deep rhythms that were claiming her body, urging her to release the hot currents seething inside her. He called to the liquid fire he knew waited within her, fire seeking the bursting, incandescent instant of release. Gently he moved aside the last barrier and heard his name as a trembling sound on her lips. He touched her with exquisite care, bringing her to the edge and holding her there until she was shaking and crying his name with each breath.

"Yes," he said hoarsely, all teasing gone as he bent to her again.

Nicole tried to say Chase's name, to ask what was happening to the body she thought she knew so well. She could not speak. She could not even breathe as he caressed her. All the hot, fierce currents that had gathered in her had burst free, tearing her body from her control, turning her into a creature of fire. She burned wildly, deeply, and she burned for him, his name a shattered cry on her lips as wave after wave of ecstasy burst through her.

Chase gathered Nicole against his body and held her until the sweet burning began to subside, leaving her dazed within the strength of his arms. She took a deep breath

which caught several times as her body slowly began to
return to her conscious control. Blindly, softly, she kissed
Chase again and again, trying to tell him things for which
she had no words.

"I didn't know—" she said, only to have her voice break
on an unexpected aftershock of pleasure.

He smiled and kissed her, controlling the hunger that
still pressed hotly, violently against the lavalava he wore.
His skin was as hot as hers, as burnished with sweat, and
his breathing was broken; but he had no intention of taking her. He had promised himself that he would simply
pleasure her and then release her, taking no more from her
than the knowledge that he had given her something to
balance the agony of the morning at his brother's house.

"I'm glad it was good for you," Chase said, his voice
dark, deep. "Very, very glad."

He smoothed back the thick, silky mass of Nicole's hair
and kissed her forehead. He continued stroking her back
slowly, gentling her, bringing her wholly back to herself
after her wild flight. When he felt the long, deep sigh of
her breath against his neck, he brushed his lips across her
cheek and then simply held her. She made a murmurous
sound of contentment and nestled closer, savoring the
peace of lying with him as much as she had savored the
sweet violence of fire sweeping through her. Both the fire
and the peace were wholly unexpected. She could not absorb them deeply enough into herself.

For a long time Chase lay quietly with Nicole in his
arms, watching the silver spirals of blossoms drifting down
from the moonlit sky. The petals touched Nicole's hair, her
cheek, the womanly curve of waist and hip. Fragile petals
settled on the tousled midnight of Chase's hair, on the
muscular swell of his shoulder, brushed fragrantly over the
mat of hair on his chest.

Finally, reluctantly, Chase knew that it was time to release the velvet woman who had trusted him enough to
drink both sweetness and fire from his hand.

"Wake up, butterfly," he whispered. "It's time for you to go home."

He picked up the long lavalava and dressed her, wrapping her in black silk, trying to control the fine trembling of his hands as they inevitably brushed her warm flesh. He smoothed the unbuttoned blouse into place on her arms slowly. Too slowly. But it was so tempting to hold onto the excuse to touch her.

Chase thought he would be able to keep from caressing her until his hand accidentally brushed the fullness of her breast. When the peak hardened instantly in response, he found himself bending over and touching it once with the tip of his tongue, and then twice, three times. Nicole smiled and turned to give herself to his loving once again.

To sit up and stop touching Nicole was the most difficult thing Chase had ever done. He closed his eyes for a moment, blotting out the vision of her nipple glistening from his caress. With hands that trembled he began to button her blouse.

Her hands moved behind his, unbuttoning.

"Nicole," he said, his voice gritty. "This is hard enough as it is."

Her hand smoothed up the length of his muscular thigh, sliding beneath the lavalava, finding and caressing him. "Yes, it is, isn't it?" she murmured. Her smile was as fiery and sweet and intimate as her hand stroking his rigid flesh.

Chase shuddered and made a sound deep in his throat. "Oh God, butterfly," he said hoarsely, capturing her hand. "Don't."

"I didn't know that you liked to play keep-away, too," she whispered, moving her fingers slowly, keeping them pressed between his hand and his hot male flesh.

Chase knew he should pull away, stand up, run, do anything but what he was doing—slowly, hotly teaching her how to please him, guiding her hand beneath his until he was shaking and there was nothing left for her to learn.

"You once said we would fit together very well," whispered Nicole, pulling aside the folds of black silk that wrapped her hips. "You were right."

The thought of being sheathed within Nicole made fire twist through Chase. "You don't have to," he said. "It won't be any better for you this way than—"

Nicole stopped trying to make him understand with words. She threaded her fingers deeply into his hair and pulled his mouth down to hers. Chase hesitated, then groaned and thrust into her mouth at the same instant that his hand found the softness between her legs. His fingers moved slowly, finding and stroking the fiery heart of her desire until she came undone, melting over him as he came to her and slid his aching flesh deep within her.

She cried out at the beauty of being joined with him again. Her cry was more exciting to him than her curious, caressing hand had been. He held her and himself utterly still, suspended in an agony of pleasure, savoring every instant of her trembling beneath him. When he could stand it no longer, he began to move slowly, deeply, letting her measure him again and again, feeling her passionate acceptance in her soft cries and in the satin flesh closing hotly, sleekly around him.

Gradually she began to move, dancing in slow counterpart to the man inside her, stroking him with every sinuous motion of her hips. He groaned as the sweet pressure of her around him shifted and changed, caressing him completely. He held onto the languid, deeply sensual dance until he felt control slipping away. Then he came to her without reservation, moving powerfully, feeling his own gathering tension echoed in her body. He tried to hold back, afraid of hurting her—and then it was too late to do anything but thrust into her as fire burst through him, shaking him. Her nails dug into the clenched muscles of his buttocks as she burned out of control again, crying her wild pleasure against the rigid muscles of his neck.

"You were wrong," she said finally, her voice ragged. "It was better this time. You were inside me."

Chase groaned and held Nicole even more tightly, more deeply, letting her heat and sweet flesh surround him. Her breath caught and fire welled up again, consuming both of them.

It was a long time before they could bring themselves to undo the sweet tangle of arms and legs and gently caressing hands. It was even longer before Chase pulled Nicole to her feet and slowly walked up the trail to her cottage with her. They shared a languid, slippery shower that ended abruptly as Nicole discovered ways not only to please Chase, but to drive him over the edge of his control. This time when he lifted her and told her to wrap her legs around him, she didn't hesitate. She wanted it as much as he did, aching to have him inside her while the shower poured hotly over their joined bodies.

But nothing was as hot as the fires they called forth from each other. As dawn came he was locked inside her once more, drinking the wild cries from her lips, coming apart even as she did, sharing the ecstatic burning.

When Chase could breathe again, he bent and licked a silver drop of moisture from between Nicole's breasts. She smiled and caressed his thick, tousled hair.

"Do you have any more doubts about your ability to please and be pleased?" asked Chase, nuzzling the soft flesh he had come to know so well during the long, consuming night.

Her hands paused in his hair, and then she laughed softly, moving her hips against his body, glorying in his sensual response.

"No," she sighed, drifting downward into sleep even as she spoke. "If either of us pleased any more, I think we'd die of it."

Chase smiled sadly, thinking what a sweet death it would be. He brushed his mustache over the rosy peak of her breast and watched it tighten, savoring for one last moment Nicole's velvet sensuality.

"Then spread your wings, butterfly," he whispered very softly as she fell asleep in his arms. "You're free."

Chapter 13

Li-sa soon?'' asked Benny.

Nicole smiled despite the emotions twisting through her. She couldn't think of Lisa without thinking of her father and thinking of Chase brought anger and regret and pain. Nicole closed her eyes and saw again the note that he had left on her kitchen table among the sketches of swollen buds and volcanic deserts. Every time she closed her eyes, the note was there, burned into her mind:

> If I stay, I'll ask more from you than a butterfly should have to give. Your body, your mind, your love, your future.
>
> I would give you the same in return.
>
> I know you don't want that. Not from me. You've found your wings, and what gorgeous wings they are. I don't blame you for wanting to fly to a man you can trust.

I regret hurting you more than you'll ever know. It
cost more than I thought I had to give—a chance to
love.

Then why didn't you stay? asked Nicole silently, futilely, because she knew the answer: *All or nothing at all.*

That was what she had. Nothing at all. She had tried to
imagine herself with another man, touching and being
touched with the intimacy she had known with Chase. She
had gone cold at the thought. She didn't want another
man. She wanted Chase.

And she was terrified of that wanting. She had survived
Ted's monumental insensitivity to her mental and physical needs. Instinctively she knew that if Chase were ever to
tire of her or misuse or misunderstand her as Ted had, she
wouldn't recover. Ted hadn't been able to destroy her because she hadn't given enough of herself to him.

If she gave any more of herself to Chase, she would be
lost. Already he was a part of her, as deeply embedded in
her as her own heartbeat. It had happened so quickly, so
irrevocably. She had trusted Chase instantly, instinctively.

And she had been wrong.

*No. Not wrong. Just too quick. If I had waited, he
would have known I wasn't hunting Dane. Then there
would have been no morning after, no need to fear trusting Chase.*

*If wishes were horses, beggars would ride. There was a
morning after. I am afraid.*

And I miss Chase. Oh, God, how I miss him!

Nicole realized that Benny was watching her, waiting
patiently for her answer. With an effort, she pulled her
mind away from the conflicting emotions that had all but
immobilized her for the three weeks since she had awak-
ened and found Chase's note lying on top of the sketch of
the jacaranda bud.

"Lisa's coming in on the afternoon flight," said Nicole. "Didn't Bobby tell you yesterday morning?"

Benny nodded.

She forced herself to smile again. "Nothing has changed since then. Dane will pick up Lisa at the airport, and she'll go hiking with us tomorrow."

"Kamehameha Iki?" asked Benny hopefully.

"I don't know. That depends on the reports from the observatory. Kilauea has been pretty lively the last two weeks."

Benny shrugged. To him, active volcanoes were simply part of the world, like big waves and heavy rains. "Kamehameha Iki," he said firmly. "Li-sa like much-much. You Pele. We safe."

Nicole smiled and ruffled Benny's hair affectionately. "What a lot of words," she murmured. "You must miss Lisa."

"Li-sa mine," said Benny matter-of-factly, turning toward the garden doors.

Nicole stared after the boy. Even Bobby had remarked on the attachment of the two children; a mutual admiration society had begun instantly and had deepened every day. It had given both Lisa and Benny a confidence in themselves as people that delighted Nicole even as it gently amused her.

The cottage seemed very empty without Benny.

Why isn't Chase coming back to Hawaii with Lisa? Doesn't he miss me at all? How can he ask me to marry him, make love to me as though I were truly Pele and then walk away?

There was no answer but the one implicit in the note. He loved her enough to want her to be happy—and he believed she wouldn't be happy with him because she couldn't trust him. He had shown her that she could trust herself, and then he had left her so that she could find a man to trust. To love. It was all there in the note, as were regret and pain and loss. She had all the answers. She just didn't like any of them.

Especially the knowledge that in the end she had hurt Chase as badly as he had hurt her in the beginning.

The thought went through Nicole like a torrent of molten lava, burning her until she wanted to scream or cry. But she could do neither. She wanted to be with Chase, to hold him, to comfort him and herself.

Oh God, Chase, I didn't mean to hurt you!

But she had.

Desperately Nicole looked around the cottage and tried to think of all the ways there were to kill time until the picnic tomorrow. Sketching paper crumpled and fired in frustration at the corners of the room testified to her restlessness last night. She was afraid that by the next morning, there would be an even bigger mess.

She was right. By the time Benny and three other Kamehamehas appeared at her door the next day, wadded-up sketching paper studded the cottage. Failed watercolors that had been torn to confetti added color and variety to the floors and furniture. Benny took one look at Nicole's smoldering amber eyes and decided that even one word on the subject of her housekeeping would be too many. His sister Mira wasn't that wise.

"What happened?" she asked.

"Nothing," said Nicole tersely.

"Oh." Big black eyes measured the mess. "I used to tell Mom the same thing," Mira said. "She didn't believe it, either." Mira hesitated. At fifteen, she was old enough to know that adults sometimes needed to be left alone. "We don't have to go hiking today," she offered tentatively.

"I've been looking forward to it," Nicole said flatly. "I need to get out."

Benny smiled with relief and hustled his sister and cousins out the garden door before Nicole could change her mind. She sighed and looked at the drifts of paper. They reminded her of the luau, when jacaranda blossoms had lain in fragrant windrows around the chaise and Chase had made her feel as beautiful as the night. More beautiful.

The sound of a child's excited laughter came as a relief from Nicole's seething thoughts. She reached the front door just in time to open it and catch a small, energetic body in her arms.

"I missed you," said Lisa, hugging her. "Is Benny here?"

Nicole smiled despite the pain lancing through her as she realized again that Lisa's eyes were the same clear gray as Chase's. "He's in the garden. Where's Dane?"

"He and Daddy let me off at the gate. They'll pick me up there later."

Numbly Nicole released Lisa, who raced off to the garden, calling Benny's name in a high, clear voice. Nicole barely heard. All she knew was that Chase was back; he had been only a few yards away—and he hadn't even said hello.

Why? Doesn't he want to see me?

The answer came swiftly to Nicole, like a knife twisting. *Did you want to see him again after you ran out of Dane's house?*

Nicole closed her eyes and swayed slightly, knowing only that Chase was within reach and she had to go to him. She had to know if he had meant what he said in his note: *A chance to love.*

"Nicole?"

She blinked and focused on Mark. "Oh. Hi, Mark. Is everyone here?"

"All six of us. Sandi, Judy, Lisa, Tim and Steve. We all crammed into the car with Dad and Uncle Chase. But don't worry. We made lunch at home. Uncle Chase told us not to mess up your kitchen."

"Oh," she said again, unable to think of anything else to say, knowing only that she had to see Chase again.

Mark looked at her oddly. "You feeling okay?"

"Sure. Fine. Just a little—slow." She gestured at the litter of paper. "I worked late last night."

Mark's eyebrows climbed as he took in the mess. "Who won?"

"Not me," said Nicole, her mouth turning down at one corner. *And not Chase. We both lost. We're still losing.*

"You sure you're up to a hike?"

"First Mira, now you. I must look like death warmed over."

Tactfully Mark changed the subject. "Uncle Chase told me to tell you to be sure to stay clear of the southwest rift zone. It's not official yet, but they're going to close that part of the mountain any time now."

"So it's finally singing in harmony," said Nicole absently.

"Huh?"

"Harmonic tremors. Swarms of them. That's how they know the magma is moving up inside the mountain," she said. Then she shook her head and forced herself to concentrate on something besides her consuming need to see Chase. "We're going to Kamehameha Iki. It's nowhere near the Great Crack," added Nicole, referring to the fourteen-mile-long fissure that lay like an open wound down Kilauea's southwest side. "Is anything happening on top yet?"

Mark shook his head. "That's where Dad and Uncle Chase were going to go later today."

"I'll pack a radio," decided Nicole, turning to rummage in her kitchen drawer for the tiny portable radio she rarely carried. "If the mountain goes, it will be on the news. We'll hurry back and drive up for ringside seats."

On the bus the kids were still talking excitedly about the prospect of finally seeing the fabled mountain blow.

"Nah, it won't blow," said Mark. "Not like Mount Saint Helens. Uncle Chase told me that the lava that comes out of Kilauea is usually thin and fast, so it doesn't get stuck inside the mountain's throat and build up pressure like that mainland volcano did. Poor old Saint Helens literally blew its top. Kilauea just sort of lets it all bubble out quietly."

That started an argument about just what constituted "quietly." Were fountains of fire eighteen hundred feet high "quiet"? As several of the kids had parents who worked at the observatory, there were plenty of opinions to go around. Nicole listened with half her attention while she herded everyone off the bus, counted noses, and kept on counting from time to time while the children hiked along the very faint trail that their summer picnic jaunts had made through the forest.

Most of Nicole's thoughts were on Chase and on what she would do when the hike was over. The thought of not seeing him was too painful to consider. She had missed Chase unbearably in the past few weeks. Each succeeding day had been worse, not better. Yet the thought of going to him and giving herself wholly to him was frightening.

What if he doesn't want me after all? What if that's why he didn't come to see me?

Nicole stumbled and barely caught herself on the rough ground. The thought of being rejected by Chase was numbing.

Trust him. Trust yourself. Take this chance for love.

Nicole made the rest of the hike on automatic pilot, her mind locked between trust and fear. As usual, it was warm on the mountainside. As usual, it rained for a time. As usual, the small pool in the center of the kipuka felt like Eden reborn. What wasn't usual was the sudden, sharp leap of the earth beneath their feet, followed by several minutes during which the ground trembled slightly. At the first earthquake Lisa gave a startled cry and tried to run toward Nicole, only to trip and fall.

"Everyone sit down," said Nicole as she gathered Lisa into her arms. "There may be aftershocks or even more quakes." She sat down herself and bent over the little girl who was huddled in her lap. "Are you okay, honey?"

Tears trembled in Lisa's eyes. "My ankle hurts."

Nicole looked at the ankle. It was scraped, bleeding and swelling slightly, but Lisa could move it. Nicole smiled reassuringly as she turned on the radio and held the speaker to her ear. After a few minutes of moving the dial to the various stations she could receive, she lowered the radio and looked at the children.

"Nothing about the volcano," she told them. "I'll try again in a few minutes."

The ground shivered and trembled very faintly beneath them. Nicole wished desperately that there was someone nearby who knew more about Hawaii and volcanoes than she did. This might be perfectly normal behavior preceding a perfectly normal eruption in the southwest rift zone. Or it might be that a disaster was taking shape around her and the children. The earth seemed to vibrate beneath her feet, but the motion was so subtle now that it was more sensed than felt.

Nicole's instincts stabbed her with sudden, sharp warnings. *Get out. Get out.* She didn't question the instinct to flee. She couldn't. It was simply too powerful.

"I think," said Nicole as casually as she could, "that if we don't get going, the best seats at the observatory will be overrun by tourists."

Nicole helped Lisa to her feet. The girl limped but was able to walk. The children didn't argue about leaving the kipuka early. They picked up their lunches and began walking. Lisa's limp got worse with each step along the rough mountainside. Nicole watched her anxiously. The little girl was still keeping the pace, but it was obvious that she wouldn't be able to much longer.

As she watched Lisa, Nicole listened to the radio. She flipped from station to station until she found one where an excited announcer was talking about earthquakes and Kilauea. What she heard made her heart stop, then beat with redoubled speed. Kilauea was in full eruption. The earthquake had closed old fissures and opened new ones all around the section of the mountain where she and the children were.

Suddenly the wind shifted, blowing down, rather than up, the mountain.

"Something's burning," called Mark from his position at the middle of the column. "I can't see it, but I can smell it."

The children agreed loudly. Nicole held up her hand for silence, listening intently to the radio. What she heard made her mouth go dry. Mentally she calculated the distance to the road as she listened to the announcer's excited description of Kilauea coming apart and pouring rivers of incandescent stone over its flanks.

Then she heard that the road to the caldera had been cut in several places.

For an instant Nicole closed her eyes and prayed that Chase and Dane were beyond the reach of fire. With an effort, she put her fears for Chase out of her mind. There were ten children with her, depending on her to lead them to safety. She could afford to think of nothing else.

"Benny," called Nicole, making sure her voice carried to the front of the line, where Benny was confidently leading them through the trackless forest of fern and tall ohia. "Can you get high enough in a tree to see where the smoke is coming from?"

Benny didn't bother to answer. He simply sized up the trees around him, accepted a boost from one of Mark's friends, and scrambled up until the branches were too thin to support his weight. He looked around once, twice, three times, as though memorizing the land.

"Mountain burning!" he said, his voice high.

Nicole felt hot, then cold. It was what she had expected, but she had hoped fiercely for better news.

"Can you see any lava?" she called.

"Smoke," called Benny.

"From burning trees or is it in great big plumes going all the way to the clouds?" asked Nicole, keeping her voice calm with an effort.

"Trees."

"Can you see a way down to the road?"

Benny hesitated a long time. "Sorry-sorry, Pele. Big line smoke between."

"Can we get to the old pahoehoe flow that's halfway to the road?"

"Yes-yes," said Benny eagerly.

"Is there fire in that direction?"

"Smoke everywhere," he said simply, moving his hand in a circular motion.

"Do you see any helicopters or small planes?" Nicole asked, for the radio announcer had said that rescue operations were being mounted as quickly as stranded people were spotted from the air.

"No."

"Come down," called Nicole. "Thanks. You've helped a lot."

Nicole turned and faced the children, who were waiting anxiously in front of her. She saw that Sandi had moved to stand next to her older brother. Mark bent over and said something as he took her hand reassuringly. The gesture was so like Dane that Nicole wanted to smile and cry at the same time. She took a deep breath, knowing she had to stay calm.

"The radio announcer said that Kilauea is splitting some new seams," Nicole told the children. "We're supposed to go to a road or a clear area where we can be spotted from the air. Then a helicopter will come and get us. Benny, you take the lead again. Mark, help Lisa up onto my back."

"I'll carry her," he offered quickly.

Nicole shook her head. "Thanks, but it's not that far." *And I'm stronger than you. I won't be a year from today, but it's not a year from today. It's now, and we're trapped on a burning mountain.* Nicole kept her thought to herself, for there was no reason to hurt Mark's pride. "If I need help over the rough spots, I'll yell for you." She smiled over her shoulder at Lisa. "Hang on tight, honey, but around my shoulders, not my neck. Ready?"

Lisa nodded.

"Benny, I want you to keep going until you're in the center of the pahoehoe. Then sit down and wait for the helicopter," said Nicole. "Stay together. If it gets real smoky, tear up your shirts and breathe through them. Don't double back for me if I fall a bit behind," she added casually. "Lisa and I will be fine. Mark, you bring up the rear of the kids." She saw the quick concern for her and the objection forming on his lips. "I'm counting on you, Mark," she said quietly.

He wanted to object, but a single look at Nicole's face silenced him. He fell into place at the end of the line as Benny took the lead.

The walk through the forest with Lisa on her shoulders seemed endless. For the first time in her life, Nicole was grateful for her unusual size, as well as the years of dancing and hiking that had conditioned her body. Lisa might have been small, but she wasn't a negligible weight. The path Nicole was walking over was little more than a few crushed ferns leading between trees, shrubs and bigger ferns.

The wind shifted to blow from behind her, bringing acrid smoke, warning of the burning lava coming down the mountain.

Nicole coughed and kept walking, hoping for another shift of wind. She could no longer see the children ahead of her, nor hear them, but she could follow their faint trail. The forest gradually changed, thinning out and then getting lush again according to rhythms of old lava flows.

The air got no better. Every shift of wind brought smoke swirling down the mountain in billows, making Nicole and Lisa cough. Nicole listened for the sounds of fire overtaking her, but could hear nothing more than the roaring of her own blood in her ears. The forest was too wet and lush to burn easily unless the lava got close enough to dry and heat the plants to flash point. Smoke, however, was a different matter. Both volcano and burning forest produced smoke in abundance.

Vegetation thinned dramatically, signaling the presence of a geologically recent lava flow. Even after hundreds of years, plants had made few inroads on the glassy surface of the pahoehoe that had flowed like burning syrup down the mountainside, filling crevices and hollows. Mark stood at the edge of the shiny flow, looking anxiously toward the thick forest beyond. When he spotted Nicole he ran over and lifted Lisa from her back.

"Hang on, squirt," he said.

Lisa wrapped her arms around his thin shoulders. Nicole smiled wearily.

"Everyone's in the center waiting for you. A small plane flew over twenty minutes ago."

"Did it see you?"

"It wagged its wings."

Nicole closed her eyes, almost dizzy with relief. Until that moment she hadn't admitted to herself how frightened she was. "Thank God," she breathed.

There were no trees or tall ferns to shield the view of the mountain. Long lines of smoke writhed skyward, marking outbreaks of lava. The molten stone itself was still hidden, revealed only by the fires it set among the lush green forest. Nicole watched in reluctant fascination as the smoke crept lower and lower down the mountainside.

A small helicopter sank out of the murky sky and landed gingerly on the uneven ground. The pilot glanced from the ten children to the tall woman standing braced against the backwash of the rotors.

"Load 'em up!" he yelled.

Nicole looked at the two-man helicopter and then at the pilot. Neither of them said any more. She simply stood at the door and boosted children inside until they were packed in the helicopter like fish in a can. Mark was the last one in. He turned to help Nicole, only to find that she wasn't there anymore.

"Nicole?" he called. Understanding came as he felt the helicopter shudder up to full power. "Nicole! Come back! There's room! You can have my place! *Nicole!*"

The pilot's hand clamped around Mark's arm, pinning him in place as the machine lifted slowly from the ground. Mark watched helplessly as the overloaded helicopter labored higher and higher into the sky until Nicole was no longer visible. Behind her, farther up the mountain, the world was on fire. By night, the lava would look like a wild network of liquid red and gold. By day, it looked like a black, many-fingered hand wreathed in smoke.

And the hand was reaching down toward the solid island of pahoehoe where Nicole waited alone.

"I'll come back for her, boy."

Mark turned and looked into the pilot's compassionate eyes. Nothing else was said during the short flight to Hilo airport, for the pilot spent most of the time talking on the radio, telling people that he had found ten children and was bringing them in.

As soon as the helicopter touched down, Mark spotted the tall figures of his father, his uncle and Bobby running across the apron. Mark helped everyone out of the helicopter before carrying Lisa the few feet to her father's waiting arms.

Chase took Lisa's light weight with a feeling of gratitude that made his throat ache. He enveloped her in a hug. She returned it with all the strength of her small arms.

"She's okay," Mark assured him. "Just a sore ankle."

Chase nodded, looking over Lisa's black head for the fiery hair that had haunted his dreams.

The helicopter was empty, no one near it but the pilot, who was hauling a fuel line toward the machine at a dead run. Chase looked all around the apron, then turned back to Mark. Tears were streaming down the boy's face.

"There wasn't—enough room!" said Mark, his voice breaking. "She wouldn't let me—trade places! It was b-burning—behind her!"

The breath went out of Chase as though he had been kicked. With a terrible effort, he kept his voice even as he unwrapped Lisa's arms from around his neck. "Go to Uncle Dane, baby," he said, kissing his daughter, handing her into Dane's arms. "He'll take you home."

"I want Nicole," said Lisa suddenly, bursting into tears.

"I'll get her," promised Chase.

The pilot looked up as Chase approached. "That your wife back up on the mountain?"

"I'm working on it," Chase said roughly.

"Hell of a woman," said the pilot, pumping fuel with grim haste. "She saw right off there wasn't enough room. Didn't say a word. Just stuffed the kids in the cockpit and jumped back out of the way. The boy damn near bailed out after her. Had to hold him." The pilot jerked back on the fuel line. "That should do 'er. It's not real far, for a bird. Pure hell on foot, though."

"I'm coming with you," said Chase.

"Too dangerous," the pilot said bluntly. "That old mountain is coming apart all over."

"We're wasting time," snapped Chase, swinging into the passenger seat.

The pilot grunted. "Good enough. I can use another pair of eyes. Smoky as hell out there. Might miss her."

The helicopter obtained a clearance instantly and leaped into the sky. Within moments the panorama of the burning mountain unfolded before Chase. His trained eye quickly picked out the pattern beneath the chaos of writhing smoke. From a point just over halfway up the mountain, long pseudopods of molten lava spilled out, setting fire to the forest wherever they touched. There were several major fissures and many minor ones. Between the fingers of lava, slivers of green forest were encircled. Some

burned. Some did not; potential islands of life were forming as he watched.

"How the hell did you find the kids?" asked Chase,
appalled at the murky chaos beneath.

"Observatory plane spotted 'em. She had 'em parked in
the middle of a batch of pahoehoe. No trees to burn or to
hide them."

The helicopter veered to the right and then skated down
on a long descent, coming closer to the rivers of burning
stone with each second. Heat rising from the lava buf-
feted the helicopter, but the pilot held his course.

Chase bit back the impatience hammering in him, the
fear that he was too late. Silently he cursed himself for not
being with Nicole.

*You were going to have it all your own way. You were
going to heal her and set her free and then wait for her to
come flying back to you. But she can't fly. She's trapped
down there, and you're trapped up here in this bloody tin
can.*

"How much farther?" asked Chase, his voice harsh.

"Under that smoke, somewhere."

Chase swore savagely.

"Going down for a closer look," said the pilot. "Keep
your eyes peeled."

The engine noise changed as the pilot shot down through
the smoke, one eye on the compass and the other on the
altimeter. Chase stared out into the murk, seeing a blur of
forest unreel dizzyingly beneath the helicopter. After a few
minutes the pilot switched directions and flew another leg
of an imaginary grid. The forest raced by, green on green,
smoke swirling wildly as Eden burned.

Chase felt sweat gathering along his ribs and rolling
down his spine as he thought of Nicole, alone down there.
They were dangerously close to the treetops and he still
could barely see. The air was acrid and occasionally laced
with cinders and sulphur. The thought of Nicole trying to
breathe that soup made his hands clench helplessly. The

knowledge that volcanic gases were often poisonous was a knife turning in his heart.

Hurry, he yelled silently to the pilot. *Hurry!*

And then Chase saw a shimmer of red-gold in the midst of old black lava.

"There! Two o'clock!" shouted Chase, pointing.

The pilot switched directions, spotted Nicole and swooped down like a hawk.

Nicole lay face down, her hair whipping out like a banner over the dark rock.

Chase leaped from the helicopter before it touched the ground. He ran over to her, calling her name. When she turned slowly toward his voice, he pulled her into his arms and buried his face in her hair. She coughed terribly, unable to speak, clinging to him as he carried her into the helicopter.

They were barely strapped in before the helicopter shot upward, tunneling through the smoke toward the clear air of Hilo.

Fountains of burning lava danced against the night sky, sending dazzling rivers of liquid stone down Kilauea's seamed flanks. When the lava cooled, it darkened, forming a lid on the seething rivers. As melted stone poured over the rugged land, the lid was broken many times, revealing the burning rock beneath in patterns that were like captive lightning. The sight was both savage and beautiful, a view back through time to the birth of the land.

Nicole watched in awed silence from a safe vantage point. It wasn't only the distance from the incredible upwelling of liquid stone that made her feel safe, it was Chase's arms around her and his voice murmuring in her ear, telling her what was happening to the mountain beneath her feet.

"There's a new Great Crack pouring out lava for half the length of the mountain. One of the lava tongues has gone all the way to the sea," he continued, brushing his lips over Nicole's fragrant hair. "The island will be a little bigger come morning."

The fountains gushed higher for an instant, pulsing with rhythms alien to man, incandescent with the violence of creation. Nicole shivered.

"Afraid?" asked Chase softly, nestling her closer against his chest. "Don't be. Every last person who was trapped on Kilauea has been rescued. No one was even hurt. You saw Lisa tonight. She's running around like a little gazelle." He laughed softly. "So is everyone else on the island, trying to find the best place to watch the mountain dance."

"It's—incredibly beautiful. Unearthly."

"It's the beginning of everything," he said, kissing Nicole's hair, breathing in her scent. "Without it, there would be no land, no trees, no ferns, no flowers, nothing but the sea. Eden was born in fire, and only fire keeps it alive."

Nicole shivered again and leaned back against Chase. She was sitting cradled between his legs, her back against his chest, his arms around her, his breath stirring warmly on her neck. It was as though the last three weeks had never happened, as though he had never gone to the mainland, as though she had never huddled in the middle of black stone and prayed that she would live to see him again.

In the hours since he had pulled her into the helicopter, he had said nothing to her about his absence, asked nothing of her with his return. He had simply held her, watched her reunion with the worried children and then had asked everyone to come up the mountain with him again after dinner, saying that he didn't want them to be afraid of something so beautiful. When the children had finally tired of the spectacle, Dane and Janet had taken them back down the mountain, leaving Nicole and Chase alone.

"Chase?" asked Nicole, her voice suddenly uncertain.

His arms tightened around her. He didn't want to hear her next words, her hesitant thanks for rescuing her and then a plea to be freed again. He couldn't let her go. Not now. Not ever. He would take whatever she could give and try not to ask for more.

Chase lifted the silky mass of Nicole's unbound hair and let it fall over his shoulder and down his back like a fiery cape. The red-gold lights of Kilauea gleamed within her hair, reflecting the dancing fountains of creation. Chase's mouth found the soft skin of her neck. He tasted her delicately, testing the smooth flesh with his teeth and tongue. He heard her breath catch, felt the tiny tremors of her response. When his palms found the full curves of her breasts, she sighed and let her head fall back on his shoulder.

"Yes, butterfly," Chase murmured, "come to me. Drink the sweetness from my hand."

Nicole felt her whole body tighten beneath the long black muumuu she wore. Chase's hands moved lovingly from her shoulders to her thighs, pressing against her, urging her even closer to his heat, caging her gently between his legs. Restlessly, hungrily, Nicole's palms moved over the masculine textures surrounding her, enjoying the hair-roughened, flexed power of his legs. She turned and looked over her shoulder, hoping to capture Chase's lips.

His eyes were closed against the moonlight and the dancing fires. His expression was harsh, intensely male. He was absorbing every instant of touching, every tiny movement of her hands, everything about the woman half-reclining against him. As she lifted herself toward his mouth, she felt his hands slide beneath her muumuu, gliding up her legs until he had captured the softness waiting between. Her breath came out in a startled moan as fire radiated through her, consuming her. Her hips moved slowly, telling him how much she enjoyed the intimate caress.

A thick sound wedged in Chase's throat as he felt Nicole's silky movements beneath his hands. He stroked her for a moment longer before sliding his fingers higher, seeking the tempting peaks of her breasts, finding them, tugging sweetly at them until she moaned and arched into his hands. He shuddered deeply, wanting her with a force that was both pain and pleasure. His hands swept up her body, peeling away the soft black folds of cloth, leaving her wearing nothing but a dark lace triangle that couldn't conceal the fiery hair beneath.

An instant later Nicole was naked and Chase's hands were teasing her breasts again. She wanted to turn and capture the hot, hungry mouth that was buried in the curve of her neck, but the sensation of his hands caressing her nipples was too exquisite to end by turning to face him. His fingers looked dark against her pale flesh, hard, exciting.

When his hands drifted down her body and nestled between her legs, Nicole gave up any thought of trying to turn in his arms. Her breath came out in a broken cry of pleasure that was his name. Chase heard and smiled against her neck, biting her nape even as his fingers found and caressed the taut focus of her desire.

Nicole's whole body tightened with the depth of the response Chase drew from her. Her nails swept the length of his bare legs, only to be frustrated by the barrier of his hiking shorts. She could feel his hunger pressing against her back, just as she could feel the first, shivering waves of heat take her, melting her.

Chase felt the fire sweeping through her softness, fire that overflowed at his touch, and he made a husky, triumphant sound.

"I've spent three weeks trying to figure out how to get you to fly back to me," he said, biting her neck, feeling her untamed response as she strained against his imprisoning, caressing embrace. "I thought of using Lisa, of telling you how much Lisa loves you, needs you—but Lisa will be grown up in a few years, and I'll just be beginning to know how much I need you, want you."

"Chase, I—" Nicole's voice broke as his hands moved skillfully, taking her to the edge of fiery release, holding her there.

"I'll take whatever you want to give me," said Chase, holding Nicole tightly against his hungry body as he stroked her. "Just don't fly away from me. Stay and drink from me. Let me drink from you. Don't ask me to let you go. I can't."

Nicole cried out as she tried to hold back from the fiery waves of pleasure melting her. She trembled as her hands closed over his, stilling his caressing fingers. She turned slowly in his arms, stroking his hard, hungry male flesh with every languid movement of her body. Her hair spilled over both of them, veiling them in fire.

She unbuttoned Chase's shirt, pushed it aside and sighed as she tasted his hot, salty skin. Even as her teeth scraped lightly over his nipples, she finished undressing him. Then she stroked him hungrily, holding him between her hands, enjoying every bit of his passion as he shuddered and moved with her touch.

"I love your taste," Nicole said, "your textures, the heat of your body. I love your words when you talk about the land and your smile when Lisa falls asleep in your arms. I love *you*." Her voice trembled with the emotions that were sweeping through her, melting her body into his. She looked up into the silver flash of his eyes in the moonlight and said, "Be part of me, Chase. Now. Always."

As he bent to take her lips, he gave her the words that burned within him even more wildly than his passion for her.

"I love you, Nicole. I'll die loving you."

He caught her mouth in a consuming kiss even as he fitted their bodies together deeply, becoming part of her, completing both of them.

Across the narrow valley, fountains of molten stone danced and pulsed as the fires of Eden burned, washing the lovers in the incandescent light of creation.

OFFICIAL SWEEPSTAKES INFORMATION

1. **NO PURCHASE NECESSARY.** To enter, complete the official entry/order form. Be sure to indicate whether or not you wish to take advantage of our subscription offer.

2. Entry blanks have been pre-selected for the prizes offered. Your response will be checked to see if you are a winner. In the event that these are not claimed, a random drawing will be held from all entries received to award not less than $150,000 in prizes. This is in addition to any free, surprise or mystery gifts which might be offered. Versions of this sweepstakes with different prizes will appear in Torstar Ltd. mailings and their affiliates. Winners selected will receive the prize offered in their sweepstakes insert.

3. This promotion is being conducted under the supervision of Marden-Kane, an independent judging organization. By entering the sweepstakes, each entrant accepts and agrees to be bound by these rules and the decisions of the judges which shall be final and binding. Odds of winning in the random drawing are dependent upon the total number of entries received. Taxes, if any, are the sole responsibility of the prize winners. Prizes are non-transferable. All entries must be received by August 31, 1986.

4. This sweepstakes package offers:

1, Grand Prize	: Cruise around the world on the QEII	$100,000 total value
4, First Prizes	: Set of matching pearl necklace and earrings	$ 20,000 total value
10, Second Prizes	: Romantic Weekend in Bermuda	$ 15,000 total value
25, Third Prizes	: Designer Luggage	$ 10,000 total value
200, Fourth Prizes	: $25 Gift Certificate	$ 5,000 total value
		$150,000

Winners may elect to receive the cash equivalent for the prizes offered.

5. This offer is open to residents of the U.S. and Canada, 18 years and older, except employees of Torstar Ltd., its affiliates, subsidiaries, Marden-Kane and all other agencies and persons connected with conducting this sweepstakes. All Federal, State and local laws apply. Void in the province of Quebec and wherever prohibited or restricted by law. Winners will be notified by mail and may be required to execute an affidavit of eligibility and release which must be returned within 14 days after notification. Canadian winners will be required to answer a skill testing question. Winners consent to the use of their names, photograph and/or likeness for advertising and publicity purposes in conjunction with this and similar promotions without additional compensation. One prize per family or household.

6. For a list of our most current prize winners, send a stamped, self-addressed envelope to: WINNERS LIST, c/o Marden-Kane, P.O. Box 10404, Long Island City, New York 11101.

SSR-A-1

AMERICAN TRIBUTE

Where a man's dreams count for more than his parentage...

Look for these upcoming titles under the Special Edition American Tribute banner.

CHEROKEE FIRE
Gena Dalton #307—May 1986
It was Sabrina Dante's silver spoon that Cherokee cowboy Jarod Redfeather couldn't trust. The two lovers came from opposite worlds, but Jarod's Indian heritage taught them to overcome their differences.

NOBODY'S FOOL
Renee Roszel #313—June 1986
Everyone bet that Martin Dante and Cara Torrence would get together. But Martin wasn't putting any money down, and Cara was out to prove that she was nobody's fool.

MISTY MORNINGS, MAGIC NIGHTS
Ada Steward #319—July 1986
The last thing Carole Stockton wanted was to fall in love with another politician, especially Donnelly Wakefield. But under a blanket of secrecy, far from the campaign spotlights, their love became a powerful force.

AM-TRIB-1R

AMERICAN TRIBUTE

American Tribute titles now available:

RIGHT BEHIND THE RAIN
Elaine Camp #301—April 1986
The difficulty of coping with her brother's
death brought reporter Raleigh Torrence
to the office of Evan Younger, a police
psychologist. He helped her to deal with
her feelings and emotions, including love.

THIS LONG WINTER PAST
Jeanne Stephens #295—March 1986
Detective Cody Wakefield checked out
Assistant District Attorney Liann McDowell,
but only in his leisure time. For it was the
danger of Cody's job that caused Liann to
shy away.

LOVE'S HAUNTING REFRAIN
Ada Steward #289—February 1986
For thirty years a deep dark secret kept them
apart—King Stockton made his millions while
his wife, Amelia, held everything together.
Now could they tell their secret, could they
admit their love?

Silhouette Intimate Moments

COMING
NEXT MONTH

DOUBLE ENTENDRE—
Heather Graham Pozzessere

During a murder investigation stretching back to World
War II, soon-to-be-divorced reporters Colleen and Bret
agreed to work together. The dangers that followed brought
to light their problem and its only solution: love.

SING ME A LOVESONG—Barbara Faith

Laura's father and Jacques Duvalier were exactly
alike . . . stars adored by women and not above casual
flirtation. Yet despite the warning signs she allowed his song
to penetrate her heart.

THE RELUCTANT SWAN—Anna James

Happy in her seclusion managing a bird sanctuary, Sara
avoided any association with her parents' past Hollywood
notoriety—until biographer Cal Webster arrived and showed
her the possibility of sharing her heart without losing
everything.

FOR OLD TIMES' SAKE—Kathleen Eagle

Erin returned to Standing Rock Indian Reservation to solve
the mystery of her sister's death. But when Hunter Brave
Wolf, publisher of an Indian-owned paper, helped her trace
the murderer and rekindled their old romance, she knew she
could never leave again.

AVAILABLE NOW:

FIRES OF EDEN
Elizabeth Lowell

AFFAIR ROYALE
Nora Roberts

THE FIND OF A LIFETIME
Susanna Christie

HONOR BOUND
Erin St. Claire